SAC... ...MENTO PUBLIC LIBRARY

D0253549

Praise for *N...*

"Palmer proves that love and passion can be found even in the most dangerous situations."

—*Publishers Weekly* on *Untamed*

"You just can't do better than a Diana Palmer story to make your heart lighter and smile brighter."

—*Fresh Fiction* on *Wyoming Rugged*

"Diana Palmer is a mesmerizing storyteller who captures the essence of what a romance should be."

—*Affaire de Coeur*

"The popular Palmer has penned another winning novel, a perfect blend of romance and suspense."

—*Booklist* on *Lawman*

"Diana Palmer's characters leap off the page. She captures their emotions and scars beautifully and makes them come alive for readers."

—*RT Book Reviews* on *Lawless*

For a complete list of titles available by Diana Palmer, please visit www.dianapalmer.com.

THE MORCAI BATTALION: THE PURSUIT

DIANA PALMER

If you purchased this book without a cover you should be aware that this book is stolen property. It was reported as "unsold and destroyed" to the publisher, and neither the author nor the publisher has received any payment for this "stripped book."

ISBN-13: 978-1-335-58016-0

Recycling programs for this product may not exist in your area.

The Morcai Battalion: The Pursuit

Copyright © 2018 by Diana Palmer

All rights reserved. Except for use in any review, the reproduction or utilization of this work in whole or in part in any form by any electronic, mechanical or other means, now known or hereafter invented, including xerography, photocopying and recording, or in any information storage or retrieval system, is forbidden without the written permission of the publisher, HQN Books, 22 Adelaide St. West, 40th Floor, Toronto, Ontario M5H 4E3, Canada.

This is a work of fiction. Names, characters, places and incidents are either the product of the author's imagination or are used fictitiously, and any resemblance to actual persons, living or dead, business establishments, events or locales is entirely coincidental.

This edition published by arrangement with Harlequin Books S.A.

For questions and comments about the quality of this book, please contact us at CustomerService@Harlequin.com.

® and TM are trademarks of Harlequin Enterprises Limited or its corporate affiliates. Trademarks indicated with ® are registered in the United States Patent and Trademark Office, the Canadian Intellectual Property Office and in other countries.

www.HQNBooks.com

Printed in U.S.A.

Dear Reader,

This book is a continuation of my Morcai Battalion series, which, with the publication of this one, now comprises five novels. I never dreamed the first one would ever be reprinted, much less that I would be allowed to do more. It truly is a dream come true.

Thanks to everyone who helped me along the way, especially Tara and Mary-Theresa, and all the kind people who encouraged me. When I started the Morcai Battalion in late 1964 as nothing more than a short story for a writing course, I thought that my characters would lie dormant forever after. But there was more to be written than I knew at the time.

As they say, it's not the destination, it's the journey. And what a long and fascinating journey it's been! To all of you whom I met along the way, thank you for your encouragement, kindness and prayers. Writing is a lonely business. But the richest reward it brings is not money or fame; it's friendship. Thank you for yours.

I am your biggest fan,

Diana Palmer

To my friend, editor Carly Silver at Harlequin, who has been so kind and supportive over the years. Thanks for everything!

CHAPTER ONE

IT WAS THE most boring voyage of Mekashe's recent life. He'd been sent to represent the Cehn-Tahr government at a meeting of security experts who dealt with the safety of heads of state. Since Mekashe was captain of the Cehn-Tahr emperor Tnurat Alamantimichar's Imperial Guard, he was the obvious person to attend.

But he was used to military routine, and this was far from that. It was an A-class cruise vessel, intended for use by the general public. Because it was more expensive than most transports, the people aboard tended to be from the highest level of their respective societies. It wasn't commonly known, but Mekashe was a royal, a great-nephew of old Tnurat. His relationship to the emperor was why he was given the position of Imperial Guard Captain. Clan status denoted position. So when his best friend, Rhemun, followed Dtimun as the commander of the Holconcom, Mekashe was given Rhemun's former position as captain of the guard. Clan status was the most important facet of the Cehn-Tahr's rigid class culture.

Despite the relaxed atmosphere of the ship, which was uncomfortable, Mekashe did enjoy the observation deck. He could look out and see comets and meteors and distant stars as the huge vessel plowed its way through space. It was a novelty in his life, because the Imperial Guard was composed mostly of ground troops, elite infantry. The Holconcom, captained by his best friend, Rhemun, was more like space cavalry. The Holconcom was the most feared fighting force in the three galaxies, a specialized commando battalion on the flagship Morcai with both human and Cehn-Tahr personnel in an almost-equal mixture. Rhemun was bonded to the Morcai's former Cularian medical specialist, Dr. Edris Mallory, and they had a son, Kipling. The boy was almost as talented with the Kahn-Bo fighting style as Mekashe, and he outclassed his father, Rhemun. He was so good that Mekashe—fleet champion in Kahn-Bo—had to work very hard to best him.

He thought about families. He had been mildly infatuated with Edris Mallory and spent much time talking to her, learning about human culture. Rhemun had been jealous. That was in the time before, when Rhemun was forced by Clan structure to take command of the Holconcom and captain the flagship Morcai. He had hated humans, and Dr. Mallory came in for a lot of harassment from him. That changed when she ran from a particularly painful argument and wound up at the lawless Benaski Port, hiding from everyone. She was attacked by a brothel owner while defending two little girls and left for dead. Rhemun had sent several members of his squad after the perpetrator, who was left in pieces. After that, he and Edris bonded. It had been a sad day in Mekashe's life, because he adored the little blonde physician. But he was happy for his friend.

It was odd that he liked humans so much. In past times, Cehn-Tahr had been prejudiced toward out-worlders. Ahkmau, the infamous Rojok prison camp, had changed all that. A combined crew of Cehn-Tahr and humans had been captured and held in the hell-ish concentration camp. Many had died regaining their freedom. It had drawn the two very different races close and led to the formation of the Morcai Battalion. The integrated group was a sentinel of racial tolerance in a sea of interstellar prejudice. It had done much to change attitudes in the three galaxies.

Now humans were family to the military Cehn-Tahr. Many of Mekashe's comrades were as fascinated with the species as he was himself.

Mekashe had dreamed for most of his life about a blonde human female with exquisite features. But unlike Edris Mallory, who was short and delicate, Mekashe's dream female was tall and willowy, and kindhearted. He had the gift of telepathy, which he shared only with the Royal Clan, of which he was part. Cehn-Tahr never publicized the ability among outworlders. In fact, they never spoke of their culture to anyone outside Memcache, the home planet of the Cehn-Tahr.

He wondered about the prophetic dream. Only Caneese, the bonded mate of the emperor, had such a great gift for seeing the future. It had not arisen in any other member of the Clan. But Mekashe often saw things before they happened. So the gift was at least present in him, if not as formidable as Caneese's ability.

He was probably just dreaming, he thought, amused at his own weakness. His position gave him status among the Cehn-Tahr. Captain of the Imperial Guard was no small government job. It put him among planetal leaders, like Field Marshal Chacon, former field of the Rojok Army, who was now Premier of the Rojok Republic, having displaced the despot who had ruled after Mangus Lo. The depravity of the former Rojok government was something that Chacon was still having to live down. The death camp at Ahkmau had been hidden from everyone, even from Chacon, until he was forced to go there to save the Cehn-Tahr emperor's daughter, Lyceria. In the course of that rescue, he had helped the humans and Cehn-Tahr of the Morcai Battalion to escape execution, as well. Now, in an irony of fate, Chacon was bonded to the emperor's daughter. They were expecting their first child very soon. Gossip said that Chacon, that powerhouse of might, was pacing the floor and worrying himself to death, like any other prospective father. His passion for his mate had raised eyebrows, because Rojoks and Cehn-Tahr were traditional enemies. Now all sorts of new bonds were being formed. Homogenous cultures were becoming galactic ones, with the mixing. It produced some beautiful children. Kipling, Rhemun's son, was one of those. He had long, curly blond hair—his father had long, curly black hair— and human features, but he had his father's cat eyes that changed color with emotion. It was an exotic, fascinating blend of traits.

Mekashe would have liked a son, but he had found no Cehn-Tahr woman with whom he wanted to bond. The dreams of perfection, of that blonde phantom, haunted him. Probably, he reasoned, it was only a dream, and he would never meet…

"But I know it was this way!" a soft, feminine voice wailed, interrupting his thoughts. "I can't believe this! Why isn't there a map of the ship, or a holo, or anything…! Oh! Hello," she said as she stopped just in front of Mekashe. "Sorry, I was just talking to myself. I do that, far too much. I'm lost. I'm lost! I was supposed to meet my father for dinner, and I can't find him or the dining room or anything! I'm just hopeless!"

Mekashe's eyes had turned from the solid blue of introspection to the soft, twinkling green of amusement as he listened to her. She was substance out of his dreams. He could hardly believe it. She was tall and willowy, with perfect, beautiful features. She had blue eyes and wavy blond hair pulled up into an elegant hairdo with glittering jewel accents. She was wearing blue—a pale, soft blue gown that left her arms and her nape bare, but covered her completely from neck to toe in front and draped in soft folds down to her jeweled high-heel shoes. She was the most magnificent creature he'd ever seen in his life.

"I'm so sorry," she blurted when he didn't speak. She wondered if he spoke some other tongue than hers. Her high cheekbones colored red. "I apologize for…" she began loudly, as if he might be hard of hearing rather than raised in a separate language.

He held up a hand and smiled. "No apology is needed," he said in a deep, soft tone, in unaccented Standard. "The ship is extremely large and there are no virtual hubs to help you find your way. Where do you want to go?"

She studied him with utter fascination. "Did your eyes just change color?" she exclaimed, her eyes wide and unblinking on his golden-skinned face. He had eyes oddly like a cat. She was afraid of cats. But he was a man. He was a gorgeous man. She could overlook the eyes. They weren't really catlike at all, she thought.

He chuckled, or what passed for one in a Cehn-Tahr. "Yes," he said. "It is a characteristic of my race. The colors mirror moods." This much he was allowed by custom to discuss. The color changes were well-known.

"What is green?" she asked, truly interested.

"Amusement," he said softly.

"Oh!" She sighed. "I was afraid that I'd offended you!"

"If so, my eyes would be dark brown, not green," he replied.

"Are you an alien?" she asked. "I'm sorry, but I've never been off Terravega until we boarded this vessel. I saw a blue man just now!"

"Altair," he said. "Possibly Jebob. The eye colors are different, but they both come from the same ancestry."

"That's fascinating!"

So was she. He was entranced. She'd never been off-world. Never seen an alien. He'd been all over the three galaxies and had seen races that were even now almost unreal.

"Would you like me to escort you to the dining room?" he asked politely.

"That would be so kind of you!"

He managed a smile. It was foreign to his culture, but he studied human traits and often emulated them. It was a holdover from his infatuation with Edris Mallory.

"It would be my pleasure," he said, and bowed slightly.

She caught her breath. He was gorgeous. She'd never seen anyone so handsome, alien or human.

Unknown to her, he read those thoughts with delight. The attraction was mutual, it seemed.

"Are you on holiday?" she asked as they walked past bulkheads that lined the outer structure of the spacegoing ship.

He chuckled. "I am returning to my home, after attending a conference. I would have taken a shorter route, but my...employer said that I needed the downtime. So it will be weeks before I reach my destination."

She smiled. "Most people benefit from an occasional holiday. I know my poor father does. He was a college professor on Terravega—that's where we're from. He taught political science."

"An interest of mine," he replied.

She made a face. "I hate politics," she murmured.

His dark eyebrows lifted in an almost-human manner. "What subject do you prefer?"

"Medicine!" she said enthusiastically. "I wanted so desperately to be a surgeon, but my mother, God rest her soul, was horrified, even though she was a physician from the time she was out of secondary school."

"Why?" he asked gently.

"She said that I was far too innocent and sheltered for such a brutal profession." She sighed. "Besides that, the only career path I could find led through the military. When I mentioned that, Daddy got involved, and he and my mother blindsided me." She didn't add that she despised the military, so she hadn't fought them very hard.

He frowned. "Blindsided?"

"They joined forces to oppose me, before I knew what they were about," she translated with a laugh like tinkling bells. "I suppose they were right. I've never seen alien planets before, or been in space. This is such an adventure!" She looked up at him with soft blue eyes. "Have you been in space before?"

He'd lived in it most of his life, but he hesitated to admit that. "Yes. A time or two," he prevaricated.

She smiled. "I'd love to hear about it sometime." She flushed and averted her eyes. "I mean, if you'd like to talk to me. I'm daffy. I drive Daddy nuts. Most people avoid me because they think I'm scattered."

He stopped walking and just looked down at her. "These idioms." He chuckled. "I must confess that I need a translator." He said it softly, so that he didn't offend her. "The humans I've known used very few."

"I'm notorious for them, I'm afraid. What I mean is that I'm easily diverted and I don't concentrate well. Daddy says it's a sort of attention deficit disorder, but he doesn't believe in drugs, so he refused to let them give me any to correct it." She grimaced. "I suppose I sound like a lunatic…"

"I think you sound quite fascinating," he said quietly, and his eyes began to take on a soft, light brown color.

"Your eyes changed color again," she remarked, fascinated. "You aren't angry?" she added worriedly, because he'd said that brown meant anger.

He chuckled, or what substituted for laughter in a Cehn-Tahr. "Yes. The colors can become confusing when several emotions are involved." He nodded toward a door to avoid telling her that the soft brown meant affection. It was too soon for that. "I am not angry. The colors are more complicated than I can explain to you at the moment. The dining room is through here," he said, diverting her.

"I forgot to tell you my name. I'm Jasmine. Jasmine Dupont. Our ancestry, they say, is French, from ancient Earth. It's where all Terravegans come from."

"I am called Mekashe." He gave it the formal pronunciation.

"Mekashe." She flushed a little as she said it, and smiled delightedly. She hesitated. "Would you like to meet Daddy?" she blurted out, and flushed again, a darker pink. "I mean, if you'd like to, if I'm not imposing…"

"I should like it very much. Jasmine." He made her name sound exotic, foreign, thrilling.

She laughed. "Thank you…?" She hesitated, afraid that she was going to mess up the pronunciation.

"Mekashe," he repeated slowly. He gave it the pronunciation that a stranger would use on Memcache, because names were pronounced in many different ways among the Cehn-Tahr, depending on length of relationship, Clan status, position and so forth.

"Mekashe." She studied his strong, handsome face. "Do names have meanings among your people? I mean, my name is that of a flower on Terravega."

Even more fascinating. She reminded him of a flower, delicate and beautiful. "They do," he replied. "I was born on the day of a great battle, which ended well for my people. My name, among my own people, translates as 'He of the warrior blood.'"

"Oh." She hated the military, but she wouldn't mention that, not when she found him so attractive. She laughed then, lightening his expression. "I love it!"

He cocked his head. He smiled. She entranced him.

They stood staring at each other until another passenger came barreling out the door and almost collided with them. Jasmine staggered, but he didn't reach out to steady her. He ground his teeth together. If he touched her, even in an innocent way, it might trigger a mating behavior—especially considering the attraction he already felt. He saw her mild surprise at his lack of help, and he grimaced. He wasn't even allowed to explain it to her. One didn't elaborate on intimate customs among outworlders.

"There are reasons for my actions," he said, compromising. "I wish I could explain. But I can't."

"You aren't allowed to touch human females. Right?" she asked with certainty.

His eyebrows arched almost to his hairline.

She cleared her throat. "Sorry. Daddy says I'm always putting my foot into my mouth, figuratively speaking. I just plow right in, instead of thinking about what I'm saying. I sometimes offend people because I'm so impulsive."

"I'm not offended," he said gently, and smiled. "But I can't confirm or deny your supposition."

She laughed softly. Her blue eyes sparkled like jewels. "Okay."

She turned, reluctantly, and led the way into the dining room.

It was vast and like a maze. There were booths, formal tables and a bar all sharing the same general open space. Jasmine's father was seated at a formal, small table near the wall where the bubble port opened onto glorious space. A comet was passing by and her father had touched the viewscreen that doubled as a force shield, to magnify the comet in order to study it.

"He loves space," she told Mekashe as they walked. "He wanted to be a starship commander, but his health was bad. Back when he was a child, genetic engineering was out of fashion, so he had a bad heart and poor eyesight. He still has both. I'm afraid he doesn't move with the times at all. I do worry about him."

Mekashe was even more curious now.

Malford Dupont was forty-two, thin and graying, with a receding hairline and a stubborn chin. He seemed fascinated with the comet and oblivious to the two people approaching his table.

"Daddy?" Jasmine called softly.

His head jerked toward her and he blinked. He laughed. "Sorry, I find the comet absolutely fascinating. This tech is beyond anything I've ever known," he added, indicating the many functions of the screen that permitted magnification of space objects. His eyebrows lifted as he noted his daughter's companion.

"I got lost, again." Jasmine laughed. She looked up. "Mekashe helped me find my way here. Mekashe, this is my father, Dr. Malford Dupont."

"Sir," Mekashe said formally, and bowed. "A pleasure to make your acquaintance."

Jasmine's father stood and bowed, as well. "And mine, to make yours. Mekashe. You're Cehn-Tahr," he added, as if fascinated.

Mekashe nodded, a very human mannerism.

"Of all the coincidences." The other man chuckled. "In fact, Jasmine and I are en route to your home planet, Memcache. I was chosen to be the first human ambassador to the Cehn-Tahr."

Mekashe smiled. "I knew of the emperor's plan to allow such an embassy, but I had no knowledge of the person who would occupy the position. I am doubly honored to meet you. I hope that you and your daughter will be content on my planet."

"It really is a coincidence." Jasmine laughed, bubbling over with joy that her new friend lived on the very planet where her father would be stationed.

Mekashe smiled. "A delightful one."

"Won't you join us for dinner, young man?" the ambassador asked politely.

It was difficult to find a reason to refuse. He didn't want to. But the Cehn-Tahr were not vegetarians, and they ate most of their meals in a form that would offend human sensitivities. "I would have enjoyed it, but I have a prior commitment. Perhaps another time? Since we all seem to be equally confined on this vessel for a matter of weeks, we may find many opportunities to speak together."

"A true pleasure," Ambassador Dupont said, smiling. "Do you play chess, by any chance?"

Mekashe chuckled. "In fact, I do. I was taught by a human physician." He didn't mention that the physician was a clone, Dr. Strick Hahnson, who was a founding member of the Morcai Battalion. He didn't want to mention his military ties just yet. Better to let them see him as just an ordinary citizen of an alien world.

"I would enjoy a match. Perhaps tomorrow morning? As they reckon mornings aboard ship, at least," Dupont added.

"Just past the breakfast hour would suit me well," Mekashe said.

"I'll see you then."

"I wish you both a good evening." Mekashe bowed once more, gave Jasmine a lingering smile and left them.

Ambassador Dupont looked concerned as he watched Mekashe walk away.

"Is something wrong?" Jasmine asked when she sat down across from her father.

"We know so little about the Cehn-Tahr," he told her with an apologetic smile. "But I've heard rumors that they're easily offended. So you must be careful about the subjects you discuss with him. No politics. No religion."

She wrinkled her nose. "I never discuss politics. That's your department, Daddy, not mine," she said with a grin. "And religion is something I never discuss outside the family."

"Good," he replied. "I'm twitchy, I suppose. The first human ambassador ever to be invited to Memcache. I'm afraid of making a mistake and shaming our government." He made a face. "There were plenty of people who thought I was a bad choice in the first place. 'An academic,' they said in horror, 'what does he know about politics and interplanetary relations?'"

"I think you're wonderful," she said. "And you'll do fine. I promise I won't complicate things for you.

But Mekashe is very good-looking," she added with downcast eyes. "He doesn't even seem to think that I'm flighty." She looked up. "Maybe they don't have flighty people where he comes from."

He chuckled. "From all that I hear about them, and it's precious little, they're a pristine and moral people with a very strict society."

"The emperor's son is married to a human physician," she related. "Well, a former physician—Dr. Madeline Ruszel. There was a flash piece about her on a newscast I watched on the Nexus. She was fascinating."

"A true pioneer. A brigadier general—" he laughed "—and in command of a battalion of female troops. One of my colleagues almost fell over when the announcement was made. In the history of the Cehn-Tahr, there's never been a female in the military."

"They say the emperor indulges her." She sighed. "What a life she's had. And now she has two sons with her bonded mate!"

The ambassador didn't mention one other thing he'd been told in confidence, that there was some hush-hush genetic structuring to permit that mingling of very different DNA strands. He knew that the Cehn-Tahr had never mated outside their species before. On the other hand, Chacon, the famous Rojok field marshal, now head of the Rojok government, had bonded with the emperor's daughter, Lyceria. There were also rumors that the leader of their notorious Holconcom had bonded with a human female, as well.

It gave him comfort, because if the government on Memcache had that tolerant an attitude about racial mixing, it meant that he wouldn't have to walk on so many eggshells in the performance of his duties.

Just the same, he was uncomfortable about his only child. Jasmine was a sweet and kind young woman, but her tongue ran away with her at the best of times. It would be a disaster if she blurted something out that offended the emperor. He'd heard horror stories about old Tnurat's temper and the ease with which he took offense at any slight from outworlders.

But that might be an exaggeration. Until he actually met the people he'd be interacting with, it was just as well to ignore rumors and gossip and stick to facts.

"You're so serious!" she chided.

He laughed self-consciously. "I suppose I am. I'm just nervous. I've never done anything quite like this. The president of Terravega himself nominated me for the position and forced it through the houses of government. I don't want to let him down. I was given the post over several far more qualified professional politicians. The decision didn't sit well with them," he added with a sigh. "I suppose they'll be hoping that I'll trip and break my neck, leaving the job open for one of them."

"You'll be fine," she repeated, smiling. "You're so smart, Daddy. It's why they gave you the job. You get along well with people, too. Diplomacy is one skill I've never been able to conquer. I keep hoping, but my tongue just flaps at both ends." She laughed. "There I go again. Mekashe said he'd need a translator because of all the idioms I use."

"Cehn-Tahr speak most alien tongues, even the rare dialects," he replied. "I think he was just teasing you."

"I wonder what he does?" she said aloud. "I mean, he dresses well and this is an expensive form of travel…"

"We'll have plenty of time to find out in the weeks ahead," he assured her. "Meanwhile, eat your dinner before it gets cold."

She sighed as the table opened up and hot platters of food that they'd ordered from the foodcomp appeared as if by magic. The table folded back into itself with utensils and plates neatly placed and food arranged in the center.

"It's magic." Jasmine laughed as she watched. "I'd heard about these foodcomps, but I confess, I didn't quite believe the gossip."

"Tech is gaining ground in the galaxy," he agreed. "I've heard some amazing things about Kolmankash on Memcache. It's the most famous tech development center in the three galaxies. They say the tech there really is like magic."

"What sort of tech?"

He shook his head. "Nobody knows. The Cehn-Tahr don't share intimate knowledge of their culture with outworlders. All we get are whispers."

"Maybe Mekashe would take us there one day, to see the tech for ourselves," she said dreamily.

He raised both eyebrows. "Let's live one day at a time and not rush things," he said.

She sighed. "Okay. But it's hard."

"Many things are. And that's the truth," he agreed as he watched his coffee cup fill itself.

THE NEXT MORNING, Jasmine dressed with great care, in a very correct leisure gown of flared pale yellow skirts and a modest bodice that laced in front, with tiny sleeves that just covered her shoulders. Her bare arms were softly rounded, her nails manicured and trimmed. She wore her hair long, instead of in its usual high coiffure. It curled and waved down her back and fell around her shoulders in a pale blond cascade. She wore tiny aqua waterstones hooked in her earlobes, and used the lightest hint of a floral cologne. She hoped she looked good enough to impress a certain handsome alien.

She and her father had finished breakfast and were lounging in the recreation center at a wall table when Mekashe joined them.

He wore a very correct suit, with a banded shirt of

blue and white, and slacks that outlined his powerful legs. He smiled as Jasmine almost ran to meet him.

"You look very nice," he commented.

"So do you!" she burst out without thinking, and then flushed at her own boldness. "Daddy's got the chessboard set up already," she added quickly, to hide her self-consciousness.

"Good morning," the new ambassador greeted, standing long enough to give Mekashe a formal bow, which was returned.

"Daddy was chess champion of the college where he taught," she said.

"Indeed. Impressive," Mekashe said politely.

"Well, reputations are easily destroyed, I'm afraid." The ambassador chuckled. "I daresay you'll beat the socks off me without much effort."

"Socks." Mekashe looked blank.

"They're worn on the feet with shoes. Casual shoes," Jasmine explained. "A very ancient sort of apparel. It means that you'll win."

"An odd manner of expression. Apologies," he added with a smile.

"None needed," the older man assured him. "Most idioms are odd, and I've come across them in an amazing array of human languages."

"Truly, we find them in alien tongues, as well," Mekashe said. He chuckled, or what passed for chuckling in a Cehn-Tahr. "There are several dialects of Rojok, including a quite ancient one which was never spoken by a human until Dr. Edris Mallory came along."

"Dr. Mallory?" the ambassador asked softly.

He nodded. "She was a Cularian specialist before she bonded with a Cehn-Tahr of my acquaintance."

Jasmine's eyes widened. "I've heard many stories about Dr. Madeline Ruszel, but they don't mention Dr. Mallory in the flash reports."

"As you may have already gathered, we share very little of our culture with—" he hesitated to offend by saying "outworlders" "—other cultures," he said instead.

"I'm quite good at keeping secrets," the ambassador said, smiling. He glanced at his child a little warily. "My daughter, however…"

"I can so keep a secret," she said, and made a face at him. "Well, really important ones, at least. I'm so excited that we're actually going to live on your planet!" she added to Mekashe.

He smiled. "I think you will find it quite beautiful."

"Does it look like Terravega?" she asked at once.

He shook his head. "We have no pressure domes, nor is there a need for them." He cocked his head at her. "If you would like to see Memcache, I can arrange for a holo of it in one of the rooms."

"I would love that!" Jasmine enthused.

"You are also welcome to view it," Mekashe told the ambassador easily, and smiled again. "It will help you to understand us if you see the manner in which we live."

"But you said that you couldn't share things with people outside your culture," Jasmine began, puzzled.

"An ambassador and his family would hardly qualify as people outside," he said gently. "Since you will be living among us. The taboo only applies to those who have no connection with us."

"I see." She beamed.

He was entranced by her beauty. He had thought her gorgeous the night before, but in the artificial light of "day," she was even more exquisite. Her hair fascinated him. It was long and curling and glorious. He ached to touch it.

He cleared his throat as he seated himself across the chessboard from the human. "So," he began. "Who goes first?"

JASMINE ENJOYED WATCHING the match. Mekashe won with staggering ease, but the ambassador was good-natured and didn't seem to mind.

Meanwhile, Jasmine was filling her fascinated eyes with their guest. She'd never been so entranced by a male of any species. He had thick black hair. It had a definite wave to it. He kept it short, but she could imagine that if it had grown long, it might have the same curl that her own did.

He had a very muscular physique. She wondered

what he did for a living, because he didn't seem the sort of man to be a diplomat or even a sedate aristocrat. He had the hard, honed look of a man who made his living in ways that might not fit in parlor society.

She wondered at the quick look Mekashe gave her while she processed the thought, almost as if he read her mind. She laughed to herself. She'd never read that any of the Cehn-Tahr were telepaths. She was being fanciful.

"You're quite skilled, young man," the ambassador mused.

Mekashe laughed. He was, by human measure, over two hundred and fifty years old. The ambassador, in his forties, had no idea of the true life span of the race he was going to live among. Nor was it Mekashe's place to tell him so much, not yet, at least. He could share images of Memcache, since the ambassador and his daughter would live there. He could even share common knowledge, like the ability of Cehn-Tahr eyes to change color. But anything more intimate was taboo.

"You have great skill yourself," Mekashe replied. "But I have been playing for a longer time than you might imagine."

The ambassador lifted an eyebrow and smiled secretly. He'd been told by Admiral Lawson that the Cehn-Tahr had somewhat modified life spans, and they put human age in the shade. He didn't share the knowledge.

Mekashe read it and averted his eyes, so that he didn't give away his telepathic abilities. "Another match?" he asked.

The ambassador chuckled and started setting up the pieces.

MEKASHE LEFT THEM just before luncheon was served, with the excuse that he had to report to his employer through the Nexus.

"What sort of work do you do?" Jasmine asked innocently.

"I am attached to the political wing of my society," he said evasively, but with a smile. "My employer works at the Dectat."

"I see." She had no idea what a Dectat was.

"You seem disappointed," he teased. "Did you think I might be secretly a pirate?"

She gasped and laughed out loud, beaming up at him. "Oh no. At least, I would never have said so…!"

"Liar," he teased gently.

She flushed delightfully. "You just don't seem like a man who does a desk job. That's all," she told him.

He wasn't. She'd read him quite accurately, without knowing a thing about him. A good omen, perhaps.

He studied her with aching eyes. He wanted desperately to touch her, at least to brush that amazing hair with his fingertips and see if it was as soft as it looked. He couldn't. There was no way…

He had a thought. Hahnson might know a way. The human physician had, in times long past, been bonded with a Cehn-Tahr female. Mekashe knew nothing about the relationship, but he did know that it had existed. He could contact Hahnson. It would not be taboo to speak with a man who had Cehn-Tahr citizenship and who was best friends with the emperor's son about a delicate subject like that.

"You look odd," Jasmine remarked.

"I've had a rather delightful thought," he mused.

"Can I know what it is?"

He shook his head and smiled. "Not just yet. There is a lecture on comet patterns on the observation deck this evening. I plan to attend. If you and your father wish to join me…"

"We'd love to come!" she interrupted, certain that her father would find it fascinating. And she could be with Mekashe again.

He read that thought with utter delight. "Then I'll see you on the observation deck just after dinner."

"I'll be there. With Daddy," she added reluctantly.

The reluctance she displayed about her father's presence made him feel warm inside. He made her a soft bow and left her, his mind whirling with possibilities.

CHAPTER TWO

MEKASHE HAD TO go through channels to get to Dr. Strick Hahnson aboard the Holconcom flagship, Morcai. That meant he had first to speak to its commander, his best friend, Rhemun.

"What are you doing aboard a commercial vessel?" Rhemun asked as the holon was initiated and his friend was standing in the room with him in a three-dimensional figure that could be interacted with. The avatar had the same flesh-and-blood reality as its original. They locked forearms in a show of affection.

"I have a problem," Mekashe confessed, laughing. He reverted to his true form in the communication, not the almost-human-looking one he shared with outworlders. His true form was larger, taller, more massive than the camouflaged one. He had a face just a little more catlike than the familiar humanoid one that he showed to strangers, with a broad nose and a thick mane, and ears that were placed slightly differently than a human's. There was no visible fur and he had no tail, as cats did. But the resemblance to a galot—the sentient cats of Eridanus Three—was notable, even if Cehn-Tahr were humanoid enough not to raise eyebrows in a crowd.

"What sort of problem?" Rhemun asked.

"One of the heart," came the amused reply. "I told you when we were boys, about the visions I had…"

"…of a tall, willowy blonde human female, yes, I recall." Rhemun gave a mock glare. "You thought it might be Edris, despite her lack of height."

Mekashe laughed. "I must confess that I did. But I have now encountered the living vision." He drew in a breath. "She is magnificent," he added. "Beyond my dreams."

Rhemun cocked his head. "And this is a problem?"

"We have only just met," his friend replied, dropping into a chair beside Rhemun's desk. "I do not wish to rush things. The emperor forced me to take a civilian mode of transport," he began.

"Yes, because you refuse R & R and he thinks you push yourself too hard. Your lieutenant is performing admirably in your absence."

"Just as well, because I now have no desire to rush home. However, she will be coming with me when I arrive." He grinned at his friend's surprise. "Her father is our new Terravegan ambassador."

Rhemun burst out laughing. "Now, that is a true coincidence," he remarked.

"As I thought, also." He drew in a long breath.

"So, as you see, I must go carefully forward. I feel an attraction that I do not wish to get out of hand. I want to approach Hahnson for advice," he added. "But for that, I must have your permission. And your promise of silence."

"The emperor will know," Rhemun began.

Mekashe pulled out a small, glowing white ball. It would conceal thoughts from a telepath, even one as formidable as old Tnurat. "This is an innovation on the original design," he confessed. "I must not announce my feelings to the emperor just yet."

Rhemun understood. "There will be no issue," he said. "The emperor reveres humans since Madeline Ruszel has given him two beautiful grandchildren."

"Still, I must not rush things. I belong, as you do, to the Royal Clan. There are rumors, and only rumors, that too much mixing with the humans might provoke difficulties in the Dectat."

Rhemun smiled. "Not as long as Tnurat rules. Did you not hear that he punched the president of the Dectat for an altercation with Dtimun over Ruszel's rescue when her ship crashed on Akaashe?"

Mekashe chuckled. "I did, indeed. That is a long-standing feud."

"Both are stubborn."

"Good leaders."

"Agreed." Rhemun got up. "You have my permission to speak to Hahnson, and I promise not to mention it until you give me equal permission." He chuckled. "Will that do?"

"Indeed it will."

"I wish you great good fortune with the ambassador's daughter. And I look forward to meeting her, as well."

"How is Edris?" Mekashe asked.

"Recovering very well. Would you like to see our daughter?" he added.

"Yes!"

Rhemun pulled out a miniature holo and held it up. There was a tiny, black-headed baby in the cradle of her beaming mother's arms. Edris, looking as lovely as ever before, and Kipling, their son, standing beside his mother, grinning.

"This is Larisse," he said with pride.

"A delightful child! She will look more like you than Kipling does, I think," Mekashe commented.

"I think so, as well. She is the light of my life already, as my son and my mate already were." The little girl was only the second female born into Clan Alamantimichar in thousands of years. Princess Lyceria was the first.

"I rejoice in your good fortune," Mekashe said. "And I look forward to rejoicing in my own!"

"Speak to Hahnson. I'll see you before you leave, yes?"

"Of course!"

STRICK HAHNSON LOOKED more like a wrestler than a physician. He had been with the Morcai Battalion since its creation, in the horror of the Rojok death camp, Ahkmau. At least, his original had been. The true Hahnson was tortured and killed by the Rojoks, who were trying to find an almost fatally ill Dtimun hidden in the camp by his cellmates. Dtimun had cloned the physician for Captain Holt Stern and Dr. Madeline Ruszel as recompense for snatching them out of the Terravegan Strategic Space Command and into the ranks of his newly formed Morcai Battalion. It had been a bittersweet reunion. Stern, too, was a clone. In the old days, the two of them would never have been able to return to Terravegan society because they were clones. There was a terrible prejudice there. But the emperor, out of gratitude for their help in saving his son, had given all the humans of the Morcai Battalion Cehn-Tahr citizenship. The clones of the Holconcom, and the human ones, had meshed quite well together.

Hahnson looked up, surprised to see Mekashe walking into his lab. He grinned and locked forearms. "What a nice surprise," he enthused. "How in the world did you get here without the ship alerting everybody?"

"The holon," Mekashe said easily, and with a smile. Hahnson was one of only a handful of humans who knew about the holon tech. "I have a very personal matter to discuss."

"Still amazes me," Strick said, walking around the Tri-D3-d image to study Mekashe. "I can even touch you," he added, doing it, "and you feel real."

"It suffices, when mates are separated," the other male remarked wickedly.

"Well, sit down. How are you liking your new job? And why are you here?"

Mekashe took out the white noise ball and put it on the table. "New tech," he told Hahnson. "It can even block the emperor. You did not hear me say this, because I am not here."

"Absolutely," Hahnson agreed, grinning.

"You were bonded to a Cehn-Tahr during the end of the Great Galaxy War, were you not?" Mekashe asked, very solemnly. "I apologize for bringing up such a painful subject," he added quickly when he saw the look on Hahnson's face.

"It was a long time ago." Hahnson took a deep breath. "I have all the memories of my original, including that one. She was a suicide. After all the years in between, it still is an agony to remember."

"A suicide?" Mekashe asked, stunned.

"You didn't know. It's all right. Only a very few people do." He sat down. "It's something I don't talk about. But, yes, we were bonded."

"Which is why I'm permitted to discuss something quite intimate with you," Mekashe hastened to add. "You know what rigid rules of culture permeate our society."

"I do," the other male said.

Mekashe locked his hands together and studied them. "I have met a female. A human." He managed a faint smile. "For many years, I had a vision of such a human. I knew her, without knowing her, almost all my life. I thought at first that Edris Mallory was her personification. But in my visions, the female found me equally attractive, and Edris had eyes only for Rhemun." He lifted his eyes to Hahnson's. "Now I have met the true female, the one from the visions. She is everything I knew, all that I expected. But the attraction I feel for her is growing too quickly. I have no desire to frighten her or shock her. Like most humans, she has no idea about the mating rituals, how deadly they can be to other males. I want to touch her." He bit off the words and made a face, like a grimace. "But I dare not. I was wondering, hoping, that there might be some bit of medical tech that could permit touch without the danger of triggering a mating behavior."

"I think I have just what you need," Hahnson said, moving to his medicomp. "In fact, you're in luck, because this is cutting-edge tech, only just released. It was meant for diplomatic use, but I understand that it has been employed covertly for a number of other reasons."

"What does it do?"

"It coats the skin in nanobytes," Hahnson said. He pulled up a top secret vid, showing the range of protection it encompassed. "It's undetectable, much like certain poisons developed on old Earth millennia ago."

"And it can be trusted not to fail?" the alien asked with some concern.

Hahnson shook his head. "Well, as far as we know." He hesitated. He was the physician for the human element aboard the Morcai, not their resident Cularian expert who specialized in Cehn-Tahr, Rojok and other alien species. But he heard from Tellas, Edris Mallory's former assistant, that Mekashe had physiology much like Dtimun, who was the product of generations of genetic improvement.

"Something disturbs you," Mekashe perceived.

Hahnson shrugged. "It's probably nothing," he said after a minute. "You know that there can be issues between different species, especially in intimate contact."

"Yes, I know of this," Mekashe said easily. He smiled. "It is not a concern."

What he meant was that he knew Rhemun had no difficulty in mating with Edris, and he also knew that Dtimun and Madeline Ruszel had mated and produced two children. He had no idea that Rhemun's branch of the Clan had no genetic modification or that Madeline had to undergo genetic modification to mate with Dtimun.

Hahnson, who assumed that the other Cehn-Tahr had made him aware of the issues, just smiled. "Okay, then. I'll just create a few vials of the tech so that you won't run out. How long is this trip going to take?"

"Several weeks," Mekashe said with a wistful sigh. "I look forward to getting to know Jasmine."

"Jasmine. A lovely name."

"She is a lovely creature," Mekashe replied softly. "I have never encountered such a being in all my travels. She has no hauteur at all, no sense of superiority. She is humble and sweet and—how did she put it?—scattered."

Hahnson's eyebrows went up and he chuckled while he worked. "I like her already."

"Her father seems quite nice," he added. "He will be the first Terravegan ambassador to Memcache. An intelligent man, with a background in history and politics. He was a professor of political science on Terravega."

Hahnson frowned. "An odd choice for an ambassador."

"I thought this, as well. Most political figures are, well, less than brilliant."

Hahnson grinned. "And, in fact, some of them are stupid."

"I would put the former Terravegan ambassador in that class without fail," Mekashe recalled. "Although Taylor was never allowed to set foot on Memcache. Dtimun hated him."

"So did most of the humans in the Holconcom, especially after he denied permission for us to launch a rescue effort when Madeline Ruszel's ship went down on Akaashe."

"Those were dark days. Taylor was executed for treason for his collusion with the Rojoks during the war. I did not mourn. Those were dark days."

"Very dark," Hahnson replied. "Madeline was special. She is special. She and Stern and I served together for ten years. We'd have gladly died for her. Ambassador Taylor not only refused permission to search for her crashed ship, he recalled all Terravegan personnel from other services. We actually had to mutiny to stay in the Holconcom and go with Dtimun to save her."

"A noble undertaking."

Hahnson smiled. "Noble, indeed." He finished programming the medicomp and glanced at his companion. "Did you know that Chacon himself went to negotiate with the Nagaashe for Madeline's release?"

"Chacon and also the emperor, if gossip serves," Mekashe replied.

"Absolutely. She had powerful allies, even back then. She saved the emperor's life on Ondar."

"We heard about that from Rhemun," Mekashe said. He chuckled. "He was fascinated with her even before they met. Dtimun had some small jealousy of him, in fact, before Komak was born."

"It wouldn't have mattered. Madeline was crazy about the CO almost from the beginning." He shook his head. "You can't imagine the shock when she and

Dtimun came aboard the Morcai after their trip to Benaski Port to save Chacon's life, and Madeline was pregnant. Talk about gossip that went on for days…!"

"I imagine it was intense."

"Very, especially under the circumstances," Hahnson agreed, not understanding that Mekashe had no idea what he meant. "In the history of the Cehn-Tahr, there had never been a child born of a human mother and a Cehn-Tahr father."

"Because of the racial laws," Mekashe agreed.

"Well, that, too," Hahnson conceded. He tossed the vials into a vacuum bag and passed it to his former crewmate. "That should be more than enough. But just in case, you can flash me and I can have more couriered to you aboard the passenger ship. You know to watch for signs of allergic reaction, right? Any swelling, redness, sore throat, rash, things like that."

"I have an amazing constitution." Mekashe chuckled. "I am never allergic to anything."

"That isn't what they say," his companion replied, tongue in cheek. "Wasn't there something about you and a flagon of synthale in a bar somewhere on Kurkason…?"

Mekashe cleared his throat. "That was a long time ago. During an unfortunate hunt that ended out on the rim. I was younger."

"Ah. That would explain it. A few broken bones,

a diplomatic incident—the emperor had to intervene with the local authorities…?"

Mekashe almost blushed.

Hahnson grinned. "Sorry. Couldn't resist it. You guys are so formidable that it tickles us humans when you slip, even though you very rarely do. We don't feel so inferior."

"Humans are hardly inferior," Mekashe retorted. "We have different areas of advantage. Ours is strength and speed. Yours is compassion and tenacity."

"Thanks," Hahnson said.

"It makes for an interesting combination, the humans and Cehn-Tahr in the Holconcom," Mekashe replied. "I miss the unit," he added gently. "While it is a great honor to command the kehmatemer, the emperor's personal bodyguard, I miss pitting my skill against Rhemun's in the Kahn-Bo."

"I think he misses it, too. But his son, Kipling, is almost as formidable as you are, on the mat."

"Kipling and Dtimun's son, Komak, are almost old enough to join the military. Although, between us, I think Kipling will be the greater warrior. Komak enjoys more cerebral pursuits. I think he may make a scientist, like his grandmother the empress."

"She is formidable."

"Yes, indeed." He held up the vacuum pack. "Thank you for this."

"You're most welcome. I wish you great good fortune."

Mekashe frowned slightly. "You sounded as if more than the racial laws kept Ruszel and Dtimun apart," he began.

Just as he said it, the alert sounded. Rhemun's deep voice came over the intership frequency, in Cehn-Tahr, announcing a mission and calling for all hands to report immediately to their stations.

"It doesn't matter." Mekashe shrugged it off with a smile. "Thank you, again."

"My pleasure. We'll talk again."

"Certainly."

HE STOPPED BACK by the command deck to say his farewells to Rhemun.

"I miss the excitement of these engagements," he confessed to his friend, who was forwarding new orders to his officers over the vid screen.

"I sometimes miss guarding the emperor." Rhemun chuckled. "But we must do what our Clan status dictates."

"We must. Thank you for allowing me access to Hahnson. I'll be in touch."

"Keep well."

"And you."

MEKASHE SWITCHED OFF the holon, after he retrieved the vacuum bag from the device, where it was captured just before his departure from the Morcai. The technology was amazing, even to the Cehn-Tahr who had used it for generations. It was almost undetectable as apart from reality. The ability to touch and taste, to physically interact with other humanoids, was like magic.

He was grateful, because he'd never have been able to make the trip in real time to rendezvous with the Morcai and retrieve his precious cargo before the passenger ship docked at Memcache. And he didn't want to waste a single second of this new and exciting relationship he was beginning with Jasmine.

HE USED A trace of the nanotech on his hands and face and hoped fervently that it would work as intended. He couldn't afford to trigger a mating behavior, not now. He did wonder at what Hahnson had said, about the racial laws being in addition to some other concern about interspecies mating. But he put it out of his mind. Surely it was insignificant.

He went out to meet Jasmine and her father, dressed in a modern suit that was adapted to Cehn-Tahr standards. It was of a soft fabric that emphasized the powerful muscles in his arms and legs, and of a soft blue color that highlighted his pale gold skin and thick, jet-black hair.

Jasmine almost ran to meet him when he came into the lounge area. She was dressed in a very becoming soft blue dress that fell to her ankles. It flowed around her slender body. Like the other dress he'd seen her wear, it was extremely conservative, with a high neckline and long sleeves, in a floral blue pattern.

"How well we match," Mekashe teased.

She flushed and her blue eyes twinkled. "Yes, we do."

"A good omen," he added in his soft, deep voice. "Do you like opera?"

Her lips fell open. "Oh, I love it!"

"I arranged to get tickets for the performance tomorrow evening of a Terravegan opera company. They are performing something called *Madama Butterfly*." He frowned. "Does it have something to do with a form of insect...?"

She laughed, delighted. "No. I'll explain it to you," she said. "If that was an invitation, I would love to go. With you," she added.

His heart lifted. "I can get another ticket, if your father...?"

"Hates opera," she said at once, and flushed at her boldness. "He likes music, but he prefers instrumentals."

His smile broadened. "Then he won't mind if I escort just you?"

"I'm certain that he won't," she said. "I'm of age, you know," she added quickly, in case he thought she had to have her parent's permission. After all, eighteen was considered adult status now, with the small wars ongoing in the three galaxies. Most of the regular space navy and army recruits were themselves eighteen. A politician had written the current law, with the justification that if a soldier was old enough to die for his political affiliation, he was old enough to be considered an adult and served liquor in a bar.

Mekashe had never considered her age. She seemed not much removed from that of Princess Lyceria, who was also young at barely seventy years. He didn't realize that humans had life spans far abbreviated from that of Cehn-Tahr, who could live for hundreds of years. In fact, Mekashe himself had seen two hundred and fifty years.

They stood in the corridor, staring at each other, smiling, while passengers walked around them with amused, hidden smiles.

"I suppose we're blocking traffic," Mekashe said after a near collision with a very heavy passenger. "We should go."

"Yes...!" She caught her breath as he reached for her hand and slowly closed his big one around it.

The contact was electrifying, but it didn't produce any unwanted urges to attack other males. Apparently, Hahnson's nanotech worked well.

Mekashe smiled at her look of surprise. "In special cases, we can touch humans," he said after a few seconds. "The racial laws forbidding it have been repealed. However, I had to make certain requests," he added nebulously.

Her fingers, cool and shivery, closed shyly around his big hand. He felt very warm. She studied his hard, handsome face. "You're very warm," she said hesitantly.

He smiled. "My body temperature is somewhere around three degrees warmer than that of a human. You feel nicely cool to me."

"How fascinating," she exclaimed. She studied him. "You look like a human with what we call a golden tan," she added. "Except for your eyes changing color, you don't look any different from us."

A misconception, he thought, and a large one. But he didn't correct it.

"Have you seen a lot of aliens?" she asked after a minute.

He nodded. "Many."

"Do they all look like you and me?" she wanted to know.

He pursed his lips. "There is a species of giant serpent, which we call the Nagaashe, who are the height of a two-story building. They are vegetarians. They have blue eyes and they purr."

She caught her breath. "I'm deathly afraid of serpents," she said, shivering. "They're very dangerous."

"The Nagaashe belong to the Tri-Galaxy Council," he told her. "They are sentient and telepathic."

"Amazing!"

"There are also species with tentacles instead of legs, and a rare sort of giant spider that feeds on salt water and plankton."

"All I've ever seen were other humans," she told him wistfully. "I'm so afraid that I'll embarrass Daddy by blurting out something unforgivable in company. I'm very unsophisticated."

"I find you charming, Jasmine," he said softly. "And I cannot believe that you would ever be an embarrassment to anyone, least of all your parent."

She smiled broadly. "Thanks."

He cocked his head. "Do you have other family?" he asked.

"You mean siblings?" She shook her head. "No. My mother was killed in an accident. Daddy never wanted to remarry."

He studied her soft, beautiful face and thought that he knew how that felt. He'd never known love between a male and a female, but he was certain that if Jasmine became his consort, he would never be able to look at another female, no matter what happened.

"You aren't going to have to leave, before we get to Memcache?" she asked worriedly as they walked slowly toward the recreation area.

"No. Why?"

She glanced up and away. "Well, I don't really know anybody else aboard, and Daddy's always got his nose stuck in a virtual book. It's very lonely." She flushed.

He chuckled and his big hand tightened around hers.

"Ouch!" she said suddenly.

He loosened his hold. "Too tight? Forgive me," he said.

Her hand felt incredibly bruised, but she only smiled and said it was all right. She noticed that he was more careful when he claimed her hand again. She'd never known someone so strong.

He felt guilty when he saw her discomfort. He hadn't realized that he was hurting her. Perhaps humans were a little more fragile than he'd expected. He'd speak to Hahnson about that the next time he saw him.

They joined Dr. Dupont at one of the tables and listened with fascination to a virtual lecture about the periodic comets in this region of space and their relationship to the dark matter surrounding it.

Jasmine tried very hard to concentrate on what was said, but her hand was oddly painful. She wondered at the strength in Mekashe's hand. Her hand felt bruised, but she wasn't going to mention it. She knew that he hadn't meant to hurt her. He was very strong!

AFTER THE LECTURE, they walked out in the corridor and Mekashe grimaced as he had a flash on his communications ring.

"I must speak with a colleague below," he said, not wanting to mention that Tresar, a fellow member of the Royal Clan and a member of the emperor's Imperial Guard, like Mekashe, asked to see him. Tresar disliked morphing into the human form that Mekashe used so easily, so he stayed in his true form and out of sight. He would never venture farther than the gym. "I hate to leave so soon. But tomorrow night, the opera?" he asked Jasmine.

"I'll look forward to it," she said with breathless enthusiasm.

He glanced at her father, glad to see that he was smiling. "Perhaps another chess match tomorrow?" he asked.

The ambassador chuckled. "Of course!"

"Then I'll see you both tomorrow," he said, glancing at Jasmine with a smile as he left, very reluctantly.

She watched him until he was out of sight.

THE NEXT MORNING, Jasmine was waiting in the corridor when she spotted Mekashe. She went to him, excited, almost running. "Good morning!" she said, laughing with pleasure.

"Good morning," he replied huskily. "Did you sleep well?"

"I barely slept at all," she said breathlessly, looking up at him with wonder.

"Nor did I," he replied. He reached for her hand and cradled it in his, very gently this time.

They stood looking at each other until they were jostled by other guests and realized they were blocking the way to the dining room.

Mekashe laughed as he turned and drew her along with him to the table where her father was sitting. He could hear her heart beat, it was so loud. It made him feel joyful to know how attracted she already was.

Ambassador Dupont was waiting for them with a chessboard already set up on the table. "Good morning," he said to Mekashe, and chuckled when he noticed his daughter holding hands with their guest.

"Good morning." Mekashe let go of Jasmine's hand reluctantly and sat down at the table with the new ambassador. "I have looked forward to this game. Few of my acquaintances are familiar with it."

"I have the same issue. It's nice to find someone who shares the interest."

"Daddy, Mekashe is taking me to the opera tonight. Okay?" Jasmine asked hurriedly.

"Of course." Dr. Dupont grinned at her. "Do I hear a gown request forming in your mind?"

She flushed. "Well, my old one is outdated," she began.

He tugged his credit chip out of his pocket and handed it to her. "Have fun," he said, waving her away.

She laughed. "I'll buy something beautiful," she said. "I won't be long!"

Ambassador Dupont watched her go with twinkling eyes. "She was dreading this move. Thank you for giving her something to look forward to," he added. "She's been painfully sheltered and I've pretty much thrown her into the deep end of the swimming pool. She'd never seen an alien before we boarded this vessel."

"She seems to be doing remarkably well," Mekashe said.

"That's because she hasn't seen a race that she considers frightening yet," the professor said with a sigh. He shook his head. "I showed her a vid of the Vegan delegation and I thought she was going to have heart failure. And they're very humanoid."

"She will adjust," Mekashe said gently.

"She'll have to. I just pray that she doesn't say anything impulsive and cause offense. Of course, on Memcache, there are people just like us, so there shouldn't be any surprises."

Which meant that Jasmine didn't know, nor did her father, that the Cehn-Tahr weren't what they appeared. He felt a momentary twinge of fear at the thought that Jasmine might find him frightening. But then, he was facing problems before they appeared. It was stupid.

"You may go first," Mekashe told the professor with a smile.

The other humanoid chuckled. "Fine. Queen to queen's pawn four," he said, in the classic opening move.

JASMINE STOPPED BY the surgery on her way to purchase the dress. She hadn't wanted to mention how painful her hand really was, where Mekashe had held it the night before. She hadn't slept because it felt so badly bruised. She hadn't wanted to say anything about it to Mekashe, who would be horrified to know that he'd caused her so much pain. She couldn't bear to hurt his feelings. But the pain was really bad and she was going to have to let a doctor look at her hand.

"I slammed a drawer on it," she explained to the surgeon on call with a faint grimace. "Is it a bad bruise?"

"It's a bad break, young woman," the older man said quietly. "No worries, I can fix it. But you must be more careful. Even with our modern tech, broken bones can be tricky, especially the tiny ones in the hand."

"I'll be careful," she promised.

She was shocked. She hadn't realized how strong Mekashe's hands were. She knew that he hadn't meant to hurt her. But the injury made her nervous. If just holding hands could cause such damage, what about anything more?

CHAPTER THREE

BUT MEKASHE DID realize he'd been too aggressive with her, when he noticed that she gave him her other hand to hold, not the right one. The virtual ball he carried in his pocket, to protect against unexpected telepathic intrusions, blanked out Jasmine's thoughts. However, he'd seen the pain in her expression when she drew back from him the night before and he'd noticed her discomfort this morning. It was disturbing, especially when she rejoined them with a dress in a bag and let slip that she'd seen the ship's surgeon.

"Oh, it was nothing," she lied. "I slammed the drawer on my hand last night, but the doctor mended it," she added quickly, and chided herself for blurting out the news of her visit to the surgery. Mekashe looked drawn and worried. "I'm okay. Really!" she added to reassure him.

He started to apologize, but she only laughed and said she wanted to try on her new dress. She left them staring at the chessboard.

MEKASHE WAS CRESTFALLEN. He wanted very much to hold Jasmine. But it might take extra precautions, especially now that he knew he'd damaged her hand.

He used the communicator this time, instead of the holon, to speak to Hahnson directly.

"My strength has always been an issue," he told the physician. "Even among my friends, when I was a boy, I had to be careful. But I bruised Jasmine's hand because I was overly...stimulated." He hesitated. "Is there some way, some covert way, that I can lessen her impact on me, just for a little while?"

"Dravelzium," Hahnson said easily. "Two ccs, in the artery at your neck," he added. "The ship's surgeon should have the chemicals necessary to prepare it. Would you like me to speak to him for you? I won't mention the woman," he added, smiling to himself.

Mekashe relaxed. "That would be kind of you. As you know, we have issues with outworld physicians. Not with you," he said, with a brown-eyed smile, which denoted the affection that all Cehn-Tahr had for the Morcai's medical chief of staff.

"That's only because I belong to the Holconcom," Hahnson teased.

Mekashe hesitated. He was having second thoughts. "It may provoke questions..."

"I was just thinking that myself," Hahnson replied, interrupting him. "You hold a high position in the Cehn-Tahr government, and she's the daughter of the first Terravegan ambassador to Memcache. I'm certain the ship's surgeon wouldn't gossip, but the confidentiality rule sometimes escapes people who work in the infirmary."

"A thought that presented itself." Mekashe grimaced. "Is there another way?"

"I can send you an injector and several of the discs for it," Hahnson said. "It's not difficult to do. I'll send detailed instructions with it. Do you have access to a holo printer?"

"I have one in my quarters. The emperor insisted when he made me promise to take the scenic route home. Any urgent documents could be forwarded to me without the risk of hacked communications."

"A novel solution. I'll forward the whole package directly to you. We won't have to involve the ship's surgeon." Hahnson sighed. "I fear that he might ask some serious questions. Humans only use dravelzium to tranquilize large mammals, particularly on outlying farms."

"Which Terravegans have no part of." Mekashe chuckled. "They're all vegetarians."

"Not quite all," Hahnson replied. "I have it on good authority that Professor Dupont—excuse me, Ambassador Dupont—is quite fond of a good steak. Although I don't know about his daughter's dietary habits." He frowned. "Do you dine with them?"

Mekashe shook his head. "I hesitate to share such intimate knowledge of our culture, even with humans to whom I grow close. Our comrades in the

Holconcom already know that we eat our food raw and whole."

"It might be a conversation killer over dinner with humans who don't know that," Hahnson murmured drily.

"Of a certainty." He hesitated. "I was on leave when Dtimun had the Cehn-Tahr reveal themselves to their crewmates. Do you remember when the human contingent of the Holconcom saw us as we are for the first time?" he added. "Was it...traumatic?"

"Well, no," Hahnson said. "Not actually. But you have to remember, all of us—us meaning my original self—and you, were in the Rojok prison camp, Ahkmau, together. We had the memory of the sacrifices and horror of that place. It outweighed any surprise at the real face of the Cehn-Tahr. We were so fond of all of you by then that it wouldn't have mattered to us if you'd had two heads and three legs."

Mekashe smiled. "As we became fond of all of you. I do have memories of the prison camp, because I was a member of the Holconcom at the time, although a very junior one. It was traumatic. There were many atrocities."

"They were nightmarish," Hahnson said. He studied Mekashe's face in the Tri-D setup and frowned slightly. "Is there a more pressing reason that you need the dravelzium?" he asked delicately.

Mekashe hesitated. "I haven't experienced any of the mating behaviors," he replied. "However...I held Jasmine's hand and I think I bruised it. She is delicately built."

Hahnson smiled. "Normal humans are weaker than Cehn-Tahr. You might consider disabling some of your microcyborgs. Just to be on the safe side."

He frowned. He had no microcyborgs. Just as Dtimun had the advanced genetic restructuring, so did Mekashe. He had wholeheartedly accepted the modifications, without hesitation, in the past, when he joined the military as an adolescent, shortly before the deaths of both his parents.

The ship alarms sounded. Hahnson glanced at his computer console. "Sorry, have to run. We're chasing insurgents in the Eridanus system. I hope we can avoid Eridanus Three. Even if Kanthor's there, we could be eaten by some of his less welcoming brothers," he added with a chuckle, making reference to the giant cats, the galot, from which Cehn-Tahr had gained genetic material, including psychic abilities. Kanthor was Dtimun's childhood playmate.

"That would be unfortunate," Mekashe replied. He grinned. "In such case, you should all consume vegetables before you make port. No self-respecting galot will eat a vegetarian, on principle."

Hahnson laughed out loud. "I'll remind everybody. Listen, I'll get this package right to your holo printer. And good luck!"

"Thank you."

He cut the connection, and then worried about

what Hahnson had said. He had no microcyborgs to disable. Hahnson had no need to know about his personal physiology, because there was always a Cularian surgeon aboard ship, who dealt with the Cehn-Tahr and Jebob and even Rojok casualties that sometimes were lifted by the Morcai to medical ships. Hahnson didn't know that Mekashe needed no augmentation of his true strength. He wondered why he would need to weaken himself. Were humans so fragile?

He recalled Jasmine's look of pain when his hand had tightened on hers the night before and grimaced. Apparently, he was going to have to modify his strength in order not to harm her. Well, the dravelzium would suffice, he was certain. He just had to restrain his enthusiasm.

HAHNSON'S PACKAGE APPEARED minutes later. Mekashe opened it and read the instructions carefully to make sure he understood the proper procedure for administering the drug.

"Be careful of the dosage," Hahnson cautioned in a holomessage that accompanied the dravelzium. "Too little can be as dangerous to her, and too much can make you very drowsy. I'd start with one cc and see how it affects you. I'd do it in private, as well." Hahnson grinned. "You don't want to pass out and have her dragging you back to your quarters by a leg."

Mekashe laughed uproariously at the image that presented itself. He took the precious discs and put them in his personal safe. One could never be too careful with powerful drugs. He saved out one of the 1-cc discs for later, just before the opera. He'd never anticipated an evening so much. Already, Jasmine had become part of his life.

HE DRESSED CAREFULLY in his most formal suit, a black one that flattered his pale golden skin and black hair. He looked very correct, he told himself, smiling at his virtual reflection. His hair, thick and soft, was in a conventional cut, like the humans wore. When he transformed to his natural form, it was like a mane that swept back from his face and down his back. Like his cousin Rhemun's, it was gloriously curly, a genetic legacy from their forefathers.

Unlike Rojoks, whose hair signified rank by its length, Cehn-Tahr had only personal preference to consider. Mekashe had enjoyed long hair when he noticed that Dr. Edris Mallory seemed entranced by Commander Rhemun's long, curly black hair that he wore to his waist in back. But growing his hair hadn't provoked the same reaction in Edris, who was in love with Rhemun. It had been a huge disappointment to find that the pretty little blonde physician didn't share his infatuation.

Now, however, he didn't mind. He had Jasmine, who was the embodiment of dreams. He looked forward to the opera, which he'd never attended in his life. He'd heard some of his comrades bewail the experience as earsplitting misery which they endured because they were fond of their shipmates. Mekashe was going to keep an open mind. It wasn't the affair, it was the company that he was going to keep that warmed his heart.

He presented himself at Jasmine's door precisely when the ship's intercommunications hailed the six bells the Duponts had told him about.

Jasmine opened the door, and Mekashe's breath sighed out in wonder.

She was the most beautiful creature he'd ever seen in his life. She wore gold, a soft fabric that fell in folds to her ankles, with a high neckline and short sleeves. Over it was a cape of the same material, secured by a white fur collar and clasp. The fur smelled of mammal. He'd read that the humans still wore fur accessories for fashion, although these were Tri-D creations, not taken from live creatures.

"Is it…all right?" Jasmine asked worriedly, because his expression was troubling.

"You look quite incredibly beautiful," he said in a soft, deep tone. "You take my breath away."

She beamed. Her pale blue eyes sparkled like jewels. "Thank goodness. I was afraid I'd dressed inappropriately." She grimaced. "The salesman said it was rather risqué."

He frowned.

"Daring," she modified. She flushed.

"Why?" he asked, because he could see no evidence of that.

"Well…it's this." She turned around. Her beautiful, smooth back was bare to the waist.

The sight of that exquisite skin had a very formidable effect on Mekashe, who was now very grateful for Hahnson's prescription. What might have provoked an alarming behavior was tamed, so that all he did was smile.

"It is perfectly appropriate," he assured her when she turned back. He leaned down a little. "What the salesman meant is that to some cultures, a bare nape—much less a bare back—is extremely stimulating."

Her eyes widened. "Is your culture one of those?"

He nodded. "To us, a bare nape is very exciting."

She caught her breath. "Oh dear. Should I go and change?" she asked at once, not wanting to make her new friend uncomfortable.

He laughed out loud. "Most certainly not. The effect is tantalizing, but not overpowering. Shall we go?"

Her father paused behind his daughter with a rare paper book in his hand. "Leaving now? Have fun." He kissed Jasmine's cheek. "Chess tomorrow?" he asked Mekashe.

"Definitely. After breakfast."

"I'll warm up the chess pieces." He smiled and walked away.

"YOUR FATHER READS books made of pulpwood," Mekashe remarked on the way to the theater.

"Yes. He has a collection of them. They're very rare. He said that no electronic book has the feel and smell of the real thing. He paid a fortune for them."

"Paper pulp." Mekashe shook his head, smiling. "We revere our forests. We consider that they have a culture, even some form of sentience. It would never occur to us to slaughter one for a commercial product."

She stopped and looked up at him worriedly, afraid that she'd offended him.

"We consider that the culture of other species does not conform with our own, and we make allowances." He hesitated. "Did you think we might cage your father for public punishment for owning a book?" he added at her consternation, laughing.

"Well…" She smiled shyly. "I wasn't sure. We know so little of your culture."

"You will learn more, as we go along," he promised. "Now. Tell me about this thing called opera."

She enlightened him on the way to the event.

They were in line when he spoke again. "It will be a new experience for me."

"Don't you have opera?" she asked.

He shook his head. "Our music is mostly instrumental," he replied. "We have artists who paint with sound, who—" he searched for the right word "—who make visual canvases which, when touched, produce music."

"That sounds almost magical," she said.

He nodded. "We have a sector called Kolmankash, where exotic tech is produced. We have many inventions that would seem like the arcane to other cultures."

"I've heard of Kolmankash! I would love to see a canvas that sang." She sighed.

"Soon," he promised, and she beamed.

THEY WERE SEATED. The orchestra began tuning up. Mekashe wished he could cover his ears. If this was opera, he was already disenchanted and not looking forward to an evening of this assault on his hearing.

"They're just tuning up," Jasmine whispered, when she noted his almost-human expression of distaste. "It's not opera. Not yet."

He let out the breath he'd been holding. "Very well."

Her small hand slid over his big one on the seat beside her. He turned and looked down into her eyes as his own hand curled very gently around it and a jolt of feeling like an electric shock went through his body in a hot wave.

She felt it, too. He didn't need to be telepathic to know that. Her eyes were full of her feelings. He could hear her heartbeat, quick and unsteady. He could hear her breathing stick in her chest. He could feel the ripple of sensation go through her at the contact. If he was entranced, she certainly was. His eyes met hers and neither looked away.

He was grateful for the dravelzium. Without it, he'd have carried her out of the theater to the nearest closed room. In his long life, he'd felt the sensation only a handful of times, mostly with totally inappropriate females. This one would be eminently acceptable to his culture and his Clan. He was certain of it. An ambassador's daughter, especially the first Terravegan ambassador's daughter, would be thought of as an aristocrat. And he was also certain that the racial element would not present a problem. Jasmine was so beautiful that no one would protest at the coupling.

The clapping of other concertgoers interrupted the eye contact. They both laughed self-consciously and turned their attention to the stage.

The orchestra began to play. Mekashe was fascinated by the arrangement of notes. He'd never been exposed to human music. The humans aboard the Morcai used earphones when they listened to virtual music, so he hadn't heard any. But this was worthy of Kolmankash itself.

"Beautiful," he whispered.

She relaxed. She knew that he'd been reluctant. Probably he'd been told that opera was a form of torture, because some human men felt that way about it. She was glad that he could share this with her. It was another thing they'd have in common, a love of music. This, *Madama Butterfly* by Puccini, was her favorite opera.

She felt his fingers contract. Hers tensed, but he loosened his grip immediately and shot her a look of silent apology. She smiled. At least, this time it didn't produce broken bones. He'd probably realized that he was much stronger than she was, and he was making allowances. It had to mean that he cared. She certainly did. He was the most wonderful thing in her life. The first man. The first humanoid, she corrected. She'd never even had a real date before. Her father had been very protective. But he trusted her with Mekashe, which meant a lot.

THEY LISTENED TO the opera quietly. When the female singer came to "Un Bel Di," and hit the extremely high note that only a first soprano could hope to reach, she heard Mekashe's faint intake of breath, even as tears rolled down her own cheeks. The song was so exquisite that it was almost painful to hear. Imagine, she thought, being able to produce so much emotion with nothing more than an arrangement of musical tones.

MEKASHE WAS SILENT when they filed out with the other patrons, after explosive applause and five curtain calls.

"What do you think?" she asked.

He looked down at her with a smile. "I think that I will enjoy opera very much. Is it possible to obtain a recording of this one?"

"Yes, it is. I'll gladly lend you mine until Daddy can have one sent to you from Terravega. They aren't available on the Nexus, I'm afraid."

"I would be most grateful," he replied.

She looked down at their linked hands. He was very strong. The grip didn't hurt, but it was firmer than it should have been. She wondered if he'd been around humans much. He seemed surprised that she was so fragile, compared to him.

"Am I hurting you?" he asked at once, when he saw where her gaze had fallen.

"Not at all," she said.

But he loosened his grip, just a little. He tugged her to one side of the crowd filing out of the auditorium, and his eyes were a solemn blue. "If I do, you must tell me. Don't be afraid of offending me—you won't. I would not hurt you for all the galaxy."

Her heart soared. She smiled up at him with sparkling, soft blue eyes. "I know that. I'll tell you," she promised.

His eyes narrowed on her face. "I had no idea that humans were so fragile," he said softly.

She smiled. "I'm afraid it's probably just me. I'm sort of fragile. I bruise really easily."

He let out a breath. "Still, I apologize for any discomfort I may have already caused."

He didn't know about the broken bones in her hand, and she wasn't about to tell him. "You're forgiven," she replied. She searched his face. "Have you been around humans much?"

He started to tell her about the Morcai, about the Holconcom, and realized that it would be breaking many protocols. Later, perhaps. "I have some small acquaintance with mostly male humans," he said after a minute.

"What do you do for a living? Or are you independently wealthy?" she asked.

He chuckled. "Among my own people, I'm an aristocrat. My Clan has wealth that we all share. But I do work, just the same. I'm a..." He searched for a word that would suffice. He couldn't reveal his true duties where he might be overheard. The captain of the emperor's Imperial Guard did not dare reveal himself to outworlders. "I'm a consultant," he added, recalling his cousin Rhemun telling Kipling that, when he met his almost-adolescent son for the first time. "For the military," he added.

"Oh. One of those brainy jobs," she teased.

He cocked his head, curious.

"A job which requires intelligence," she amended. "So sorry. I have to stop using idioms."

"Alternatively, you can teach me to understand them," he replied, smiling. "I'm a quick study. I speak many languages."

"Really!" She grimaced. "I only speak English and French."

He scowled. "What is French?"

"A dialect of old Earth, carried over to Terravega with the first colonists. My surname is French—Dupont."

He smiled slowly. "Truly fascinating. Do you know much about your ancestry?"

"A little. I know that my distant ancestors were vintners."

He scowled, not understanding the reference.

"They made wine," she explained. "They had great plantations of grapevines, red and white grapes alike, which they made into expensive wines that were sold all over the planet. And when my Terravegan family colonized, they carried on the tradition. You'll find Dupont wines still served in the finest dining facilities on Terravega. Even on Trimerius, where the military headquarters of the Tri-Galaxy Fleet are located. Daddy knows Admiral Jeffrye Lawson," she added. "They play chess together on the Nexus."

Mekashe also knew the admiral, but he wasn't going to mention it. Time enough in the future to tell her what he really did for a job. Right now, he wanted nothing more than to be with her, to learn about her.

"They have a pool party scheduled for tomorrow aboard the ship," she said slowly. She hesitated. "Bathing suits and all."

He shook his head, smiling. "What is a bathing suit?"

"People wear skimpy clothing-suits that leave the arms and legs and midriff bare on women, just swimming trunks for men that leave the chest and legs bare."

He scowled. No way could he do that. Not only was being half-nude in public considered indelicate for the Cehn-Tahr, he couldn't reveal the band of fur that ran the length of his spine to Jasmine. It might offend her, cause her to draw back from him before she got to know the person he was.

She saw his unease and grimaced. "I don't like wearing bathing suits, either," she confessed. "Mama said it was indelicate. She wouldn't let me go in swimming pools, ever, back home."

He laughed. "I would have liked your mother. I have to confess, my culture also considers public nudity—even seminudity—indiscreet."

She beamed. "I'm glad." The smile faded. "There's not much else to do on board."

"There are holorooms," he corrected. He pursed his lips. "We might have a picnic, on any planet of your choosing."

She caught her breath. "Really? They can do that? I thought they were only used for, well, for indiscreet purposes."

He laughed. "Some of them are, certainly. But we can walk in a forest on Terramer, or sit by the ocean on Trimerius. We can even go to Enmehkmehk and catch farawings."

"What's a farawing?"

"A small creature with brilliant wings. Untouchable in the real world, but they can be caught and even tamed as pets in a holoroom. You can save the program and revisit the pet at your convenience, and anywhere you might be. A chip of the capture is provided as part of the entertainment."

"I should love to go on a picnic!" She hesitated again. "How do you know about picnics?"

"My best friend is bonded to a human female," he explained. "She taught us about certain human entertainments. Sadly, opera was not one of them."

She laughed with delight. If his friend was bonded to a human, it might mean that he had no qualms about an interracial marriage. Her heart felt lighter than air.

He saw her delight and read, quite correctly, her train of thought. His was going along the same lines. He was certain already that he would not be able to give her up. She was capturing him, as surely as farawings were captured in holorooms.

"Tomorrow, then?" she asked. "After breakfast?" She grimaced. "You're playing chess with Daddy."

"Then after luncheon," he suggested softly.

Her sad expression lifted. "That would be wonderful. What should I wear?"

He wanted to tell her to keep on the gown she was

wearing. It complemented her delicate beauty. But it would be impractical. "Casual clothing," he said.

"Jeans and a shirt and boots?" she asked. "That's Western American clothing. It's the fad right now with designers. Nobody knows what they really wore, but handed-down documents mentioned boots and jeans, which we assume were pants made of some coarse fabric, and shirts that button up."

"Western American." He sighed. "I shall have to go to the virtual library."

"Not to worry. Daddy has a book on it." She laughed. "He has a book on everything!"

"A paper book."

She looked worried. "It would offend you to touch it," she guessed.

He glanced down at her. "Jasmine, a paper book is already a dead tree," he pointed out. "I only take issue with trees on my own world being used for such a purpose, which would never happen. The process of other cultures is their concern." He leaned down, his eyes searching hers. "I'm not offended."

"Oh." She was looking at his mouth. It was beautiful. Chiseled, the upper lip thinner than the lower one, wide and masculine. She'd never been kissed. She wanted to be.

He read that in her face and almost groaned. There were people everywhere.

It was too soon. He kept telling himself that as

he pulled her slowly by the hand to a hidden alcove that was, temporarily, unoccupied.

"This is too soon," he said aloud.

"I don't care…!"

She reached up as he reached down. Her mouth was soft and sweet, nectar itself. He groaned under his breath as he fought not to crush her against his body. It truly was too soon for that sort of intimacy. He framed her face in his big, warm hands and drew his lips tenderly against her soft mouth, drowning in frustrated passion, hungry for far more than this.

He drew back to see her reaction. Her eyelids were half-closed. She looked at him with something akin to awe.

He bent again, parting her lips softly this time before he possessed them. She moaned and pressed close to him.

He didn't dare take the invitation. The dravelzium was already wearing off. He'd have to make sure he kept a supply with him. He couldn't bear to hurt her.

But her mouth was intoxicating. He got drunk on the taste of her. He whispered to her in High Cehn-Tahr, the Holy Tongue that only his Clan and a few members of the kehmatemer could even understand.

"What?" she whispered dizzily.

"Synthale."

She drew back a breath.

"You go to my head like spirits," he translated.

"You go to mine," she whispered shakily. Her soft

arms reached up, but he caught them and pulled them gently down.

"Too soon," he whispered. He felt unsteady on his feet. "Some things must not be rushed," he added.

She smiled stupidly. "Okay."

He chuckled. She looked as intoxicated as he felt.

"Nobody ever kissed me before," she confessed, shocking him. "I wasn't sure how it would feel." She flushed. "It's very…nice."

"Very nice, indeed." He was immensely flattered. He would be her first, in every way. He had heard that some humans were very promiscuous, especially in the outer colonies. He was delighted to find her as chaste and discreet as he, himself, was. The Cehn-Tahr were pristine in their mating habits. Once bonded, they never strayed. Bonding was for life.

"So. Tomorrow after luncheon." She looked up at him.

He nodded slowly. "After luncheon. I'll see your father after breakfast."

She cocked her head and smiled. "Is it a cultural thing that you don't eat with other cultures?"

He smiled. "I'm afraid so. Our choice of cuisine is quite different from yours and might be offensive to your olfactory processes."

She blinked. "We might not like the smell?"

"Exactly."

She searched his eyes, so far above her own. "I

can get used to anything," she said softly. "And I mean anything, if it means being with you."

He caught his breath. It was the way he felt, too.

He bent, helplessly, to her soft mouth. This was unwise. The dravelzium was wearing off. Contact with her mouth, without the protection of nanobytes, which also wore off, could trigger the mating cycle. She knew too little about him, about what he truly was. It would be unfair to expose her to something she might not be able to accept.

He kissed her very softly and drew back before she could reciprocate. "Slowly," he said.

She managed to smile through her excited disappointment. "Slowly," she replied.

He touched her soft hair where it draped around her shoulders in a beautiful, curly curtain. "Your hair is magnificent," he whispered.

"I thought you might like it better if I wore it loose, like this."

"Yes. I do." He chuckled. "My own hair is even longer…" He stopped suddenly at her look of surprise.

He ground his teeth together. It was a bad slip. "I mean, I used to wear it long," he said, shaking his head. "You see? You intoxicate me so that I can't say what I mean."

To his relief, she laughed. "I wonder what you'd look like with long hair," she said aloud.

"I'll grow it out, just for you," he promised.

She smiled. "Will we be able to do things together, when we get to Memcache?" she asked worriedly. "I mean, will your family mind?"

"My Clan won't mind," he replied. "My parents are long dead. I have many cousins, but no close family anymore."

"Sort of like me," she said. "All I have left is Daddy."

"I like your father," he told her. "He is unique."

She smiled. "Yes. I love him very much."

He brushed her hair away from her face. "I want children," he said huskily.

She felt a wave of hunger so sweeping that it almost staggered her. "I want them, too," she whispered.

They stared at each other hungrily until a passing couple noticed them and called a greeting.

They shook themselves mentally, moved apart and called back the greeting as they proceeded toward the cabin Jasmine shared with her parent.

"I have never enjoyed anything as much as this evening," Mekashe told her softly. "It has been one of the happiest days of my life."

"Of mine, as well," she replied, searching his eyes. "I'll look forward to tomorrow afternoon."

"As will I." He smiled tenderly. "I will carry this memory of the way you look until I die…" He hesitated. "Is it permissible, for me to capture you like this?"

"Of course," she said at once.

He produced a small photographic device the size of a thumb from his jacket and captured a photograph of her.

The door opened just after he shot it.

"Daddy, would you capture us together? Is it all right?" she asked Mekashe.

"Certainly!" he said, handing the device to her father. "If you wouldn't mind?"

He chuckled. "Not at all." He triggered the device, three times. "I made multiples, in case the first didn't take." He handed it to Mekashe. "Might better check and make sure."

He did. He looked at the portrait of the two of them and sighed inwardly. They looked perfect together. Her fairness, and his black hair and light gold skin, seemed to complement each other.

"May I see?" she asked, and leaned on Mekashe's arm to look over it. He was far too tall for her to look over his shoulder. "It's perfect! Can you share it with me, on the Nexus?" she asked.

He wouldn't dare. No holos of him or any member of the Imperial Guard or the Holconcom were permitted.

"I can do much better. I'll bring you one of these with the capture in it tomorrow. Will that suffice?" he teased.

"That would be wonderful!" She looked up at him delightedly. "And you'll teach me to use it, yes?"

He nodded. "Yes, I will."

"We're going to have a picnic in the forest in a holoroom," she told her father. "So I'm afraid you'll have luncheon alone," she teased.

Mekashe frowned. "A picnic involves food?"

She looked at him. "Well, usually." She flushed. "Sorry, I forgot. I'll have lunch with Daddy, and we'll have a foodless picnic," she added with a grin.

He chuckled. "Very well. I'll see you for chess in the morning, then, Ambassador," he told her father.

"I'll look forward to it. Good evening."

"Good night," Jasmine added.

He gave her a lingering smile. "Sleep well."

He walked away. Jasmine stared after him for a minute before she went inside with her father and closed the door.

Ambassador Dupont looked at her worriedly. "You know," he began, "their culture isn't the same as ours. It's very different, from what I've heard."

She smiled. "Then I'll learn as I go along. He's... incredible. Tender and funny and smart. Smarter than me."

"Smarter than me, too, I'm afraid." He hesitated. He'd just had a virtual briefing with the head of the diplomatic department on Terravega. It included top secret information about the true form of the Cehn-Tahr and cultural differences that were unknown to most humans. Jasmine had never seen a true alien. The Altairian she'd discovered on the ship was quite human looking, except for his blue skin. The Vegans, though more alien, were mostly humanoid. But the Cehn-Tahr were very different. Not only that, they were far stronger than humans.

Jasmine was hungry for Mekashe and the reverse seemed equally true. It was more dangerous than she realized, but he'd never seen her so animated, so very happy. Was it fair to destroy her illusions? After all, it might be just an infatuation, the lure of the unfamiliar. If that were true, it would seep out on its own accord and he wouldn't have to hurt her by imparting unpalatable facts. Like the fact that Cehn-Tahr ate their food whole and raw. He understood now why Mekashe wouldn't dine with them.

Their cultures were radically different. He knew that two members of the Royal Clan had human consorts, but there were deep secrets about the bondings. He didn't know what Mekashe's Clan affiliation was. There were rumors from HQ that some clans had accepted genetic enhancements that made them extremely dangerous to humans.

Well, he could certainly discount that after tonight, he told himself, amused. His daughter looked slightly disheveled, but there was no bruising and certainly no broken bones. So perhaps Mekashe's Clan didn't have those enhancements. Perhaps the cultural differences wouldn't matter.

Still, he worried. Jasmine was so unsophisticated, and so very young. He watched her go back to her room, her mind far away on the handsome stranger from Memcache. And he hoped against hope that he wouldn't regret his silence.

CHAPTER FOUR

THE NEXT MORNING, Jasmine was almost floating on a cloud, anticipating the afternoon with Mekashe. She went through her closet, looking for something pretty enough to wear for him that was also casual.

She could have gone to the boutique for another outfit, but she hesitated to run her parent into more debt, especially in the early days of his new, lucrative profession. So she settled for a pair of long pants, jeans they were called, in some knotty fabric that was wispy and cool, and a button-up blouse with short sleeves. The jeans were blue, a dark color, and the blouse was white with a blue pattern. The well-fitting garments gave her an even more youthful look, especially with her hair down, but age had never been a problem with Mekashe. She supposed it didn't matter to him, any more than his, whatever it might be, mattered to her. At that, he looked to be in his late twenties or early thirties. Older than her, but not by that much. Feelings, she decided, were far more important than minor details.

She relived those kisses all night long and barely

slept. She loved the warm, hard touch of his mouth, the hunger and passion she sensed in him. She wondered what would come next in their relationship. Whatever it was, she knew that it was leading to something permanent. He'd mentioned children, not something a man with a casual passion in mind would care about. She thought of children with black hair and eyes that changed color to mirror moods, and she was fascinated. Her children would be unique.

She knew that Dr. Madeline Ruszel had bonded with a Cehn-Tahr and had two children. She wished she could access more information about the woman on the Nexus, but it was impossible. Apparently the Cehn-Tahr were secretive about any part of their culture. Mekashe had told her as much.

She laid out her outfit and wished she had an excuse to crash the chess match, to see Mekashe again. But it would look contrived. No, best to let him have his time alone with her father. It was important that they liked each other.

AMBASSADOR DUPONT WAS distracted as they played. Mekashe wondered why. He was reluctant to bring it up, but it concerned him.

"Jasmine is looking forward to the picnic," the older man said with a smile, melting his companion's concern. "She's spending the morning picking out just the right clothing to wear." He glanced up from the chessboard. "She said that you were less than enthusiastic about the swimming party."

Mekashe grimaced. "We consider such things indiscreet." His solemn blue eyes met those of the ambassador. "Our culture is quite pristine."

"I know." The other man hesitated. "The head of our service shared a few facts with me, about your culture, things he thought were important enough to tell me before I arrived on Memcache."

Mekashe sat back. His eyes studied the other man. "That was wise. It will help you to adjust. But it may be more difficult for Jasmine, especially since she has been so sheltered from alien races."

"My fault. And I wish there were time to remedy it." He sighed. "There were no holos, you understand. We aren't permitted to share such things on the Nexus, even in our diplomatic service. I know that the Cehn-Tahr are even more careful about such things than we are. That was why you offered to give Jasmine the capture on a device, rather than flash it to her for the Tri-D reconstituter, yes?"

"Yes." He reached into a pocket and handed the capture device to the ambassador with a smile. "I will let you keep it for her, until we return from the holoroom." He didn't add that the giving and acceptance of a gift was a notorious trigger for the mating cycle. It was much too soon for that to happen.

"I'll do that." The ambassador pocketed it. "The

differences between our species seem wider than I first realized."

"I'm afraid they are." Mekashe's face was solemn. "And we are careful about any information we expose on the Nexus. We never publicize details of our political, military or religious protocols, much less the names of those who serve."

The professor hesitated over a move. He still looked troubled.

Mekashe didn't need to read his mind to understand why. "You were told that we are not quite as we appear in public," he said after a minute.

The ambassador's hand jerked just faintly, the only outward sign of his concern. "Well, yes." He looked up. "Is it a great difference, or are you allowed to tell me even that much?"

Mekashe smiled. "Your status allows you to know more than a private citizen. I cannot elaborate. But, yes, the differences would be apparent, especially to a sheltered female." He frowned. "I would hope that it wouldn't matter a great deal."

"You don't have tentacles or two heads…?" It was a joke.

Mekashe chuckled. "Certainly not."

The ambassador sighed. "I don't mean to pry," he told his companion. "It makes no difference to me. I'm quite familiar with alien races through my research. My daughter, however, has never even seen a Rojok up close. They're said to share some traits with Cehn-Tahr, but they're very human looking."

Mekashe was solemn. "I'm afraid that we are far different than Rojoks." He glanced at the human. "I would never harm her," he added quietly. "She has already become…precious to me."

Ambassador Dupont smiled faintly. "I believe that feeling is very much reciprocated. Inevitably, however, you will have to tell her the truth."

"I realize that." Mekashe's eyes had a faraway look and he frowned. "But we have still a long voyage ahead of us," he said finally, smiling, "and the need for total honesty is not yet urgent."

Ambassador Dupont nodded. His smile was nostalgic. "I found my wife wandering in a garden on Trimerius, when I was in military intelligence," he said, smiling at the memory. "She was enthusing over a sunflower plant to a very bored young man. I stepped in and marveled at the flower and she found an excuse to send the other man back to his command." He chuckled. "I'm no fan of flowers, but I learned to love them as much as she did." His face saddened. "She's been gone for five years, and I still grieve. She was fragile. I didn't protest when she wanted to go on a rescue mission with a group of other physicians. The transport crashed and all hands were lost."

"I'm sorry."

"So was I. Jasmine took it very hard. It's just the

two of us. I have no other family and Martha was an only child, as well, of older parents who predeceased her."

"Your bonded consort was a physician?"

He nodded. He studied the alien curiously. "Do you have family? Or am I permitted to ask such a personal question on such short acquaintance?"

"My family is sparse," Mekashe replied. "My father was career military. My mother was in diplomatic service. They were lost in…" He started to say "in the Great Galaxy War," but that might shock the human, who had no real concept of the life span of the Cehn-Tahr. The Great Galaxy War ended decades ago. "They were lost in a regional conflict," he amended. "I have cousins, and what you would call a great-uncle." He meant the emperor, but he couldn't tell that to an outworlder. "But no close family."

"Yet in your society, Clan is life itself," Dupont said gently.

Mekashe smiled. "Yes. We consider that Clan is more important than any personal consideration. We live and die to bring it honor, to spare it from shame."

"It's a difficult concept, for humans."

"I understand. You have family, which is akin to Clan. However, our complex social makeup will be difficult for you to comprehend. A tutor may be required. It is dangerous to say or do anything that gives offense to any Clan, but most especially to the Royal Clan. Even a criticism spoken out of turn may give offense, and there are grave consequences."

"I'll adjust, I'm sure. It's just…I worry about Jasmine." He smiled apologetically. "She's impulsive, as you already know, and she often speaks out of turn."

"I cannot imagine that such a kind and gentle person could ever offend in any way," he replied. "She has grace and beauty, but it is her empathy and compassion which make her so remarkable. I have seen the combination very rarely in my life."

"Thank you. I've done my best with her. So did her mother, who loved her greatly. Martha, however, was frequently absent, due to the rigors of her profession. She discouraged Jasmine from following in her footsteps, even disparaging medical work around her. She said that Jasmine was too fragile and far too squeamish to ever fit in a surgical ward. I have to agree."

"Sometimes our strengths only appear under provocation," Mekashe remarked. "Often it is turmoil rather than calm which heralds them."

"Truly spoken. Are you certain that you want to move that pawn?" he added with pursed lips and twinkling eyes. "It might have consequences."

Mekashe, who'd been listening rather than concentrating, saw immediately what the older man meant and chuckled. He moved his hand to a bishop instead. "You very nearly had me there. If only you hadn't spoken," he added drily. "Checkmate, I believe."

"I believe in fairness, and I'm hopelessly honest," Dupont replied with a sigh. "I fear it may involve me in controversy one day. I don't prevaricate well. I'm told that this is almost a requirement in diplomatic work, of which I have no practical experience."

"Honesty is a hallmark of our culture," Mekashe replied. "It will stand you in good stead with the emperor, I assure you. He values nothing more."

"What is he like?" Dupont asked. "I mean, is he fair? Is he even-tempered?"

"He is kind until circumstances provoke him to be otherwise" was the reply. "I have found him to be of a rather mild temperament on most occasions."

Dupont was silent, contemplating his next move. "I think that you might be involved somehow in your government, Mekashe."

The alien's eyes twinkled green. "You know that I can neither confirm nor deny that suspicion."

Dupont chuckled. "Yes. I know." He sat back, shaking his head. "Well, that's another match lost. I don't seem to improve, do I?"

"You attack without contemplation," Mekashe said, and not unkindly.

"It's said that one of my ancestors knew only one form of combat—charging straight at the enemy. Perhaps I'm like that, as well."

"It can be an effective strategy. Unless your opponent is equally minded."

"Noted." He moved his captured pieces back onto the board. "Do you have time for another game?"

"One more," he replied. "Then it will be time to escort Jasmine to the holoroom. I thought perhaps she might enjoy the fauna and flora on Eridanus Six," he added. "It has exotic wildlife, as well."

"Oh dear," the other man began.

Mekashe chuckled. "I'm quite familiar with the tech used in Tri-D reproductions," he said. "In fact, I know the engineer on board who programs these. He is a Rojok, and a friend of long acquaintance. The wildlife will not be dangerous. There are protocols written into the biological software to prevent any injury. Nevertheless, I promise you that I will let nothing harm her."

"You know, even humans are familiar with the Holconcom and its reputation for fearlessness," Dupont replied. "I assume that most Cehn-Tahr males are equally competent at self-defense. Even diplomats." His eyebrows rose.

He was insinuating that Mekashe was involved in diplomatic service. It was amusing that he mentioned the Holconcom, to which Mekashe had belonged before his appointment as captain of the emperor's Imperial Guard. The human could have no idea of that, of course, because the roster of Cehn-Tahr military units was never disclosed. It was an odd sort of co-incidence, just the same.

"I can assure you that I have no fear of native wildlife on any planet, and that I would defend Jasmine with my life."

The ambassador seemed to relax as he rearranged his chess pieces.

JASMINE WAS ALMOST dancing with joy as they entered the holoroom. "I can't wait!" she exclaimed. "It's truly a reproduction of a real alien planet, with alien life-forms?" she asked.

Mekashe chuckled. "It truly is."

She hesitated. "No cats?" she asked worriedly.

His heart skipped a beat. "Why do you ask?"

She grimaced. "It's just, well, a friend of Daddy's kept big cats as pets on Terravega." She didn't notice Mekashe's expression of concern, quickly concealed. "One of them scratched me rather badly. I've been afraid of them ever since."

He paused and turned toward her, his eyes a solemn blue. "I can assure you that most felines are friendly. Few ever attack humans."

"Well, galots do, don't they?"

His eyebrows arched.

She laughed self-consciously. "I've been reading about them, on the Nexus. I couldn't find any vid captures… Why are you laughing?" she added curiously.

"Of all felines, those are by far the most danger-ous. There are no vid captures because researchers are terrified to go near Eridanus Three."

"Why?"

"Galots eat them."

Her face paled. "Really? They really eat people?"

He grimaced. "Only those who trespass," he amended. "I know one who is quite fond of hu-mans. He frequently visits the emperor's son and his bonded mate."

"I see." She wasn't smiling. In fact, she wrapped her arms around her slender body and hesitated. "There aren't any galots in there…?" she asked, in-dicating the glorious tropical forest that lay ahead of them on a stone walkway.

He turned to her. "Jasmine, I would never let any-thing harm you. Anything!"

She looked up at him with her heart in her eyes. He was already dear to her. "I'm sorry. I'm behaving like a child, I know. It's just…I've never seen alien creatures. There were holozoos on Terravega, but I never liked the idea of seeing creatures in cages, not even virtual ones."

He smiled. "Nor I."

"It's only cats," she added, wondering silently why he seemed so perturbed at her fear of felines. "I don't mind other animals. Well, I'm scared of snakes, too." She hesitated. "Lots of people are nervous around cats," she added. She shivered. "I overheard Daddy talking to another professor, several years ago, about your government's commando force, the Hol…Hol…" She searched for the word.

"Holconcom," he finished for her.

"Yes. That. Anyway, the professor said that they had a terrifying reputation. That your emperor once led them, and that they conquered other species by—" she swallowed, hard "—eating their enemies."

He seemed to pale, just a little. Her revulsion was truly unexpected, as was her fear of cats. Both could have grave consequences, down the road.

"I'm sorry," she said, noticing his consternation. "I don't mean to give offense. I'm just repeating what I heard." She hesitated. "Is it true?"

He managed a stiff smile. "Jasmine, I'm not permitted to discuss intimate characteristics of my people with outworlders. Even charming outworlders."

"Oh." She flushed. "I'm sorry. I just open my mouth and blurt out things. You aren't angry?" she added worriedly.

Angry, no. Uneasy, yes. He saw his dreams of a future with her going up in smoke, and he didn't know what to do about it. Her fear of cats was going to cause problems, especially if and when she learned the truth about the shape-shifting Cehn-Tahr and their true form.

"I'm not angry," he assured her.

"But I've made you sad," she said, frowning. She

winced. "I'm sorry. I didn't mean to spoil the afternoon…!"

"You haven't," he said convincingly. He studied her beautiful face and the sadness passed. There would be obstacles, certainly. But she could overcome her fear. She'd get to know him, get to care for him, and the differences wouldn't matter. He was certain of it.

She went close. One small hand touched the center of his chest and lingered there. "You must tell me if I give offense," she said softly, her pale blue eyes probing his. "I wouldn't hurt you for anything in the world."

"Nor would I hurt you," he said huskily.

She reached up and touched his hard mouth curiously. "I've never met anyone like you," she whispered. "You're so different. And yet I feel as if I've known you all my life."

He framed her face in his big hands. "I feel exactly the same."

They stood staring at each other and he thanked providence, once again, for Hahnson's drug that permitted him to touch her without triggering the mating cycle. It even permitted him to kiss her, which he did, softly, slowly, with exquisite pleasure.

She smiled under his hard mouth. "I love to read romantic books," she whispered. "But I didn't know what they were talking about, before, when they said that kissing was sweet. It truly is."

He chuckled softly. "You hadn't been kissed before."

"Never." She nuzzled her nose against his. "I like it very much."

"So do I." He lifted her by both elbows and his mouth ground into hers hungrily, until she protested softly. "Forgive me," he whispered, easing the pressure. "You are far more fragile than you appear."

"Only a bit," she said, recalling suddenly the broken bones in her hand when he'd closed his around it too firmly.

He'd forgotten to turn the white noise ball back on when he put it inside his pocket. He was shocked speechless when he read that thought in her mind, and relived the incident from her point of view.

He put her back down very carefully. His eyes held horror. "I hurt your hand, before…"

"It was only bruised." She smiled as she gave him the lie. He read in her mind that she couldn't bear to let him know he'd harmed her. It touched his heart. He read also, with delight, the depth of her growing affection for him. It matched what he felt for her.

But it was dangerous to leave the white ball untriggered, and he turned it on unobtrusively. The emperor had been quite firm about its use. They couldn't risk having an enemy telepath learn who Mekashe really was, not when he was vulnerable and apart from his command.

True, there was a handful of other Cehn-Tahr

below, officers returning from a mission who were also allowed R & R on this vessel. One of them was his cousin Tresar, also a member of the Royal Clan. Tresar and the others would be leaving the following week, while Mekashe had almost a month left to enjoy Jasmine's company and entice her to share his life. He thought that it might not require much enticing. She was hungry for him, as he was for her.

"We should move ahead," he said with a laugh. "Our time here is, sadly, limited."

"It's so exotic," she said almost in a whisper as she clung to his big hand and followed where he led. "The flowers are bigger than my head!"

"Rimonia," he named them. "They're used in medicines that the Rojok employ in surgery."

"So beautiful," she said on a sigh. "They smell wonderful."

"Those are divulga." He indicated a small purple flower that grew on an odd, fat vine. "An herb used in certain meat dishes."

She made a face. "I don't eat meat," she said.

"I had heard this about Terravegans."

"It doesn't apply to all of them. Daddy still likes his steak," she said with distaste. "I've tried and failed to get him on a vegan diet."

It was another difference between their cultures that he hoped would not present a problem.

She glanced up at him. "You like meat, too, I suppose?"

He chuckled. "Sadly, yes."

She sighed. "Well, I don't think any of us has the right to dictate food choices to other people," she said after a minute. "I eat what I like and I let other people do the same. Except for Daddy. I worry about him."

"He seems quite healthy."

"He is, now. But he had a rare virus that caused some serious problems last year. He's still not quite over it. It's not contagious or anything, but he's supposed to be careful what he eats, and his protein is limited. He hates fruits and vegetables."

So did Mekashe, but he didn't mention it.

"What a beautiful planet," Jasmine said as they moved along the path. "Does it really look like this?"

"Yes," he assured her. "At least, the prime continent does. There are others which present very different flora and fauna." He frowned. "Odd," he murmured, looking around. "The plants seem overgrown here."

"They do?"

He nodded. "In a holo, space is limited, so species are regulated as to growth. It indicates a glitch in the matrix. I must remember to report it to the program manager."

"I'm sure it's nothing important," she said. "Oh goodness!" she exclaimed as they arrived in a clearing. "You had it set up already!"

And he had. There was a cloth spread on the grass, along with a hamper of foods designed to appeal to a human palate. There were fruits and edible flowers, even a form of nectar that was beloved by Terravegans.

He chuckled. "I asked your father about your food preferences before I approached the programmer."

"How sweet of you!" She plopped down on the grass and poured a glass of nectar. But when she sampled it, there was a sting to the liquid. She made a face. "It's supposed to be sweet, but this has a sour note."

"Another glitch. I'll make a note of it."

"You don't have to do that. It's not really important," she said, smiling as he dropped down on the cloth beside her. "Do you eat fruits?" she added, offering him one.

He forced himself to take it, but he only stared at it.

She sighed. "Don't tell me. You're like Daddy. You like protein."

He chuckled. "Am I so obvious?"

"Yes. But it doesn't matter," she said softly, searching his eyes. "I like fruits and you like meat. The world won't end."

He cocked his head, uncertain of her meaning.

"I mean that it makes no difference."

"I see." He smiled, but he put down the fruit.

She was watching him while she ate her fruit. "It's why you won't dine with us, isn't it?" she asked suddenly. "You don't want to offend me by eating meat at the table."

It was far more complicated than that, but he couldn't admit it. "It might be one reason," he said.

She finished her fruit. "Funny, it tastes like bananas, but it looks like a pear," she said. She sipped the nectar. It really did taste terrible, but she wasn't going to spoil the picnic by mentioning it. She wanted to be with him, and the food didn't matter.

He scowled. The programming was bad. He wondered if there were other glitches, perhaps more dangerous ones. He'd have to be careful. He couldn't risk having something happen to her.

"Can we explore some more?" she asked excitedly. "It's so different from what I'm used to!"

He chuckled, offering a hand to pull her up. Fortunately, Hahnson's dravelzium was of long duration. It felt good, touching her. "Certainly."

They strolled down a tree-lined lane. Jasmine was fascinated with the flora. "These trees look like something called weeping willows. They were prevalent on old Earth. There are holovids of them. Aren't they beautiful?"

"We have a similar tree on Memcache," he said. "In fact, I have some on my own lands."

She paused and looked up at him. "Do you have a house? Are houses on your planet like the ones on Terravega?"

He smiled. "I have a villa. It might suggest ancient stone cities to you, remnants of your own past. We build with the environment in mind. We decry the slaughter of trees to construct dwellings, so we build with stone."

"Is it a big villa?"

"Big enough to house a dozen people," he said easily. And it did, considering how many workers were required to maintain it. He lived as an aristocrat, as much because of his Clan status as his family's wealth. Not that wealth was measured as humans measured it.

"I would love to see your villa," she said shyly.

He smiled. "And you will, soon enough," he assured her. He searched her face with warm, covetous eyes. "It is a beautiful place to raise a family."

She caught her breath as she looked at him. "It's lonely, being an only child."

"Yes," he agreed, because he knew what that was like, just as she did.

"I'd like to have several children," she said dreamily. "Boys and girls. Mixed." She laughed self-consciously.

"As would I." He could picture her so easily, surrounded by children, having picnics like this with them, and him. "My life has been a solitary one."

"So has mine. I mean, I have Daddy, but it's not the same as having a big family." She stopped. "Do your people have holidays? I mean, like Christmas and New Year's and Terravegan Independence Day…?"

He laughed softly. "We celebrate the emperor's birthday and the founding of our planet. We also have religious celebrations, but they are far different from yours, I fear."

"I can adjust."

He nodded. "Certainly, you can."

She felt warm all over, on fire with hope and love and confident of a future that would contain him.

"I can hardly wait to see Memcache," she said breathlessly. "Is it beautiful, like this—"

She broke off as a giant creature confronted them on the path. It looked like a nightmare construct of galot and cremor-lizard, with scaly skin and slit pupils. It was growling. She screamed, a piercing, horrific cry that echoed around the holoroom.

Mekashe stepped in front of her. She was still screaming. "You must try to be quiet," he said firmly. He never took his eyes off the creature. "It may provoke it to attack."

"But what is that?" She sobbed, terrified. She pressed against his spine. "Please, make it go away! Oh please! It's terrifying!"

He made a sound deep in his throat. It was a growl, but she wouldn't recognize it, because the Cehn-Tahr didn't sound like domestic house cats. The cry was wild and throaty and threatening.

The creature wasn't impressed by it. The death cry that could send humanoids running away in terror had no effect whatsoever on the construct. It roared back and its entire huge body tensed.

Mekashe knew that it would charge. It was in the beast's eyes. "Go back the way we came," he told her over his shoulder. "Run. Now!"

"But what about you?" she asked, even in her terror, more concerned for him than herself.

"I will stop it," he said huskily. "Do as I say. Run, Jasmine!"

She made a husky little protest, but she did as he told her. When he was certain that she was out of sight, he shifted into his true form and leaped forward, right into the beast's chest, his furious growl echoing around them.

HE HAD A bloody sleeve, but otherwise, he seemed unharmed when he rejoined her down the path. Jasmine was terrified. "You're hurt!" she exclaimed. "I should never have agreed to leave you! I should have stayed and tried to help you fight it!"

He touched her hair gently. "Brave heart," he said softly. "But I was able to subdue it. Not without some effort, however, and this must be reported. Someone could die. All the safeguards were disabled because of the programming error."

"I do agree. But you need to be seen to first. We can go straight to the infirmary…!"

He laughed. "I can mend this myself. I carry medical supplies with me, and I am versed in their usage. You must not worry. I am only slightly damaged."

"But you need a doctor," she argued.

"I have a friend who is a surgeon," he replied. "And I have a direct line to him from my quarters. He can mend me. Truly, it is of no importance."

She relented, but reluctantly. "I'm so glad you weren't badly hurt."

"I'm sorry that our adventure ended so badly. We must try again. But perhaps in a less exotic setting," he added wryly.

"You're sure you'll be okay?"

"Very sure. You should go back to your suite. I'll call for you later. There is a musical performance by a traveling group of Altairian musicians. If you would like to see it?"

"I'd love that," she enthused. "But shouldn't you rest?"

"I will be completely recovered, and soon. Farewell."

"Farewell."

She watched him go, with sad and concerned eyes. He'd protected her, and she was proud of his courage. But she worried that he might be more damaged than he was showing.

HER FATHER WAS HORRIFIED. "The creature actually attacked you?"

"Not me," she said. "Mekashe jumped in front of me and made me leave. He stopped the beast, although he was injured." She frowned. "It was huge, with claws and fangs... I'm still not sure how he subdued it. It was twice his size."

He didn't dare tell her what he knew. "I'm sure he can handle himself," he said quietly. "I'm glad that you're all right, but that programming error should be reported."

"Mekashe was going to do that before he went to his room," she said. "He was angry."

"It could have killed someone," the ambassador said irritably. "Some programmers are just lazy. They don't want to put themselves out to correct what they see as small glitches. But those small ones can escalate into tragedies."

"I'm sure they'll get it fixed. Mekashe is taking me to an Altairian concert this evening. You don't mind?"

"Of course not," he assured her. He smiled. "I like Mekashe. Even more, since he saved you from a mauling," he added, tongue in cheek.

"He has a villa on Memcache," she said. "He said he'd love to have a big family." Her eyes were full of dreams. "So would I. We're both only children."

He had reservations about that dream coming true, but he didn't say anything. She was happier than he'd ever seen her. It wouldn't hurt to let her dream. She was so young. Time enough for reality to make an entrance.

CHAPTER FIVE

MEKASHE HAD WORDS with the manager of the programming staff of the holo division aboard the starliner, a Rojok engineer named Teskas, whom he had known for many years.

"As you can see—" he indicated his bloodstained sleeve "—there could have been tragic consequences."

"I do see," the manager agreed at once. "I'll have the programmer responsible suspended pending a full investigation. Sir, you don't think there might have been a malicious purpose in this, rather than a glitch?"

"No one on board knows who I am, except for you and the ship's captain," he assured the manager. "I hardly think such a method would have been chosen, in any case. And no potential assassin would risk the emperor's displeasure, not to mention Chacon's," he added drily, alluding to the former Rojok field marshal who was now the son-in-law of the emperor.

The Rojok chuckled. "I see your point. All the same, I'll keep you apprised of the investigation."

"That would be appreciated."

"I am sorry for your injury."

Mekashe shrugged. "I've had worse than this practicing the Kahn-Bo with my friend Rhemun."

"Has he still not beaten you?" the Rojok asked.

Mekashe chuckled. "No. But his son has. Repeatedly. Kipling has a natural feel for the Kahn-Bo staff. He is almost without peer in the division."

"So I hear. Keep well."

"And you."

BACK IN HIS SUITE, Mekashe attended to his injury efficiently. Then he had a quick meal of the raw meat he preferred and brooded about the future.

Jasmine was afraid of cats. That might not have mattered, had he been human. But the Cehn-Tahr had galot genes and they had many feline characteristics. If she was already afraid of cats, how badly would she react to a humanoid male who was closely related to them, and whose true form she had never seen? Added to that were her vegan background and the other small differences that kept cropping up.

He reminded himself that no relationship was going to be perfect, that even people who had things in common frequently disagreed on small issues. But her fear of cats and her distaste for meat were major issues. He saw no easy resolution.

His only hope was that as she grew to know him she would put less emphasis on their differences. He knew her feelings. They were as strong as his own. Nothing was impossible. Not even this.

He contacted Hahnson on the scramble channel, his worried expression capturing the husky physician's attention at once.

"Something's wrong," Hahnson guessed.

Mekashe sighed. "Very wrong. She's afraid of cats."

Hahnson made a face. "Still, people can overcome fear," he added. "There are drugs to make the process easier."

"She's also a vegan and has a distaste for people who eat meat."

Hahnson sat down on a nearby stool. "I see."

"She is fragile and very sheltered. She was terrified of a creature we found in a badly programmed holoroom earlier. She screamed and panicked." He looked as worried as he felt. "She couldn't stop screaming. I think it might be what provoked the attack. I got her out of the way before I shifted into my true form and dispatched the creature. I also had words with the program manager. Such a glitch could have resulted in deaths. The holo tech is similar to the holon that we, ourselves, use. It permits an interface very close to reality."

"Yes, I know," Hahnson said quietly. "I'm sorry. I thought things were going well for you."

"Thanks to your dravelzium and the new nanotech, they are," Mekashe replied with a faint smile.

"I forgot to reset the white noise ball and had a quick glimpse of her mind. She feels exactly as I do." He drew in a breath. "However, she told me that her hand was only bruised when I held it, before you gave me the dravelzium. I broke several bones," he added miserably. "I would not have harmed her for all the world."

"I'm sure she knows that," Hahnson told him. "It's likely why she tried to keep the truth from you."

Mekashe stared at his hands. "Humans are fragile."

"Yes, they are," came the reply. "But Dtimun and Rhemun overcame their problems with their strength, and you will, also."

Mekashe looked relieved. He smiled. "I've been far more careful with her. There have been no more injuries. I am more grateful than you know for your help," he added. "Without the nanotech, I would not have been able to touch her at all."

"We're discovering new things all the time. Your Lady Caneese has been responsible for many of those discoveries. She has a genius for biochemistry. And Maddie Ruszel has contributed some of her own innovations." He chuckled. "They're working on a new drug, one that's gossiped to have tremendous implications down the road for mixed bondings."

Mekashe nodded, without paying much attention to what the other man was saying. "The dravelzium has a longer duration than I thought."

"Yes, this improved formula lasts for several days instead of the scant minutes that limited its use in the past," the physician agreed. "Just don't miss a dose." He chuckled.

"I can promise you that I won't. There's another matter." He held out his arm. "I told you about the creature in the holoroom. This was the result of my confrontation with it."

Hahnson grimaced. "Those are bad bites. What sort of creature was it?"

"A very nasty construct, with a bad attitude. I dispatched it after sending Jasmine away, but it was difficult to bring down."

Hahnson programmed his drug banks and activated the holo printer on Mekashe's dresser. "Use that on it—" he indicated the packet of drugs "—and self-inject the antibiotic, as well. Even a virtual creature can carry bacteria, especially with the sort of holo used on that ship."

"Truly. Thank you for the house call," he added, chuckling.

"My pleasure. I can't let the captain of the emperor's guard die. I'd be spaced!"

"He may space me when he finds out that I'm contemplating a bonding with a human. We already have two humans bonded to high-ranking aristocrats—one of them, the mate of the emperor's son, Dtimun."

"I hardly think it will be a concern," Hahnson assured him. "You might recall that the emperor is very fond of both Dr. Ruszel and Dr. Mallory. He loves both his grandsons. Not to mention the new granddaughter that Rhemun and Mallory recently presented him with."

Mekashe chuckled. "I have to be at the christening, but it isn't for two more terran months. It will be an event to remember. The second female born into Alamantimichar in its entire existence."

"I'm going, as well," Hahnson said, smiling. He nodded toward the packet he'd just sent. "Get busy with those meds. And call me if you need anything further. You know what signs to look for if the antibiotic doesn't kick in shortly."

"Yes, I do." He checked his ring-watch. "I have to dress for the evening. I'm taking her to another concert tonight. I find that I enjoy human opera," he added. "However, this is another sort of music."

"What sort?"

He told Hahnson, who grimaced.

"Well, it's not for every ear," the physician replied. "But you may find it interesting, at least."

"It isn't a bad idea to try new things."

"Exactly." He glanced at a board beside him. "I see that Tresar and Akmaran are on the vessel with you. Tresar has a physical upcoming with Tellas in a week. Is he going to be back here by then?"

"I'll make sure that he is," Mekashe said with twinkling green eyes. "He hates physicals. But he has a condition that certainly requires monitoring."

He shook his head. "He isn't seen very much. He detests shifting into a more human form just to be around outworlders, so he keeps to our private area below. He is what you humans might call eccentric."

Hahnson chuckled. "I can think of a few better words, but I won't comment. Plus he's a member of the Imperial Clan," he added. "We can't afford to let anything happen to him. The emperor is a terror when he loses his temper, and he's doubly protective about members of his own Clan. So remind Tresar about the physical, will you?"

"Certainly."

"And let me know how the concert goes." Hahnson glanced at the board again. There was a familiar chime. "I'm needed. How are you doing with dravelzium supplies?"

"I have more than enough for several weeks. Thank you for all your help."

"I'm delighted to do what I can." The physician grinned. "I'd love to be invited to the bonding, by the way."

Mekashe laughed delightedly. "Rest assured that your name will head the list. I owe you a great deal. So does she."

"Take care."

"And you."

MEKASHE DONNED A dark suit to wear to the concert and checked himself in the virtual mirror to make certain that he was presentable. He could hardly wait to see Jasmine again.

His arm was already healing, thanks to the efforts of Hahnson. The newer meds were far superior to the old ones.

He called for Jasmine at her door. The ambassador looked up from yet another paper book, grinned, waved and walked away. Jasmine was wearing a pale blue clinging dress that outlined her exquisite figure and matched her beautiful pale blue eyes. Her long hair was soft and wavy around her shoulders.

"You look exquisitely beautiful," Mekashe said huskily.

"So do you. I mean, you look handsome!" Jasmine stuttered, flushing. "How is your arm?" she added worriedly.

"Mended," he said, delighted at her concern for him. "My personal physician attended to it, and provided an antibiotic, as well. Even the bacteria in holorooms is quite lethal in the wrong situation."

"So I've heard." She shivered delicately. "I told Daddy about the creature. I'll never forget how terrified I was." She looked up. "I was so afraid that it had hurt you. The wound on your arm was bad enough, but it could have killed you!"

"I'm quite tough," he said, amused.

"I know, but it was such a large creature," she added worriedly. She searched his eyes. "I'm so glad you're all right!"

His chest swelled at her relief, at the evidence of her fear for his well-being. Things were going to work out. He was certain of it.

"The concert starts shortly. We should go."

"Yes. Daddy, I won't be late," she called.

"Be as late as you like, and have fun. Both of you!" he called back.

MEKASHE CHUCKLED AS they walked along en route to the concert hall, Jasmine's small hand tucked into his. "Is your father ever without a book in his hands?"

"Not often." Her eyes twinkled. "This one's about chess. He's determined to beat you, even if it's only one time."

He smiled. "He plays very well. He doesn't think through the moves before he makes them."

"He's too impulsive. I'm like that, too, I'm afraid. I just jump right in without thinking."

"In some circumstances, quick action can be a benefit, especially if lives are at stake."

"My mother was wounded once, years before she died," she said solemnly. "She was tending to a wounded diplomat when insurgents attacked. She jumped in front of one of her patients and took terrible fire from a weapon burst. But her quick action saved the man, who turned out to be related to the Terravegan president. She was given the highest civilian medal for it," she added proudly.

"An exceptional act of courage." He stopped walking and turned to her. "I'm sorry. I know how it feels to lose a parent."

"I know you do." She searched his eyes. "I want lots of children," she said huskily. "So that my child isn't an only child."

He studied her quietly. "I've been thinking the same thing lately."

Her heart skipped. She was thinking about children with black hair and golden skin and eyes that changed color.

He was looking back and thinking the same thing. A little girl like Rhemun's with blond hair and palest gold skin would be exquisite, especially with the elegant shape of Cehn-Tahr eyes and their color-changing ability. But that would be a long shot.

He reached out and touched her long hair, a sensual touch that made her shiver with pleasure. She caught his hand and curled hers around it while they stood in the corridor and stared at each other until they realized they were being watched by several amused passengers.

He cleared his throat and led her down the corridor. "Perhaps we should go to the concert before we become a, how did you say it, floor show?"

She laughed, delighted. "I think we should, yes."

But when they got to the concert auditorium, the scheduled Altairian concert had been canceled and one from a Terravegan performing company was substituted.

"Oh dear," Jasmine said softly, when she read the description on the virtual billboard. "This may not be what we expected."

He noticed her consternation. "What sort of concert is this?" he asked.

"Something totally strange and fascinating, if it's done properly," she replied. "It's a form of ancient human music that came from a place called, I think, China. It was on old Earth, before the Rendering."

He frowned. "Rendering?"

She nodded. "There was a cataclysm. All the records of that time were lost due to the global destruction, but a few precious vids made it out; mostly personal recordings of the time and place and what happened. A comet struck the earth, in one of the great oceans. There were these giant waves called tsunamis that devastated several continents and destroyed major cities. The survivors were hard-pressed to find food and potable water, shelter, safety. Eventually the people recovered and technology grew exponentially after some kindly interference by other world cultures. It was kept hidden from the majority of the population, because they were afraid of outworlders." She made a demure smile. "Sort of like me."

"I'm an outworlder. You aren't afraid of me," he pointed out.

"Yes, but these were apparently much different from humans," she replied. "In fact, I believe the gossip was that they were Rojoks."

"Rojoks are amazingly humanoid in appearance," he said. "Except that they have dusky skin and slit eyes and six fingers and toes. And all of them are blond."

"All of them?"

"Yes. In the military, length of hair is used to identify officers. A field marshal, like Chacon, has hair down past his waist in back."

"Chacon." She shivered. "I've read stories about him. He was a barbarian."

"You are thinking of the emperor Mangus Lo," he corrected. "Chacon was known all over the three galaxies for his compassion in battle. He was known to stop an attack that would have devastated the opposing force to allow them to remove their wounded and dying from the battlefield."

"Really?" she exclaimed.

He nodded. "His reputation for chivalry is deserved. He is an amazing leader, even as a politician. He now heads his government, and notorious prison camps like Ahkmau no longer exist."

"I must have mistaken the names," she confessed. "Honestly, there are so many that I can't remember at all. I'm afraid that Standard and French are all I speak, and some of the news reports are in languages that don't translate well."

"Understandable."

"Still, I'm not keen on the military. Any military," she added, not noticing her companion's expression, although his hand did seem to jerk faintly in her grasp. "Soldiers kill people, in all sorts of horrible ways." She made a mock shiver. "I look forward to the day when we can do away with armies forever."

"You may have an extremely long wait," he pointed out, trying not to take offense. "The military protects us from predation by insurgents bent on destruction."

"Yes, but are there really any insurgents left?" she asked innocently. "The galaxies are going through an unprecedented period of peace."

"Peace is an illusion, Jasmine," he said quietly, trying not to voice the resentment and hurt he felt. He'd been in the military all his life, and she hated it. This was another issue they'd face down the line, when she knew what he did for a living. "There will always be regional conflicts."

She drew in a long breath. "Oh, I suppose there will," she said. "But at least that's no concern of ours, right?" She brightened, looking up at him affectionately.

"Right." He said the word without enthusiasm.

She didn't notice. She was almost ethereal with happiness. She loved being with Mekashe. He was the most handsome man she'd ever seen, and he cared for her already. She had visions of a wonderful future that included him.

They reached the doors of the auditorium and Mekashe presented a microchip with their ticket purchases verified. The man at the door noted it in his reader, smiled and gave them their seat assignments.

"Daddy and I love Chinese music." She bit her lip and looked up at him. "But I'm not sure about this performance," she added, having noted the source of the music, which was listed. She was familiar with the background of the symphony composition, which was an experimental reconstruction of what the composer supposed to be authentic music from an ancient human society. "I hope you'll like it."

He chuckled softly. "If you love it, so shall I," he replied.

FAMOUS LAST WORDS. The sounds grated on his ears like the screaming of galots in the night. There was no sense or rhyme or regularity to the rhythm, and the instruments seemed to be composed of tin drums and some odd reedlike tubes. There were also strangely shaped flat things with strings that produced an amazing reverberation but no recognizable tune.

"They say this was pieced together from bits of old vids they found in the wreckage when Earth was devastated," she said. "Two of the instruments are from some island colony and others are from a city that fell. They were found with pieces of musical script that had 'China' at the top, so the music they recovered was called Chinese."

Privately, Mekashe thought that they'd cobbled several musical cultures into one badly reconstructed one. He'd never heard such a cacophony of terrible sounds.

"Well, there was a protest from this man who lived on New Cathay, one of the very old Earth colonies," she confessed. "He said that what they'd made was a combination of Island, Scottish and New Age music and the sheet music they found wasn't Chinese either—it was torn pieces of other forms of music that they had a computer arrange. He said the computer should be shot for the appalling result, and it should be burned. He was quite vocal. Of course, his was the only protest, and nobody listened. He was very old."

"Oh? How old?"

"Ninety," she said, shaking her head. "Amazing that he could even read the article about the new music!"

From his vantage point of being over two hundred and fifty years old, he could sympathize with the human on New Cathay. He was amused at the thought of Jasmine's expression when she knew his true age. And his true form.

That bothered him. She'd already reacted badly to one alien species. But she knew Mekashe. Surely she wouldn't be afraid of him! Not when she cared so much. He forced the thought out of his mind.

THE CONCERT WAS finally over. They were filing out of the concert chamber. Mekashe was amused at some of the whispered comments about the utter horror of the various combined musical traditions.

"You know," she said after a minute, "maybe that old man wasn't so crazy after all."

He chuckled. "Perhaps not." He turned to her. "Shall we have a cup of, what did you call it, cappuccino, before we part? The dining room is still open."

"I'd like that," she said, as reluctant as he was to part for the night.

THEY SAT SIPPING the hot beverage without speaking for a few minutes, watching the stars out the window and the occasional meteor passing.

"Space is so big," she commented.

"Bigger than you can imagine," he agreed.

"You've traveled a lot, haven't you?"

"Yes. My business takes me to many other planets."

She cocked her head and studied him. "You told me that you were a consultant. But you work in some political area, don't you? That's what Daddy thinks," she added with a smile.

He shrugged, a very human trait he'd picked up from the humans aboard the Morcai. "In a sense, yes."

"I knew it!"

He smiled at her, drinking in her exquisite appearance. "You are the most beautiful creature I've ever known," he said softly.

She flushed and laughed under her breath. "I'm not beautiful."

"You are to me," he said. "All my life, I've dreamed of a tall, willowy woman with a kind heart and beauty. I was shocked when we met by accident. You were the embodiment of my dream."

She smiled as she studied him. "Sometimes dreams walk," she said.

He nodded. "They do, indeed."

"I dreamed of a tall man with jet-black hair," she confessed. "But he had no features that I could discern." She hesitated. "Although, to be honest, it wasn't so much a dream as a nightmare," she said, frowning slightly. "I was terrified of him. He burst out of what looked like a plastic human body and became something else, something very scary." She sipped her cooling coffee, unaware of Mekashe's stricken look. "I woke up screaming. That was when Mama was still alive. She tucked me back in and said that sometimes our fears manifested in dreams, and that I wasn't to worry—it was just my subconscious stepping on my brain." She laughed. "I never had that dream again."

He was sipping his own cooling coffee, feeling a sense of despair that he couldn't even voice. It was as if she knew the truth about him without ever being told.

"Why so solemn?" she asked after a minute, when he didn't speak. "It was just a dream. I'm sure yours was much nicer."

"Much nicer indeed," he said, and forced a smile. He looked around. "They'll be closing soon. We should go."

"Okay."

She finished her coffee, he finished his and he escorted her out of the room and back to the suite she shared with her father. He was very distant.

"I didn't offend you somehow, did I?" she asked suddenly.

He arched his eyebrows, human fashion. "No. Of course not! I have a project I'm working on. It occupies me too much," he added with a smile. "What would you like to do tomorrow?"

She brightened at the thought that he wanted to take her out again. "Could we do one of the tourist things in the holoroom, you know, those scripted excursions to other planets that they offer? They're monitored carefully," she said, recalling that their sad experience earlier had been in an unscripted holo re-creation. "One of them is Dacerius. I've always been fascinated by it!"

"The desert planet?" he asked, smiling. "Certainly."

"It's a desert planet?"

He nodded. "They have these great mounts called Yomuth. I'm told they resemble a small creature that inhabited human worlds called a hamster. However, these are bigger than horses and they go like the wind itself."

She caught her breath. "You've been there," she assumed. "You've ridden them!"

He chuckled. "Yes. My travels have taken me to Dacerius. They also have a subspecies of reptile called Naagashe, a tiny white serpent with blue eyes. It purrs. Tourists purchase them."

"Reptiles that purr?" she exclaimed. "That doesn't sound scary at all! Do they have them for sale?"

He laughed delightedly at her enthusiasm. "Yes, they do."

"Then I must have one! I can't wait!" She hesitated. "Can we do the tour? Will you have time?"

"I am on holiday, until the ship docks at our spaceport above Memcache," he reminded her. "And, yes, I have the time. I would make it, even if I didn't, to be with you," he added softly.

She caught her breath. "I love being with you."

"As I love being with you, Jasmine."

He tugged her close, into a recessed area adjacent to the suites, bent and kissed her with suppressed hunger. She pushed closer into his arms and tugged his head down, locking her arms around his neck.

He was more grateful for the dravelzium than ever before, because the hunger he felt for her grew daily. Without the drug, nothing would have spared her. And that was impossible. Cehn-Tahr were conventional. They must be bonded before intimate contact. But he wanted her so badly that he was ready to throw convention to the winds.

It was with a great effort that he finally managed to draw away. The taste of her was sweet on his mouth. She looked as hungry as he felt. Her face was flushed, her eyes almost closed, sensual and sweet as they roved over his face.

"I love the way you taste," he teased. "I could make a meal of your mouth."

She laughed softly. "I love the way you taste, too," she whispered.

He hugged her close, but not too close, remembering the broken bones in her poor hand. Reluctantly, he let her go.

"Tomorrow. After breakfast?"

She nodded. "Tomorrow."

He smiled slowly, taking in the picture she made with her mouth softly swollen from his kisses, her hair disheveled where his hands had grasped it. She looked as if she belonged to him. The thought made him ecstatic.

"Good night," he said.

"Good night," she replied, and reluctantly went back into her suite.

HER FATHER WAS SNORING, asleep in his easy chair with the book open on his chest. She woke him.

"Back so soon?" he asked, disoriented.

"It's after midnight, ship time." She laughed.

"How was the concert?"

She made a face. "Well, I wouldn't call it music. A rendering of Sibericus was presented instead of the scheduled Altairian concert. And Mekashe looked as if he was being drawn and dismembered between two fast horses."

He chuckled. "That's exactly how I looked when I had to listen to that horrid collection of mangled tones. Whatever they say, that isn't Chinese music. I found a vid on the Nexus, from a private collection. Remind me, I'll play it for you. It's exquisite. The real thing."

"I'd love to hear it. Daddy," she said, laying down her small purse, "how would you feel, if it became serious with Mekashe and me?"

"I like him very much," he said. He hesitated. "But I think you should let matters progress slowly. You don't have to rush into something. Not when he'll be a neighbor, of a sort, when we reach Memcache."

She turned and looked at him. He was hiding something. She always knew. "You know something that you aren't telling me."

"Perhaps," he confessed. "Nothing deadly. Just some gossip. But I like Mekashe very much, and I'd have no problem adding him to the family. If you want to."

She hugged him hard, not noticing the way he'd

worded the sentence. "Oh, thank you! I was worried that you might want me to look for a human male…"

He burst out laughing. "Jasmine, I'd only have second thoughts if your intended had tentacles. And you can quote me."

She grinned. "Okay! Good night, Daddy."

"Good night, child. Sleep well."

THE NIGHTMARE SHE had that night was the old one, but this time the man in her dreams had Mekashe's face. He was holding her, in the silence of a primeval forest. It was quiet all around, except for night sounds, and she was so hungry for him that it was almost like pain.

Then, without warning, there was an attack and Mekashe shifted into some form that she'd seen only once, in the nightmare she had as a child. He became a monster, with claws and fangs and fur, and she screamed and screamed…!

CHAPTER SIX

"JASMINE!"

She heard the voice, just vaguely. She was still caught in the nightmare, screaming until her throat was sore.

"Jasmine, wake up!"

She was shaken, gently, by both arms. She forced her eyes open and there was her father, looking concerned.

"Child, you almost screamed the room down!" he exclaimed. "What was it, a nightmare?"

She sat up, drew up her knees under the covers and rested her damp face on them. She was shivering. "It was the old nightmare," she whispered brokenly, tears rolling down her cheeks. "Except that this time, the man I was with had a familiar face. It was Mekashe. We were in a forest somewhere, being threatened by some creature. Mekashe changed into a monster, with fangs and claws and fur...!"

Ambassador Dupont swallowed, hard, and tried not to let her see how disturbed he was. It was as if she'd seen Mekashe in his true form. The ambassador knew of the shape-shifting ability, but he'd only heard about the form it took in the Cehn-Tahr species. What he'd been told about them sounded very much like the creature his daughter was describing. He dreaded having her know the truth. She was in love with Mekashe. How would it affect her, when she knew that the form he took wasn't his true one, that he was something entirely out of her experience?

Mekashe cared for her deeply. It would destroy him, if she saw him as he was and screamed like this.

The ambassador ground his teeth together. He was watching a personal catastrophe in the making, and there was nothing he could do to prevent it. He was forbidden to tell anything he knew about the Cehn-Tahr to anyone except the Cehn-Tahr himself. He couldn't even tell his own daughter; that had been made explicitly clear. Besides that, Jasmine would never keep the secret. It would slip out and he'd be sent home in disgrace. It was doubtful that he'd even be able to get employment if that happened. There was so much resentment already among politicians about his selection as ambassador. The political sector would make sure that he never worked again. It was a chilling thought.

"There, there," he said gently, as he had when she was a little girl, patting her on the back. "Everything will be all right. It was just a dream, sweetheart. Just a dream."

She smoothed back her hair and wiped her eyes.

"I'm sorry if I upset you," she said with an apologetic smile. "I'm just not used to aliens. Although Mekashe doesn't look anything like that monster I dreamed about," she assured him.

He wasn't convinced, but he couldn't let his worry show. "Where are you and Mekashe going today?" he asked, to cheer her.

She glanced at the clock display on the wall and laughed. It was, indeed, morning, if very early. "We're going to Dacerius," she said. "I've always wanted to see it."

He smiled. "So have I. They have an entire pamphlet in the databanks for anyone who's interested in the tour. It sounds fascinating. If the two of you like it, I may try it myself."

She looked worried, as if she thought he might want to tag along with them.

He laughed. Her expression was so open. "I don't want to go with you and Mekashe," he told her. "Just so you know. The time you have together is precious."

"It is," she said, and smiled apologetically. "But I really think we're going to be together for a very long time." She sighed. "I've never felt like this. It's joy beyond description."

"I had that, with your mother," he said. "She was a rare person."

"She was."

"Try to get a little more sleep," he said, rising. "And no more nightmares. That's an order."

She laughed. "Yes, sir."

"Sleep well, daughter."

"You, too."

SHE DID MANAGE to get a few more hours of sleep, without the nightmare returning. When she got up, she powdered her face, put on a light lip gloss and put on a gossamer blue sleeveless dress in a light, clingy fabric that swirled around her ankles. It made her look older, more sophisticated. And it was just right for a hot, desert climate. She'd noticed that the holorooms did an excellent job of matching climate to location. She didn't want to sweat too much.

Mekashe was punctual. He was wearing a light-weight suit, superbly cut, that enhanced his muscular form. She wondered at the strength of it; he was very fit for a diplomat.

"Why are you watching me so closely?" he teased.

"You're very…well, very muscular," she replied, smiling up at him. "Does your diplomatic service have physical requirements?"

"Many," he said, "and more than just physical ones. You look very pretty," he said, changing the subject.

"I tried to dress for the climate. I expect Dacerius is very hot."

He chuckled. "Extremely hot. The sands blow

constantly, so that it's impossible to walk around the villages without being lightly covered in yellow dust."

She laughed. "If I get covered in yellow dust, I'll look like you," she said with a shy glance. "You have the most beautiful skin color. Sorry, handsome skin color," she corrected at once.

He curled her fingers into his, sending a shock of pleasure through her. "I'm pleased that you like it."

"What do the Cehn-Tahr look like?" she asked suddenly. "I mean, do you have different skin colors, like human colonies do?"

He'd caught his breath when she asked what his species looked like. He was afraid that she'd seen or heard something that would disturb her. He laughed softly. "No. All Cehn-Tahr have golden skin and black hair. We are one race, not many."

"Then you must never have conflicts," she began.

He threw back his head and roared with laughter. "We have them constantly. One Clan takes offense at something a member of another Clan says, and there's open verbal warfare. It can be extremely unpleasant."

"What are Clans?"

He pursed his lips. "You might call them family units, but that would be a simplification. Clan is everything in my culture. We live and die to spare it shame or dishonor."

"It sounds like a very noble culture," she said after a minute.

He smiled. At least that sounded positive.

THE HOLOROOM THAT Mekashe had reserved was already programmed for Dacerius. He'd already checked with the programming manager to make sure there were no more glitches, like the one that had injured Mekashe. They arrived in a shuttle in the created environment, which made the experience even more real.

When they stepped out of it into the spaceport on the planet's surface, Jasmine caught her breath and laughed. "It's so hot!" she exclaimed.

He smiled. "True to life. Come. There are Yomuth for rent just outside. We can ride to a village and sample the native foods. And see the Nagaashe," he added when she looked dubious.

"But I'm really not dressed to ride anything," she began worriedly. "I should have worn slacks. I'm so sorry!"

He chuckled. He led her to a small cubicle in the spaceport. "It's a changing room," he said. "Clothing for the tourist attraction is provided with the holoroom."

Her face lit up. "Really? Oh, thank goodness. I would have been heartbroken if I couldn't ride!"

"Go ahead," he said, indicating the room. "I'll wait here."

"I won't be a minute!" she promised.

OF COURSE, IT was ten minutes, maybe more. She had a choice of desert outfits, so she finally chose one that was supposed to resemble ancient human desert garb—a tunic and long skirt with high boots and a wide-brimmed hat, in a khaki color. She was so fascinated with it that she lost track of time.

"I'm so sorry!" she told Mekashe when she reappeared. "I got carried away."

He scowled. "Carried…away." He nodded, not understanding.

"I lost myself in the search for clothing," she amended. "It was fun!"

He laughed. "I see. You look nice."

"It's ancient human desert wear, they said," she told him. "At least, it should keep the sand out!"

"Indeed."

She noticed that he was wearing the same suit and hadn't changed. "Won't you ruin your suit?" she worried.

He laughed. "It's made of durable fabric, and it changes color and shape according to the environment it encounters. You'll see when we get outside."

THAT REALLY FASCINATED HER. She followed him out the spaceport doors and into the desert sun. His suit turned pale tan and amended itself into desert wear, much like the Dacerians themselves wore.

She laughed with delight. "That's so incredible!"

"We have rather advanced tech on Memcache," he said simply. He caught her hand in his. "Now. Let's find a Yomuth shop!"

THERE WERE YOMUTH in all sorts of colors. Some were white. Some were tan. Some had patterns. But Jasmine fell in love with a black-and-white one with huge blue eyes. He rubbed his head against her and she was entranced.

"They're quite affectionate," Mekashe said. "This one, then?" He gave the merchant his chip and paid for the animal for a whole day.

"Mount up," he told her, indicating a large, high stone edifice with steps.

She knew immediately what it was for. She climbed to the top and let Mekashe seat her on the soft blanket that served as a saddle. He moved into place behind her, linked a long arm around her waist, took the reins and urged the mount forward.

The Yomuth was fast. It took to the road with a spring and a grunt and galloped down the long, winding desert road.

"This is fun!" Jasmine called.

"Yes, it is." He chuckled. He turned the animal toward Hakar, a small village a mile from the spaceport. It had a famous bazaar in real life, which was re-created in the holoroom.

"It's so hard to believe that we're in a room," she

exclaimed as she looked around at the endless horizon.

"Technology has made many advances over the years," he agreed. "One does get the feeling of actually being in the chosen place."

"Is it like this? Really like this?" she wondered when they reached the village and he was handing her down to the mounting stone in place beside a stable.

"More or less," he said. He smiled down at her. "Of course, on the real planet, there are raiders and some rather fierce predators. Those won't be re-created here."

"Thank goodness. I couldn't bear to see you hurt again," she confessed huskily.

His heart soared. He smiled at her and felt himself almost airborne.

"Is that where they sell the Nagaashe?" she asked excitedly, when she saw another group of tourists gathered around something serpentine on a raised table.

"Yes, it is. This village is famous for them. Of course, these are virtual Nagaashe, Jasmine," he emphasized. "The sale of real ones is taboo." He didn't tell her why, that the blue-eyed serpents were both sentient and telepathic. The small ones from Dacerius were sold on the black market, but their possession was illegal on most civilized worlds.

"Why?" she asked curiously.

He smiled. "I'll tell you later. Look." He pointed

to a table where the little Nagaashe were slithering around.

She moved closer. She was shocked when one of the little creatures rushed toward her.

She jerked back, but Mekashe caught her shoulders and held her in place. "No. Don't run," he whispered. "It likes you! It wants to be picked up."

"Oh." She stopped struggling and moved closer. The tiny serpent coiled just in front of her, swayed back and forth and emitted a purring sound. "My goodness!" she exclaimed.

She cupped her hands and the little creature slid into them and coiled and purred even louder. She laughed like a happy child as she lifted it to her face. It leaned forward and rubbed its head against her cheek, vibrating and purring.

"It's so sweet!" she exclaimed.

"They make loyal pets," he said. "There have been stories about them, legends, for many years. The virtual ones have a shape-shifting ability. They can grow to enormous size and actually protect their owners from attack. It's why they're so sought after as pets."

"Do the real ones do that?" she asked.

"No. The true Nagaashe are as tall as a two-story building. They are both venomous and aggressive when attacked. They have a large colony on Eridanus Three, where they live undisturbed. The virtual ones are patterned after the real ones, but with the shape-shifting function programmed in."

"That's fascinating."

He smiled. "Yes. They have other traits that are only revealed to the owner, and each is different and unique. They can never be used against the owner. But they are quite protective, and they survive to a great age, like their living counterparts."

"How long do they live? The real ones?" she asked curiously.

"We have no true figures, but some are rumored to be thousands of years old."

"My goodness!"

The little Nagaashe purred some more.

"I have to have him," she said huskily. "I don't even care what it costs."

He laughed. "I will give him to you…"

"No, you won't," she said firmly. "Daddy gave me plenty of mems to spend, and I'm buying him myself." She looked up at his surprised expression. "You're so kind to me, Mekashe. You've treated me to so many fascinating trips. I can do this one thing for myself."

He sighed. The giving of a gift was a prelude to courtship. It would bring on the mating ritual. He didn't mind. He planned to bond with her. But perhaps she was right. It might be just a little soon for something so profound. With that thought in mind, he'd given her the capture device through her father. He'd asked earlier if she had it, and she assured him that her father had passed it along. She seemed enthralled with the capture of the two of them together.

"Can you ask him how much the Nagaashe is?" she asked Mekashe.

"I can." He spoke Dacerian like a native. The shopkeeper replied, and Mekashe translated for Jasmine.

"That's very reasonable, for something so precious!" she said. She reached into her pack and pulled out a sack of mems. She handed it to the merchant and Mekashe explained that she wanted the merchant to take out what was needed for the serpent and return the rest, which he did.

"And now you're mine, you precious thing," she whispered to the little serpent. "You're just so precious!"

Mekashe was delighted at her pleasure in the little pet. It would keep her safe, too, protect her against any threat. It might shock her when she watched it transform, however. He'd have to make sure she understood that it wouldn't look like the tame, affectionate little creature she was holding, if it changed into its larger form to meet the threat.

She turned to him suddenly, worried. "We're in a virtual place," she said. "I won't be able to take him out of here, will I?"

He chuckled. "If that were the case, the holorooms would go unvisited. The Nagaashe will be replicated outside the instance and waiting for you, nicely packaged, when we leave."

She let out the breath she'd been holding. "Oh,

thank goodness," she said heavily, rubbing her head against her pet's. "I'm already attached to him. It would hurt to have to leave him behind."

"I can assure you that you won't," he said, smiling. "And now, how would you like to sample Dacerian fare? You can bring the little serpent inside with you," he explained with a laugh when she paused at the doorway of the small restaurant.

"Oh, then, that's fine! What is the food like?"

"Much easier to show you than tell you, but I think you may find it delightful," he commented as they went inside and were seated.

She looked at the menu and hesitated. "Can you tell me what it says?" she asked. "Better yet, can you just order something for me?"

"What sort of fare do you prefer?" he asked.

"Nothing that comes from an animal," she replied quickly. "Just vegetables or fruits."

"Certainly."

SHE ATE HEARTILY, delighted with the taste of the native plants. "Aren't you eating?" she asked worriedly.

He smiled. "I think you know that I prefer meat. But I won't eat it in front of you."

She smiled back. "That's so sweet. But I wouldn't mind, really," she said hesitantly. "Sometimes we have to compromise."

"I agree. But I had a large breakfast and I'm

truly not hungry," he said, smiling warmly. If she was willing to compromise, perhaps the road ahead wouldn't be so rocky after all.

After she finished her small meal, with her virtual Nagaashe tucked safely into her pack, they mounted the Yomuth again and headed to the next tourist attraction. It was a desert camp in the old style, with a campfire and huge tents in which the inhabitants lived.

There were animals being roasted on spits in the campfire and Mekashe tugged Jasmine's hand as she went toward it.

"That will not make you happy," he told her quietly. "We should go along to the rest of the camp. They use flint knapping techniques to work stone weapons. It will be interesting."

She looked up at him, puzzled. "But I've heard of campfires. I've never seen one. They say that the Holconcom used to tell stories of Dr. Madeline Ruszel around them, before she was bonded to your emperor's son."

"That is true," he replied, smiling. "She was legend among the kehmatemer, the emperor's Imperial Guard, long before she left the Holconcom to bond with Dtimun."

She caught her breath. "She was Holconcom? But she's a woman…!"

He chuckled. "You see, Dtimun and the emperor were involved in a feud that lasted many decades.

When the Morcai Battalion was first formed at Ahk-mau, where military humans and Cehn-Tahr were imprisoned, it was Dr. Ruszel who saved Dtimun's life. Dtimun had Ruszel assigned as Cularian medicine specialist aboard his flagship, the Morcai, and she became the first and only female human ever to serve there. The emperor was furious, but Dtimun's authority aboard the Morcai was absolute. Later, she saved the emperor's life during a small conflict on an away mission, and earned his respect."

"She must have been an exceptional person," Jasmine remarked, fascinated.

"She still is," he said, smiling.

Her pale blue eyes were full of concern. "Those are facts that most Terravegans don't even know. You won't get in trouble with anyone, for telling me?"

He shook his head. "Your father will be privy to much information that is never shared with outworlders. I am, how do you say, anticipating your residence on Memcache. You are not an outsider," he added huskily, with possessive eyes.

She moved a step closer to him. "I'm glad. I love it, that we'll be near each other on your planet. And we can see each other?"

He nodded.

"And…go places together?"

He nodded again.

She moved closer still. "I can't wait," she whispered. "It will be a whole new life."

"For both of us," he whispered back.

Around them, the villagers were smiling and laughing softly. Mekashe cleared his throat and stepped back.

"We seem to be attracting attention," he explained.

She noticed. Her face flamed. "Sorry."

"You have nothing to apologize for. But we should move on."

"Yes."

It was a perfect day. When sunset came to the planet, it was time to board the shuttle and travel back to the ship—or at least, enter the simulation that created the experience.

Mekashe walked Jasmine back toward the rooms she shared with her father. They were holding hands and both reluctant to part.

"It grows harder to leave you," he said huskily when they reached the door.

"For me, as well," she replied, looking up at him hungrily.

He pulled her into the small alcove and kissed her with such passion that she caught her breath and shivered.

He drew back at once. "Did I hurt you?" he asked

quickly. He'd used an extra dose of the dravelzium, to make sure, but perhaps…!

"You didn't hurt me," she said. Her breath was jerking, like her heart. "It was…beyond words."

He understood then, and he laughed softly. "Perhaps we both improve with practice," he teased.

She laughed. "Perhaps we do."

"Where shall we go tomorrow?"

"You choose, this time," she said.

He pursed his lips. "Memcache?"

Her breath caught. "Could we? But isn't it taboo?"

"Not for an ambassador's daughter," he replied easily. "But if it makes you more secure, I will ask the approval of my government first."

"Please," she said. "I couldn't bear to get you into trouble."

He beamed. "In that case, I'll do it tonight."

She reached up a small hand and stroked his hard cheek. "I don't know how I lived, until you came into my life. Everything before this is gray and still. When I'm with you, it's explosions of color and light and joy."

He brought her palm to his mouth and kissed it hungrily. "You have a way with words," he said. "I could not have put it better. I feel the same."

She searched his eyes. They were a somber, quiet blue. "I don't think I could live, if anything happened to part us."

His heart jumped. "I promise you, nothing will. And I never give my word lightly."

She drew in a breath. The nightmare she'd had was disturbing. She thought about sharing it with him, but she would have felt ridiculous. So she smiled instead and walked reluctantly into the rooms she shared with her father.

"Good night, then."

"Sleep well," he said gently.

He stood, watching her, until she was out of view.

WHEN HE GOT back to his quarters, he turned off the white noise ball and called to the emperor, who was instantly inside his mind.

The emperor chuckled. "So this is the one, then?" he teased.

Mekashe laughed, too. "I'm afraid so. She is human…"

The emperor scoffed. "So are my son's mate and your cousin's. All my grandchildren have human blood. It enriches our culture. Even the Dectat approves. You will find no barriers here."

Mekashe let out a sigh. "I have lived my life alone," he said. "No female has ever appealed to me, except in the way of friendship. This one—she burns me."

"A beautiful young woman" was the reply. "I have read the dossier on her father, which included one on her. She has a kind heart, which is far more important than beauty, although she has that in abundance. She will grace Alamantimichar," he added, naming the great Royal Clan to which he and Mekashe both belonged.

"I am gratified that you have no objection."

"You have spoken with Dr. Hahnson?" came an unexpected question.

Mekashe blinked. "Well, yes. I have been using dravelzium," he began.

"Never mind," the emperor replied, amused. "I understand. If you know the obstacles, that is enough. Take care. I look forward to meeting her at the reception, when all of you arrive on Memcache."

"I had not thought to enjoy such a long R & R," Mekashe mused.

"And I was certain that you needed one," the emperor retorted. "As you can see, my decisions are usually correct."

He laughed. "Indeed they are, sir. I will see you in three weeks."

"You are sorely missed. But enjoy your time with her. Your duties will be rigorous when you return, I fear. We are entering into another bout of diplomacy with the Altair delegation. It will require much travel."

"I will not mind."

"Rhemun is considering a different position," the

emperor added. "This is something that might concern you. But we can discuss it when you arrive."

"Yes, sir."

"Take care."

And he was gone.

MEKASHE WONDERED WHAT was going on with Rhemun. Now that he was comfortably bonded, with two children, he might be encountering resistance from Edris Mallory about his spacegoing duties aboard the Morcai. Rhemun headed the Holconcom, which faced many dangers.

He wondered if Rhemun was considering a post nearer home. His heart leaped. That would place Mekashe in command of the Morcai, of the Holconcom. It had been the dream of his life, that position, but he would never have begrudged it to his best friend, Rhemun. Clan status dictated position. Mekashe was next in the chain of command, if Rhemun relinquished command of the Holconcom.

If he was appointed, he could not refuse. But Jasmine would have issues with that. She still didn't know what he really looked like, or what his position was in his government. She didn't like the military. Mekashe was in command of the kehmatemer. How would that sit with a female who had pacifist leanings? Even worse would be the Holconcom with their fearsome reputation.

"Mekashe, put these concerns out of your mind

and rest," came an amused old gravelly voice into his thoughts. "And turn the white noise ball back on! Enemies thrive even on cruise ships!"

"Yes, sir!" he replied, chuckling.

He turned the device back on, shaking his head. The emperor was right. He could do nothing about the future. *Karamesh*. It was written. He turned away from the viewport and went to bed.

JASMINE'S FIRST VIEW of Memcache took her breath away. Mekashe, watching her reactions, felt joy surge through him.

"It's more than I ever imagined," she whispered. "It's…perfect!"

They were in the middle of a forest that resembled bamboo forests on old Earth. The ground was sprinkled with pretty blue and gold flowers in an assortment of shapes and sizes. A silver ribbon of water curled lazily through it with small waterfalls made by natural stone barriers slowing it.

She reached out and touched the water. "It feels so real," she exclaimed.

"The programmers are quite good. Most of them." He glanced at her. "Come this way. I want to show you something."

She followed him to a clearing. There, among flowering shrubs and fountains, was the most majestic, beautiful stone house she'd ever seen. It had towering columns with designs on them, and the sound of wind chimes were all around them.

"What is this place?" she asked, breathless with delight.

He smiled. "It's my home," he said simply.

CHAPTER SEVEN

JASMINE'S HEART SKIPPED wildly as they walked down a paved walkway, past a huge ornamental fountain that featured a cat sitting in the bowl, with water pouring from his mouth.

She stopped, disturbed.

Mekashe grimaced. He took her hand in his. "My culture reveres cats, I'm afraid," he said gently. "You will have to adjust to this. There are statues of cats in most private homes and in many public buildings."

She took a deep breath. She turned and looked up at him. "I'll do my very best. I promise."

"If you are exposed to the things you fear, they become less troublesome," he said softly, searching her eyes. "I know that we have many differences. But I think that we can overcome them."

She moved a step closer. "I think so, too."

He stepped back and made a sound deep in his throat.

"Oh dear," she mused. "Have I stepped on another taboo?"

He chuckled at her wording. "In fact, you have. We permit no overt displays of affection in public."

"I see." She moved back a step and grinned at him. "Okay."

He smiled. "You adjust quickly."

"I certainly do." She hesitated. "Mekashe, you're sure you won't get in trouble for this? I mean, taking me to your home?"

"I have permission from the highest authority on Memcache," he said. "I will not get in trouble."

"In that case, can we go inside?" she asked. "I love this architecture!"

"So do I. This home has been in my family, in my Clan, for generations. I love every stone in it."

She ran her hand over one of the smooth columns and caught her breath. "It's warm!" she exclaimed. "But it looks like marble!"

He frowned. "What is marble?"

She went into an elaborate description of the stone building material that humans had brought from old Earth. They'd located quarries of a similar stone on Terravega.

"We build with it, but it's only for the aristocratic families," she said sadly. "Daddy and I live in a wooden house, with fancy gingerbread boards and high eaves. It's painted white, and we think it's charming. I'll have to show you a capture of it."

"I would like to see it," he said. He searched her face. "If we had the schematics, I could have my friend who manages the programming unit aboard this cruise ship re-create it."

"I'd have loved that," she said. "But I'd have no idea how to obtain them."

"Nor I," he confessed. He pursed his lips. "Perhaps we might ask your father if he knows someone who could do such a favor for him."

"Now, that's what I call an idea," she teased.

He smiled. "Meanwhile," he said, catching her fingers in his, "we can explore my reality."

The inside of the great house had many rooms. All were open, airy, with small balconies that overlooked the stream on one side and the mountains on the other. The trees, which looked like ancient bamboo, reached high into the sky, which was an odd shade of blue. She remarked on it as they watched the wide stream flow lazily over a series of natural waterfalls from a balcony.

He laughed softly. "The color of the sky comes from the source of power that we use. This is close enough to our main city that you can see the plasma discharges in the sky. It was one of your people, Dr. Madeline Ruszel, that made a treaty with the Nagaashe possible. They have abundant resources of Helium three, which we use in our reactors."

"The Nagaashe?" she asked, puzzled. "They have a culture?"

He didn't feel uncomfortable telling her about them, since the Nagaashe were not Cehn-Tahr and the secrecy laws did not apply. He turned to her. "The true Nagaashe, the counterparts from which your virtual one is taken, have an ancient and great civilization on Akaashe, their planet. They are sentient, as tall as two-story houses on your world, and they have advanced psychic powers. They saved Dr. Ruszel's life when her vessel crashed on Akaashe during a rescue operation, by calling for help."

She searched his eyes. "She couldn't mend herself?"

"Her wrist scanner was broken, beyond repair, and she had fatal injuries," he said, recounting the story that most Cehn-Tahr knew by now, especially members of the Royal Clan, who were her relations by bonding. "The Nagaashe had affection for her already, because she had rescued a Nagaashe child on Memcache. As a result of her interaction with them, a treaty was made, which all the diplomats on Memcache had not been able to accomplish in a century," he added with a deep chuckle. "Needless to say, there was an uproar in the Dectat."

"She must be a fascinating person," Jasmine said. "I'd love to be able to meet her, but she's royalty, isn't she? I've read about royalty. You have to be an aristocrat even to be allowed into their presence…"

He drew her gently to him. He'd used a dose of dravelzium covertly to keep from injuring her. "You will be able to meet her when we arrive on Memcache," he said softly, bending to brush his mouth over hers. "You forget that your father is now an ambassador. He will have access to the emperor, something that no humans, except Ruszel and the human members of the Holconcom, have ever been privileged to accomplish."

She caught her breath. "There are humans in the Holconcom, besides Dr. Ruszel?" she exclaimed.

It was a dangerous slip of the tongue. He amended the taboo statement. "The humans and our Cehn-Tahr were both apprehended by Mangus Lo during his rule on Enmehkmehk, the Rojok prime planet. That was before your government rescinded its mutiny charges against the humans for participating in Ruszel's rescue, before they were allowed to go back to Terravega." He was lying, but not really. He was insinuating that the humans had gone home. They hadn't.

She pressed close to him, resting her face against his chest. "Your culture is very complicated," she said softly.

"It is. But it is an ancient one, rich in legend and accomplishment. We govern almost a hundred and ten worlds, most of which revere the emperor and have representatives in the Dectat."

"Your emperor sounds as fascinating as Ruszel," she murmured against the soft fabric that covered his broad, muscular chest. Odd that he felt so much bigger, broader, than he looked.

He didn't hear her thoughts because the white

noise ball was still functioning. But he did feel her breath stir, her heartbeat quicken against him. He was feeling similar emotions. He wanted her. They were alone. No one would know.

His own breath quickened at the thought. They could bond very soon. It would not matter. He could mark her...

He drew his thoughts back, quite forcibly. He did not dare step over that invisible line. He would disgrace not only her, but her father, as well. When he returned to Memcache, there would be no white noise ball to shield his mind from the emperor or Dtimun or Rhemun, his friend. They would all know what he'd done. It would shame the Great Clan.

He laughed softly and drew away, but not before he touched his lips to hers in a long, sweet, tender kiss.

"Very soon," he whispered, "I will have a question to ask you."

Her heart was racing like mad. "Very soon," she whispered, her pale blue eyes shimmering with joy, "I will have a positive answer."

He hugged her close, careful not to be too enthusiastic, and then released her, taking her small hand in his. "There is an aviary in the room that faces the mountain. We keep birds here."

"In cages?" she asked hesitantly.

He smiled. "We keep the injured ones," he amended. "We have a worker who cares for them, tends to their wounds, and releases them when they are healed. It is against the law to contain any wild thing."

She caught her breath. "I'd love to help do that!" she exclaimed. "My mother would have loved it, as well. She was a physician, a very good one. She tried to discourage me from medicine. She thought I was too soft, that I would never be able to cope with the horrors she had to see." She looked up at him. "But I think she was wrong. I know I could do it, if I really wanted to."

His hand linked into hers. "You will have no need to work here. As you can see—" he indicated the spacious villa "—we will be quite self-sufficient. And I have my position, as well, which provides anything else I might need."

She cocked her head. "You won't tell me what that profession is."

"I promise you that I will, at the correct time," he said with a smile.

"All right."

HE LED HER past a huge bedroom with a circular bed and many live plants and a balcony that opened to the outside. The furnishings were in natural colors, greens and browns and tans. She noticed a lounging chair and what looked like a telescope.

"That's your room," she said at once.

His eyebrows arched.

She laughed self-consciously. "I'm sorry. I'm being presumptuous."

"You are not. And it is my room. For now." His eyes promised a future that set her heart beating wildly again.

He ground his teeth together. The bed was very tempting. But he fought the inclination and tugged her toward the area in the back of the house, which was outfitted like a human animal treatment center. It had expensive equipment, and the cages were the largest, most natural she'd ever seen. They were like being outdoors. Even trees grew in the ones which contained a variety of colorful birds. Some sort of force field seemed to be used as walls.

"We use force technology to keep them inside. It isn't like hitting what you call a window," he added. "It is a soft repelling, which doesn't hurt them."

She smiled and shook her head. "This is like an animal hospital," she exclaimed as they walked among the cages. Besides the birds, there were some small rodent-like creatures and a larger, colorful lizard with a long tail, who came right to the front of the cage and wagged his tail like a dog. He even panted.

"Brulius," he commented. He pushed his hand very slowly through the force web and patted the great lizard on the head. The tail wagged even more. "Good boy. Very good boy," he said softly, as he withdrew his hand.

"A lizard who acts like a dog," she exclaimed.

"A trilerius," he told her. "Native to Memcache."

"He's so cute! I'd love to…!" She stopped dead. In the farthest cage was a solid black cat, bigger than a man, with glittering green eyes and white fangs that displayed as he lowered his ears and growled at her.

"I forgot. We have a virtual galot here, to protect the injured animals from predators. We have only a small family of true galots on Memcache," he began. "They live in the mountains, near my cousin's home…" He didn't need to add that all the animals in the facility were virtual, as were their surroundings.

She screamed. And screamed. The birds went wild. The lizard shot up a tree. The virtual caretaker made a sound like a sob.

"Let's go. Quickly!"

He drew her out of the enclosure. She was crying wildly, shaking. He ground his teeth together. This was a bad omen. The worst. Because he had as much in common with a galot as he did with a humanoid.

"Jasmine, you must stop screaming," he said sternly. "Even virtual animals can attack if they are provoked!"

She was still shaking. "Please. I want to go," she cried wildly. "I have to get out of here! I'm sorry, but I can't… I just can't…!"

He led her to the exit, his heart falling in his chest. He didn't speak. He couldn't find the right words. She had no idea what his true form was. How could he ever tell her, show her, if she acted like this with just a virtual galot?

They were outside the instance. He folded her in his arms and held her while she cried. It was a long time before she was calm enough to leave the area and go back to her suite.

"I'm so sorry," she said. Her eyes and her nose were still red. "I'm terrified of cats. I don't know what to do. Maybe there's a medicine…"

"We can research that," he said heavily. "I'll ask my physician."

She nodded. "I spoiled our day," she said sadly. "I'm an idiot."

Her sorrow lessened his grief. He touched her hair, her beautiful blond hair, which she always wore long around her shoulders, just for him. She wouldn't know, but his own mane curled down to his waist in back, much like his cousin Rhemun's. It was longer than hers, although the sensor net he used camouflaged that aspect of him.

"There will be other days. We still have three weeks," he teased softly.

"Three weeks," she agreed. "Then we reach Memcache." She searched his eyes and smiled. "I can't wait!"

He smiled. "Nor I." He drew a strand of her soft hair through his fingers. "We will find a way to deal with your fears. I promise."

She relaxed a little. "Okay." She stood on tiptoe

and kissed his hard, chiseled mouth. "Sleep well. I'll see you tomorrow?" she added worriedly, as if she thought he might not want to see her again, after her panic attack.

He bent and brushed her mouth with his. "Of course you will. Good night."

"Good night, Mekashe."

He left her there, loving the way his name sounded in her soft voice. One day, he'd be able to teach her the familiar pronunciation, as well. He'd have to do something about the galots his worker treated at the villa. Normally, she would never encounter one, so it wasn't going to be a big problem. Except that he had feline traits of which she was unaware. His heart dropped again.

HE CALLED HAHNSON again and discussed the problem.

Hahnson was supportive, but not encouraging. "People can overcome phobias," he assured his friend. "But it isn't a simple thing. Often counseling is necessary as well as medicine. I think your physician on Memcache will be of much help," he added, his eyes twinkling. "It's not a big problem. Really."

"She's never seen me as I truly am," Mekashe said heavily. "It is a thing I truly fear."

"We all got used to the way you Cehn-Tahr look," Hahnson said. "Nobody fainted or asked for reassignment after Dtimun had all of you in the Holconcom shift into your true appearances. It was because we knew you and had great affection for you." He smiled. "Jasmine loves you. It won't matter to her, any more than it mattered to Madeline Ruszel when she saw Dtimun in his true form for the first time."

He relaxed a little more. "At least there's hope," he said.

Hahnson laughed. "There's always hope. Even when the world seems to end," he added gently. "Get some sleep and stop worrying. I'll do some research for you."

"That would be much appreciated."

"And you're very welcome."

IT WAS LATE the next "day" when Mekashe went to call on Jasmine. There had been a sudden death among the kehmatemer. One of its youngest members had died in a sporting accident on R & R, to the shock and horror of its members. Mekashe was sad, because the youngest one of them had been a favorite of his. He would mourn him. But it also meant that another candidate had to be chosen. He was sent virtual résumés of Cehn-Tahr currently in the military, from which he would select a replacement. It would take some time. The unit was small. He wanted no potential conflict among the Cehn-Tahr who served the emperor.

It was on his mind when she came out, dressed in a gossamer gold gown, her blond hair clean and shining as it waved down over her shoulders, her face beautiful and aglow with pleasure.

"You look beautiful, as you always do," he said, and caught her hand in his.

"And you look handsome, as you always do," she replied gently.

"Ahem," Ambassador Dupont said after a minute, because they stood like statues.

They started and noticed him in the doorway for the first time.

"It's the Altairian folk dance group tonight," he told them, chuckling. "They finally got here, so you'll have nice music to listen to, for a change."

"What they called Chinese music was an insult to that wonderful culture," Jasmine replied. She made a mock wince. "It was horrible! They should stop performing it at all."

"I'm sure they've been told that, a few times. The Altairian group is quite good. I've been to a performance."

"Then it will be something to look forward to," Mekashe assured him. "Shall we go?" he asked Jasmine.

She held his hand and grinned at her father. "We won't be too late."

"Not to worry. I found a vid on the great cats of Eridanus Three," he said. "I can't watch that with her—she has nightmares…" He broke off and looked horrified at what he'd said.

Mekashe had some idea of why. "Phobias can be addressed successfully," he assured the other man, and he smiled. "I have that information from my personal physician," he added. He looked down at Jasmine. "It's a minor problem. Only a minor one."

Jasmine smiled broadly. "Yes, it is. I'll see you later, Daddy," she added.

He nodded, giving Mekashe an apologetic smile.

"Don't worry," he told the ambassador gently. "It isn't a problem."

"All right."

Jasmine looked from one to the other. "Whatever are you two talking about?"

Mekashe chuckled. "Chess."

She rolled her eyes and shook her head. "Chess. Goodness!"

The ambassador chuckled. "Have fun." He saw them off and went back inside. But he felt a sudden jolt of fear. How would Jasmine react to a creature who was part cat, part humanoid, because that was what he'd been told in confidence. They were close to Memcache, and the diplomatic service wanted to make sure that their representative did nothing to offend the emperor, especially if he encountered the Cehn-Tahr in their true form. He was not to react to their appearance; he wasn't to grimace or flinch or make any show of disrespect. He assured his superior that he wouldn't.

But he was less certain of Jasmine's reaction, if she encountered Mekashe in his true form. He'd heard about the young virtual galot at Mekashe's villa, as well as the cat statues and statuettes throughout the airy construction. She didn't have to hide her fear from her father, and it was formidable. It was, she confided, the only thing that really worried her about her relationship with Mekashe. She adored him, but those cat statues were going to have to be removed if she lived there.

She was almost haughty about it, and the ambassador felt sick at heart. It would not be possible for them to be removed, because they were religious artifacts. She didn't know that, but the ambassador did. Cats everywhere on Memcache. She would never adjust. He only hoped that she wouldn't offend anyone when they arrived. She was very young and sometimes thoughtless. She could give offense without realizing it, in an impulsive outburst. If that happened, his job was lost. They would go back to Terravega in total disgrace.

He worried, as he had before, about the future. But he'd never felt such foreboding as he did right now. Perhaps what he needed was something to help him calm down. He went to the small counter and brewed a cup of hot chocolate. He had to stop thinking negatively, he told himself firmly. Jasmine and Mekashe loved one another. Nothing would interfere with that. Nothing at all.

"THIS ISN'T THE way to the auditorium, is it?" Jasmine asked as they turned down a long, unfamiliar corridor.

He laughed. "It isn't. I have to stop by the cabin of a…" He hesitated. "A friend," he added finally, "to give him some news I just received from the Dectat."

"The Dectat!" She looked up at him adoringly. "Mekashe, if you speak to the highest authority on your planet, you have to do something important, don't you?"

"That will be revealed in time," he assured her with a twinkle in his suddenly green eyes, denoting humor.

"All right. I'll try to be patient, then." She tightened her fingers in his and felt the returned pressure with a warm glow in her heart.

At the end of the corridor were three cabins, one of which was the equivalent of a private gym. The sound of Kahn-Bo sticks being used in practice came from it. Mekashe knew that his cousin Tresar loved the sport and enjoyed sparring with his companions.

"I'll only be a minute. You should wait here… Jasmine!" He was too late to stop her.

"I want to meet your friend," she began brightly.

But then she saw the creature with the long stick. He'd just put it down and he made a mock attack toward his sparring partner, who'd apparently won. He extended his claws and bared his fangs and growled.

Jasmine, who'd never seen anything more alien

than the very human-looking—but blue—Altairians on board, and the less humanoid Vegans, gaped at the thing in her field of view and felt terror to her very soul.

He heard her gasp and turned to face her. He was huge. Towering and muscular, with a broad chest and muscular arms, bared to the waist, his golden skin glistening with sweat. He had a curling mane down over his shoulders, falling to his waist, jet-black and pushed away from his face, which had a broad nose and slit-pupiled eyes that were almost as black as his hair.

Tresar growled again, fiercely, and raged at Mekashe in a hissing, feline-sounding language that was actually the Holy Tongue, spoken only by intimates of Alamantimichar and the Imperial family.

"Get her out!" Tresar hissed. "Now!"

Mekashe turned to Jasmine, but she was frozen in position, all her nightmares coming to life before her as she stared at the alien.

"Monster!" she cried, sobbing in fear. "Horrible, repulsive creature! Someone should put it in a cage, and not let it out around civilized beings! Someone should kill it! It's disgusting!"

"Jasmine, say no more," Mekashe said in a curt, strained tone, as he watched the emotions play in Tresar's eyes.

"How can they let something that inhuman aboard a cruise ship?" she exclaimed. "It should be thrown out, spaced, killed!" She screamed as the creature moved toward her.

"No!" she cried, hysterical now, out of control. "Keep it away from me! Mekashe, do something! Don't let that…that creature come near me! Oh please, call the ship police, have it put in a cell…!"

"Get…her…out!" Tresar hissed and began to crouch in what was, even to an unknowing onlooker, a prelude to attack.

Mekashe caught her arm and literally dragged her out of the gym. She was still screaming. He glanced back at his cousin with anguish in his face. She had insulted Alamantimichar. Called it inhuman. Said it should be caged, spaced, killed. It was an insult that no Cehn-Tahr could permit, and it carried the death penalty.

She had no idea what she'd just done, and she was still screaming at the top of her lungs.

"Jasmine!" he said sharply, and actually shook her. "Stop! Now!"

She'd never heard a threat in his voice before. It hurt her. She was terrified. Why hadn't he done something? Why wasn't he comforting her?

She couldn't control the fear. She was shaking all over, still sobbing hysterically. "I saw that…that thing, in a nightmare." She sobbed. "It was so horrible! I've never seen anything like that…that monster! Why do they let it run loose on the ship?"

He used his ring communicator to call the infirmary and asked for an intern to come up and treat her. The response was immediate.

By the time he got her back to her father's suite, she was still hysterical, but the intern was waiting. He'd apparently alerted the ambassador, who was waiting, too.

Jasmine threw herself into her father's arms, wailing. Beside her, the intern shot something into the vein in the crook of her arm from a laserdot.

"What in the world happened?" Ambassador Dupont exclaimed.

"There's a monster down that corridor!" She sobbed. "A horrible creature with claws and fangs and a mane…!"

Horrified, the ambassador looked over her head at Mekashe and grimaced. He knew, without a word being said, exactly what she'd seen. He knew, also, that Mekashe wasn't the only Cehn-Tahr on board; that two members of the Royal Clan were said to be traveling on the same vessel with a small military contingent. Was it those that Jasmine insulted? If so, the ambassador was going to face serious charges, maybe even fatal ones, because of the insult his daughter had given them.

"What did you say to him?" Ambassador Dupont asked in a strangled tone.

"I didn't…say anything…" she managed. "Well, not anything much. I mostly just screamed."

He looked up at Mekashe, his expression questioning.

"She said that it was a repulsive monster and should be caged or killed," Mekashe said in a haunted tone. His face was rigid with distaste, his eyes almost black in anger. And the ambassador knew at once what was going to happen.

"I am most deeply sorry," he told the ambassador. "I think you can anticipate the outcome," he added heavily.

"Sadly, yes" was the reply. He drew in a breath as Jasmine began to slump. "Let me get her inside."

"I'm sorry," she murmured drowsily. "Sorry, Mekashe. I'm sorry I spoiled our day. I always do that. I'm so…sorry…"

The ambassador got her into her stateroom and put her on the bed. The intern, female, hovered.

"Can you help her undress and get into bed?" he asked softly.

The intern smiled. "Of course, Ambassador."

He thanked her, closed the door and went out where Mekashe was still standing, stunned and devastated by what had happened.

"Tresar is a great-nephew of the emperor," Mekashe said quietly. He didn't dare mention that he, himself, was also a great-nephew and that he belonged to Alamantimichar, as well. "Such an insult, even if it had not been overheard, and it was, carries a terrible penalty. I will do what I can to avoid the most extreme penalty. But the emperor will not respond well, and I think you may not remain on Memcache long."

"I am most deeply sorry. She's very young," he added in a subdued tone. "I've failed as a parent. I should never have brought her on this trip. I should have left her at home and come alone. I've been afraid since we departed Terravega that she'd react badly among alien people. This is…horrible. Just horrible. I'm so sorry, Mekashe."

"So am I, Ambassador," he said heavily. "I will do what I can," he promised. His eyes went to the closed door. It seemed profound. The way to Jasmine was closed forever. Her outburst had cost him a future with her. The emperor would be outraged. Also, Mekashe saw now what would have been her reaction to him, if he'd shifted into his true form in front of her. Dreams died, blown away into the cold darkness around them.

"I'm sorry for you, as well," Ambassador Dupont added gently. "I know how much she means to you."

Mekashe could barely manage a reply. "I cannot see her again."

"What should I tell her?"

"Nothing," Mekashe replied in a dead tone. "It is taboo to explain what she saw. And I am now forbidden by custom to speak to her again." He drew in a harsh breath. "Your reception may be quite unpleasant. You must prepare yourself for that. It is a tragedy, in many respects."

"I know what to expect. I'm still grateful that I got to know you," he added softly, and smiled. "It was a privilege."

Mekashe was touched. But he had to leave. "I enjoyed the chess matches," he replied. "And the company." He glanced toward the closed door. "Farewell."

"Farewell."

HE WENT BACK to Tresar's cabin. His cousin was waiting for him.

"I am deeply sorry for you," Tresar said apologetically. He drew the other alien into his arms and held him, rocked him, while the grief passed over him. "I should not have been careless enough to leave the door open. I did not expect company."

"You have nothing to apologize for," Mekashe said after a minute. He drew back and forced a smile. "Such an insult can never be forgiven. The fault was mine, for bringing her with me. I told her to wait outside, but she is young and impulsive and refused to listen."

"We come from a culture with rigid rules," Tresar said. "Sometimes they are cumbersome. I will at least plead with the emperor for the lightest penalty. He will grant that. He is very fond of you."

"And I of him. And you," Mekashe replied with a faint, sad smile. "The ambassador already knows what to expect. I did not tell him," he added, "but he was briefed by his superiors about our true form, and our laws."

"At least, it will not be such a shock for him. But your female companion will not understand. And he will not be permitted to explain it to her."

"I know." The two words were uttered with visible pain. He moved away. "I must speak with the emperor."

"Castarus has already spoken to him," Tresar said, mentioning one of his unit that had accompanied him on the journey. "He was outraged."

"So he should be," Mekashe replied heavily. "Such an insult cannot be overlooked. Not even by me. Especially not by me."

"I grieve for you," Tresar said gently. "I, too, lost my mate. I know the pain."

"I avoided gift-giving. There will be no repercussions because of an induced mating cycle."

"At least, that is something for which to be grateful."

Mekashe nodded. He felt the weight of grief like a living thing. He would leave the ship tonight, with the emperor's permission, and bring Tresar and the others with him back to Memcache on a military transport.

With luck, the Morcai would be near enough to rendezvous with the cruise vessel.

Mekashe told his cousin good-night and went back to his cabin to arrange everything.

CHAPTER EIGHT

JASMINE AWOKE THE next morning with something of a hangover, and a raging embarrassment for the scene she'd made in front of Mekashe. Two scenes, she amended. The first had been at his virtual home, where the equally virtual galot had been housed.

She recalled that Mekashe had asked her to wait outside the gym, but she'd disobeyed him and walked right into a nightmare. Had he known that the creature was in there? Was it sentient? It had to be, because it had spoken to him in some strange, incomprehensible tongue. Perhaps he'd had to speak to it for his job. She'd screamed her head off like a child and embarrassed him. How could she have done that? Her behavior shamed her. She'd have to do a lot of apologizing to make up for it. But he'd forgive her. She was sure of it. He wanted a future with her. He had to love her, as she certainly loved him. It would be all right. She'd apologize when he came to get her, as he had almost every morning after breakfast.

Dressed in a flattering tan skirt and blouse, with her hair brushed and her long nails polished, she went out to the dining room, where her father was already sitting at a table.

He looked devastated. She wondered if he'd had another communication from the embassy. Those messages always seemed to disturb him.

"Good morning!" she said brightly.

He looked up and managed a faint smile. "Good morning, Jasmine."

"I'm so sorry about last night," she said as she sipped fresh coffee. "I acted like a child. Mekashe is going to be irritated with me. I don't know what we'll do today, but I'm sure it will be something exciting!"

He didn't know how to tell her. He couldn't tell her the truth. He'd have to find some reason for Mekashe's sudden disappearance, something that wouldn't hurt her too much.

"I have some sad news."

She stopped with the coffee mug halfway to her lips. "What is it?"

He grimaced. "Mekashe was recalled by his superiors last night," he said. "He's very sorry, but he couldn't disobey. It's something…important, that he had to deal with."

"Oh." She felt the words. "He didn't say goodbye?"

"He couldn't," he bit off.

"Oh. Of course." She laughed and sipped her coffee. "I was out of it after the intern sedated me. I was unconscious." She brightened. "But we'll see him when we reach Memcache. Daddy, he said you'd deal with the emperor himself when you take up your duties!"

That would have been an honor, Ambassador Dupont thought. But it wasn't going to happen now. There would probably be a hearing or meeting of some sort about Jasmine's outburst, and then he'd be sent home. He recalled that some offenses against the Royal Clan could result in death. He prayed that Jasmine's wasn't one of them. When he was judged—because it would be the ambassador, not his child, who was judged—it was going to be devastating news to the embassy back home, and to the politician who'd appointed him. He was the first ambassador ever sent from Terravega to Memcache. And now it looked as if he might be the last. His superiors back home were going to crucify him.

"Daddy, you look positively morose!" Jasmine exclaimed.

"Sorry. I'm just dwelling on things I shouldn't. Here. Have some more coffee," he said, and tried to appear undisturbed. No need to upset her now. There would be ample time for that at the end of their journey.

MEKASHE DIDN'T MINGLE with the crew aboard the Morcai. He kept to his cabin and brooded, grieved, anguished over his profound loss. He was grateful that he'd kept enough sense not to present her with a gift. That would have triggered the mating cycle, and no power in the universe could have stopped it.

But losing Jasmine was like losing a part of himself. He'd had plans for the two of them. So many plans. A home, children, a future growing old together. Well, she'd grow old. That would have been a profound sadness, to watch her age and have her realize that he never did. His life span, with the genetic modifications he had accepted, would probably stretch to three or four hundred years.

Besides that, her fear of cats and her terrible reaction to Tresar when he was transformed told him that she'd never have been able to adjust to life with him. He'd been living in a euphoric dream. The return to reality was like hitting a stone wall at top speed. He was in shock.

The emperor had contacted him telepathically, disturbed by Tresar's description of the aftermath of the incident. It was easy now, because there was no longer a need for the white noise ball since he was aboard the Morcai.

"Tresar is worried about you," the emperor's gravelly voice spoke in his head. "So am I, Mekashe. You have secreted yourself away from everyone."

"Forgive me," he began.

"It is not a question of forgiveness. You grieve, as I grieved when I lost two of my sons, when my mate left me decades ago, when my only living son hated me. I survived. So will you."

"I should never have taken her with me to the gym where Tresar was practicing. I knew that he never adopted humanoid features."

"Blaming yourself will change nothing." The emperor's voice hardened. "The insult was one which I cannot forgive. You must understand. A ruler must enforce certain constants. We cannot lose face, as a Clan, because of a human's insensitivity. Such an outburst, which was overheard by a Rojok who was also using the gym, would diminish us if it was reported that we accepted such a racial slur and did nothing about it."

"I understand," Mekashe replied in a subdued tone. "I did not see her again. Her father was devastated. The embassy told him a few things about us, probably the fact that we shape-shift, as well."

"It will be difficult for him. I have already spoken to the human on Terravega who is responsible for the recall of the ambassador. He will go home in disgrace. Also, he will never be able to tell his daughter why. That is a breach of protocol which none of us will allow. She knows enough about us already."

The last sentence had a faint accusatory content. "I confided in her, because I had planned to bond with her," Mekashe said heavily.

"I had not thought to ask about the extent of your genetic modification," he replied suddenly. "Your grandparents refused it, as I recall."

"Yes," he said solemnly. "So did my parents."

"That would have made it simpler for you, had the bonding been possible…"

"I had the full sequence of modification, many years ago, when I first joined the military," Mekashe interrupted, which was a measure of his misery, because no sane person would dare interrupt the emperor.

There was a faint inhalation, just audible in the psychic connection. "Mekashe, I am not permitted to speak to you of such things, despite our Clan affiliation. But I urge you to tell Hahnson what you have just related to me. It might…comfort you."

"Sir?"

"Just tell him," came the reply. "I will see you soon."

"Yes, sir."

"And, Mekashe, on your behalf, I have lessened the penalty to expulsion. There will also be no retaliation on his daughter."

"I am most grateful."

"It is the least I can do. The law must be enforced, or the state will fail."

"I know that as well, sir. Thank you."

"Farewell, for now."

"Farewell."

Mekashe stood up, feeling morose and anguished as never before in his life. He had to do something to lighten his mood. Perhaps a strenuous match with Tresar with the Kahn-Bo might help.

He left his berth and jogged down the familiar long, wide corridor, where the Morcai's complement of humans and Cehn-Tahr worked in perfect harmony. None of the Cehn-Tahr were disguised aboard ship, not since Dtimun, the emperor's son, had commanded the Holconcom and was coaxed by Dr. Madeline Ruszel, his mate, to trust the humans with the true form of the Cehn-Tahr. Now it was accepted without comment.

But on the way to the sparring area, Mekashe slowed. The emperor had wanted him to confide in Hahnson. Why?

His curiosity drove him into sick bay, where Hahnson was just finishing a resection on a human arm that had been damaged.

"All done, Jones," Hahnson said with a grin. "And I salute your devotion to duty. Rhemun will be proud of you."

Ensign Jones flushed a little, pushing back his blond hair. He was a favorite of the Holconcom's commander, also a member of Rhemun's personal bodyguard. He was a little slow, but the whole crew liked him.

Jones looked up. "Mekashe!" he exclaimed, his expression one of pure joy.

He chuckled at the enthusiasm. "Hello, Jones. It's good to see you."

"Good to see you, too, sir. Going to give up being

captain of the Imperial Guard and come home to the Holconcom, are you?" he teased.

Mekashe just shook his head. "We never know what fate has in store for us," he said enigmatically.

"I'd better get back to my post. Thanks, Doc," he told Hahnson. He grinned at Mekashe and darted out the door into the corridor.

Hahnson closed the pressure door behind him. He turned to Mekashe. "The emperor wants me to speak to you."

"Yes. He told me."

He looked uneasy. "You might want to sit down."

Mekashe's old humor flashed in his face. "Is it that bad? Do I have some incurable disease?"

Hahnson didn't laugh, as he was expected to. He perched on the side of the raised bed and waited for Mekashe to sink down onto the stool beside it.

"I didn't realize that you had genetic modifications," Hahnson said solemnly. "I don't deal with Cularian types, as you know—that's Tellas's department, now that he has his certification."

"Yes," Mekashe replied. "I accepted the full complement of them when I joined the military, decades ago. I wanted every possible enhancement. My mother encouraged me," he added, remembering her with sadness and affection. "She was always terrified that I might not return from a mission."

"You said that when you first started going with Jasmine, that you broke her fingers."

Mekashe winced. "Yes. I had no idea. She wouldn't tell me, for fear of wounding me emotionally. She was…gentle."

Hahnson could see the pain of loss in the other male's features. He knew from what the emperor had told him that the human ambassador was going to be sent home in disgrace, along with his daughter, Jasmine. Poor Mekashe. He felt the officer's anguish.

"The emperor thought that if you knew the truth, you might be able to accept the loss with more grace," Hahnson said.

That got Mekashe's attention. "The truth?" he asked, scowling.

"I told you that I was bonded to a Cehn-Tahr female."

Mekashe nodded. "Yes, I remember."

Hahnson smiled sadly. "My original—of which I'm a clone—didn't know how strong modified Cehn-Tahr actually are, and how fragile humans are, by contrast. When we attempted to mate, she broke my spine in the first few seconds. She called for aid. Dtimun managed to find an ambutube in time, got me into stasis and transported me to a medical ship. He saved my life."

Mekashe was beginning to see the light. It was shocking. Horrible. He lowered his eyes. "I…didn't know. I had to use such caution with Jasmine, the doses of dravelzium, the nanobytes to prevent true contact…" He looked up. "I had no loss of control."

"That was fortunate," Hahnson said flatly. "Because you would have killed her, Mekashe. Modified Cehn-Tahr cannot mate with humans. There's only one case on record of a successful mating, and that was Dtimun and Madeline Ruszel's; but it was only successful because Madeline had advanced genetic modification. The sample was used up in the process, and no one has yet been able to reconstruct it."

Mekashe was looking paler by the minute. "I could never have mated with her," he said in a dull, shocked tone.

"No."

Mekashe looked up. "Your mate…that was why she commited suicide?"

Hahnson swallowed. He was a clone, but the emotional pain was just as deep. "Yes. She killed herself, when she realized the truth."

"I am most sorry for you."

"I loved her very much," Hahnson said. "I never got over it. Which is why I never mated again." He smiled sadly. "I have her memory, which is bittersweet. She was an extraordinary person."

"I think you must be, too," came the unexpected reply. "We all know what you did at Ahkmau. You saved your crewmates, including me, and our emperor's son, with your sacrifice. You made an escape possible that had never happened in the history of the prison camp." He spoke of Hahnson's original, who died in Ahkmau. This Hahnson was a clone, whom

Dtimun had created for Madeline Ruszel and Holt Stern, who were mourning him.

Hahnson looked mildly embarrassed. "Well, yes," he said. "Ahkmau is a painful memory, as well."

Mekashe was processing the information he'd been given. It was a shock. He knew that it would haunt him for the rest of his life, the memory of what he could never have. He'd loved Jasmine with his whole heart. Now he must go home to Memcache, assume his duties and maintain dignity while Jasmine and her father were ordered home. It would be done at the reception. Jasmine would be there, and Mekashe could not look at her or speak to her or indicate in any way that he had feelings for her. It would be a test of his will, his endurance.

"I thank you for your words," he told Hahnson when he rose. "The grief will not ease for some time. But knowing what could have happened, and did not, is at least a little comfort."

"I'm sorry that I can't do more," Hahnson said. "I know how you feel, if it helps."

Mekashe clasped forearms with the burly surgeon. "In fact, it does."

"If you need anything, anything at all…"

Mekashe managed a faint smile. "I need time. Just time. I will recover. So will she. She has a strong will."

JASMINE WAS COUNTING the minutes until the great ship docked at the space station above Memcache.

She was so excited that she could hardly wait for the shuttle to pick them up and transport them down to the Terravegan Embassy. She was planning her wardrobe for the social function that would introduce the new ambassador, and anticipating a joyful reunion with Mekashe.

Ambassador Dupont saw that joy and felt deep pain at her happiness because it would be short-lived. He was going to be sent home. The official at the Terravegan Ambassadorial Department had been almost beaming with pleasure as he imparted the news. There would be a public reception for the four new ambassadors, at which Ambassador Dupont would be duly snubbed, and then informed of his recall.

It was going to be humiliating, for many reasons. He was forbidden to speak to Jasmine about it, just as he was forbidden to tell her that Mekashe was the same species as the "creature" she'd been horrified by in the gym. She was walking into tragedy, happy and unknowing. He would never be able to tell her why he was losing his important position, one that was historic in the extreme.

It would reflect badly on Terravega, and no other ambassador had yet been selected to replace him. It was unlikely that one would be, at least in the near future. The insult had to be forgotten, fences had to be mended, before the emperor would even consider allowing another human to represent Terravega on his world.

All that, because he'd been lenient and overly protective of his only child, who'd had episodes of uncontrolled hysteria all her life and never been corrected. If he hadn't sheltered her, if he'd accustomed her to facing her fears without screaming and behaving like an infant, it might all have been avoided. He and his wife had been overly permissive. Now he was reaping the reward for his failure as a parent.

Jasmine was so happy that she didn't notice his reticence, or his misery. He wasn't able to hide it. But she had always looked inward instead of outward. She was used to having her own way, doing what she pleased. She tended to be insensitive to other people. She had a faint superiority complex, as well. She had wonderful traits; she was kind and gentle and pretty. But she was selfish at times. This was one of them. Her mind was purely on her own circumstances, not on anything else. She was so self-absorbed that she hadn't noticed that her father was barely eating, that he couldn't sleep, that he looked haunted. Even a fellow passenger had noted his dismal demeanor and asked if he could help. Jasmine sat at meals with him and noticed nothing.

"I wish they'd hurry up!" she said, glaring at the porters who were filing in with the luggage as they landed in the spaceport on Memcache. It had an unpronounceable name, which was written in Cehn-Tahr script on the entrance. She had no idea what it meant, nor could she read any signs that were placed around the spacious building.

Finally, the luggage was secured and placed in a hovering transport outside. In the city, their driver remarked in perfect Standard, no polluting vehicles were allowed. Only hovercars or hoverbuses were permitted, and they were strictly regulated. They shared space with pedestrians, so they had to be cautious about where they ran.

The city was beautifully rounded, contoured, and the buildings glowed with a pale blue light. The driver told them that the reactors that powered the city gave it that color. The streets were wide and paved with natural stone. Many of the buildings outside the city were also built in such a manner.

"You never build with wood, do you?" Jasmine asked.

"Never." The driver laughed. "We revere our trees. We consider that they have a living spirit, which must never be violated."

She smiled, but as her eyes found a huge statue of Cashto, the galot who was revered in Cehn-Tahr culture, she shivered. It was black as jet, muscular, with glittery green eyes and snow-white fangs. It crouched over the city, like a feral protector.

"I hate those statues," Jasmine said gruffly. "I hate cats!" Jasmine averted her eyes, an action that, accompanied by her harsh words, wasn't missed by the driver, who became less talkative and placed his attention on the road. Jasmine didn't notice, but the ambassador did. She was making a bad situation worse, with her phobias. If he'd had them seen to, by a psychologist, so many bad things might have been avoided.

THEY WERE CARRIED to a towering stone villa with a fountain out front and a light, roomy interior with ten bedrooms and an enormous sitting area downstairs, with a walk-in fireplace.

Jasmine wondered if they burned wood, but the driver had already gone.

"I'm sure that it's powered by something other than wood," her father remarked. He touched a panel on the side of the fireplace and flames appeared in it. They were actually warm, so the tech needed to power it must be formidable.

"That's nice!" she said. She looked around. The furnishings were all blue and white. There were nature paintings on the wall, and blue carpeting. "It's very pretty. It reminds me of Mekashe's villa. When do you think we'll see him?" she added. "I don't even know how to get in touch with him. He never told us where he worked."

"I imagine we'll see him at the reception tomorrow." He glanced outside. It was already dark. Their trip had taken a long time. "We should get some rest."

"I guess so. But I'll never sleep! I wish I'd bought

a different outfit to wear," she added. "This one is a year old…" She saw her father's pained expression and grimaced. "I've spent too much already," she said at once. "What I have will be fine! Really!"

She hugged him. "I'm sorry I'm such a pain," she said. "I'll try to reform. Honest I will."

"There's nothing wrong with you," he said, kissing her hair. "Your mother would be proud of you."

"She'd be more proud of you. The first human ambassador ever to serve on Memcache!" she exclaimed happily, drawing away. "It's an incredible honor."

"I suppose it is." He felt his heart dragging the floor. Tomorrow, his pride would join it there. "Bed, daughter. We have a long day ahead."

She laughed. "But a happy one. Good night, Daddy!"

"Good night," he replied, smiling.

The smile faded the minute she was out of sight. He sank into an armchair and gave way to the anguish he felt. There was no one to see the pain in his face now.

THE NEXT MORNING, it was raining. Jasmine was worried, because her gauzy blue dress would get wet. She hadn't thought to bring an umbrella. It only rained on Terravega when the technicians decided that the vegetation in the huge life domes needed water. And it was advertised days in advance that showers were coming. Here, apparently, there was no control over the weather at all.

"How do people know what to wear, when the weather isn't announced?" she wondered aloud as she joined her father in the foyer. The transport was due any minute.

"It was like this on Terravega, before the devastation," her father replied. "I remember hearing my grandfather talk about it."

"Ages and ages ago." She looked around. "I love the house."

"It's very nice."

"Do we have a cook?" she wondered. "Or do they send us meals…?"

"We can worry about that later," he said quickly, ushering her outside. The rain had stopped. "Our ride is here."

HE WAS UNUSUALLY quiet all the way to the embassy. Jasmine more than made up for his silence.

"Do you think Mekashe will be there?" she wondered aloud. "I thought he might call us when we arrived. Surely, he knows we're here!"

"He might have been unable to," her father said dully. "He was called home. I'm sure his job is the reason he didn't get in touch."

"I suppose so." She looked out the window as the small vehicle whizzed toward the towering building that served as home to the Imperial family, religious hub and political entity. It was like the building that housed the Dectat—softly rounded, glowing in shades of blue and gold.

"Isn't it magnificent?" Jasmine sighed, glancing at her father. "Honestly, Daddy," she said, exasperated. "We're not going to a funeral!"

"Is that how I looked? Sorry." He managed a convincing smile.

"I want to see Mekashe so badly," she said. "We've hardly been apart for longer than a few hours since we boarded the starcruiser. I hope nothing has happened to him," she added worriedly.

"I'm sure that he's fine," her father replied. "Probably just too occupied with his work to think about other things. Even pleasant ones."

She smiled. "We're going to meet the emperor," she enthused. "I'm so nervous! Aren't you nervous, Daddy? It's a truly historic occasion. You're the very first human ambassador here!"

And probably the very last, he was thinking morosely as they pulled up at the steps that led to the tall building.

The driver opened the door for them, but without looking at them fully. He indicated the way up.

"They're very—what's the word I want?—reserved, aren't they?" Jasmine remarked as they made it to the top of the wedge-shaped staircase.

"Very."

"There's another blue man!" she exclaimed as they started into the building.

"Jasmine," he groaned.

She caught her breath. "Oh gosh, I'm sorry—I'm still doing it! I'm so sorry!" she amended. "He's… an Altairian, right?"

"Yes," he said heavily.

"My tongue is going to be the death of me," she groaned.

She had no idea how true that might have been, the ambassador thought. "You must try and be more sensitive to the feelings of other people, Jasmine," he said quietly. "Especially here."

"I know. I'm trying. Really I am. It's just…everything is new and a little frightening." She hesitated and lowered her voice before they got to the moving staircase that lifted guests to the next level. "Daddy, you don't think they'll have, well, any of those horrible cat statues here…?"

"Grit your teeth and hold your tongue," he said under his breath as he noticed a Cehn-Tahr couple glancing at them in an unfriendly way.

She bit her lip. The aliens were absolutely glaring. "Is there something you aren't telling me?" she asked her father.

"They're religious objects," he said in a rough undertone. "It's the equivalent of trying to burn down a church back home, what you've said about the cat statues."

She gasped. She looked up at her father, wincing. "Why didn't you tell me before?" she asked miserably. "I've said such terrible things to Mekashe about them. I didn't know!"

"I wasn't allowed to tell you," he said. "It doesn't matter now. Just please try to get through the next hour without offending anyone else, Jasmine."

She felt stung by his words. He'd never spoken to her like this. She began to realize what a terrible position she'd been putting him in, with her unruly tongue.

"I'm sorry," she said again. She touched his sleeve, her face lined with worry. "I keep doing the wrong thing, saying the wrong thing. You've been overly tolerant with me," she added after a minute. "You've sheltered me too much. You should have shouted at me more."

His eyes were kind, if sad. "I love you, just as your mother did. You were our only child. We both went a little overboard with you." He drew in a long breath. "We tried to shelter you from any unpleasantness. What we forgot is that other people wouldn't. Here—" he indicated their surroundings "—if you speak out of turn, there are grave consequences." He didn't add that there already had been.

"I'll keep my mouth shut, no matter what," she said, trying to reassure him. "Truly I will."

He started to speak, thought better of it and led

"4 for 4" MINI-SURVEY

We are prepared to **REWARD** you with 2 FREE books and 2 FREE gifts for completing our MINI SURVEY!

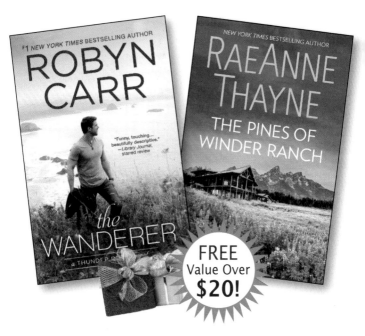

FREE
Value Over
$20!

You'll get...
TWO FREE BOOKS & TWO FREE GIFTS
just for participating in our Mini Survey!

Dear Reader,

IT'S A FACT: if you answer 4 quick questions, we'll send you **4 FREE REWARDS!**

I'm not kidding you. As a leading publisher of women's fiction, we value your opinions… and your time. That's why we are prepared to **reward** you handsomely for completing our mini-survey. In fact, we have 4 Free Rewards for you, including 2 free books and 2 free gifts.

As you may have guessed, that's why our mini-survey is called **"4 for 4".** Answer 4 questions and get 4 Free Rewards. It's that simple!

Thank you for participating in our survey,

Pam Powers

www.ReaderService.com

To get your 4 FREE REWARDS:
Complete the survey below and return the insert today to receive 2 FREE BOOKS and 2 FREE GIFTS guaranteed!

▼ DETACH AND MAIL CARD TODAY! ▼

"4 for 4" MINI-SURVEY

1 Is reading one of your favorite hobbies?
☐ YES   ☐ NO

2 Do you prefer to read instead of watch TV?
☐ YES   ☐ NO

3 Do you read newspapers and magazines?
☐ YES   ☐ NO

4 Do you enjoy trying new book series with FREE BOOKS?
☐ YES   ☐ NO

YES! I have completed the above Mini-Survey. Please send me my 4 FREE REWARDS (worth over $20 retail). I understand that I am under no obligation to buy anything, as explained on the back of this card.

194/394 MDL GMYP

FIRST NAME	LAST NAME

ADDRESS

APT.#	CITY

STATE/PROV.   ZIP/POSTAL CODE

Offer limited to one per household and not applicable to series that subscriber is currently receiving.
Your Privacy—The Reader Service is committed to protecting your privacy. Our Privacy Policy is available online at www.ReaderService.com or upon request from the Reader Service. We make a portion of our mailing list available to reputable third parties that offer products we believe may interest you. If you prefer that we not exchange your name with third parties, or if you wish to clarify or modify your communication preferences, please visit us at www.ReaderService.com/consumerschoice or write to us at Reader Service Preference Service, P.O. Box 9062, Buffalo, NY 14240-9062. Include your complete name and address.
ROM-218-MS17

© 2017 HARLEQUIN ENTERPRISES LIMITED
® and ™ are trademarks owned and used by the trademark owner and/or its licensee. Printed in the U.S.A.

READER SERVICE—Here's how it works:

Accepting your 2 free Romance books and 2 free gifts (gifts valued at approximately $10.00 retail) places you under no obligation to buy anything. You may keep the books and gifts and return the shipping statement marked "cancel." If you do not cancel, about a month later we'll send you 4 additional books and bill you just $6.74 each in the U.S. or $7.24 each in Canada. That is a savings of at least 16% off the cover price. It's quite a bargain! Shipping and handling is just 50¢ per book in the U.S. and 75¢ per book in Canada*. You may cancel at any time, but if you choose to continue, every month we'll send you 4 more books, which you may either purchase at the discount price plus shipping and handling or return to us and cancel your subscription. *Terms and prices subject to change without notice. Prices do not include applicable taxes. Sales tax applicable in N.Y. Canadian residents will be charged applicable taxes. Offer not valid in Quebec. Books received may not be as shown. All orders subject to approval. Credit or debit balances in a customer's account(s) may be offset by any other outstanding balance owed by or to the customer. Please allow 4 to 6 weeks for delivery. Offer available while quantities last.

◄ If offer card is missing write to: Reader Service, P.O. Box 1341, Buffalo, NY 14240-8531 or visit www.ReaderService.com ◄

BUSINESS REPLY MAIL
FIRST-CLASS MAIL   PERMIT NO. 717   BUFFALO, NY
POSTAGE WILL BE PAID BY ADDRESSEE

READER SERVICE
PO BOX 1341
BUFFALO NY 14240-8571

NO POSTAGE
NECESSARY
IF MAILED
IN THE
UNITED STATES

the way up to the next level and out onto the huge patio where the reception was being held.

Jasmine saw a man in a uniform, with long blond hair and slit eyes and red skin. She glanced down and noted that he had six fingers on each hand. She forced herself to smile, not to react. It was harder when one of the Serian races joined the group; they were more like dogs than humanoids, with four legs and heads that arched up from a long neck. They had fingers like tentacles and they spoke in a language that sounded more like gurgling underwater than speaking Standard.

"Goodness, they look like the dogs we keep for pets on Terravega," Jasmine said without thinking.

Several aliens, including the doglike ones, looked at her with disdain. She ground her teeth together. "I'm sorry. I'm so sorry," she whispered to her father. "I'll do better. I promise I will!"

Ambassador Dupont knew that she'd try. But even though she was making an effort not to behave badly, it was too late. Far too late.

"That's a Rojok, isn't it?" she whispered to her father, indicating the man in uniform. He was standing with a beautiful Cehn-Tahr woman; Jasmine could tell her race by her golden skin and jet-black hair.

"That's Chacon," he replied, as fascinated as she seemed to be. "He was field marshal of the entire Rojok military before he became Premier of the

Rojok Republic. He's bonded to the emperor's daughter. She's standing beside him."

"Chacon." Her voice trailed away. She remembered speaking of him to Mekashe and shuddering at the so-called atrocities she thought he'd committed. Mekashe had said that Chacon was admired even by his enemies. He looked dangerous.

"There's a refreshment table, if you're thirsty," he told his daughter, guiding her toward where a group of humanoid-looking aliens was sampling the culinary delights.

Jasmine looked around. "Do you know if there are other new ambassadors here?" she asked.

"Yes. There's one from Chacon's planet and two from the Jebob and Altairian governments."

She noticed them speaking to the emperor, who seemed pleasant and attentive.

"The emperor's very big," she commented. "He's tall, like Mekashe."

"Yes."

She turned again and noticed a squad of military standing in perfect formation near the emperor. Her heart jumped as she noticed their leader, standing at parade rest, looking straight ahead.

"Daddy! That's Mekashe!" she exclaimed. "Who are those soldiers?"

"That's the Imperial Guard," he replied quietly.

"Mekashe is standing in front of them…"

"Yes. He's their captain, apparently," the ambassador said heavily. "I knew that two members of the kehmatemer were aboard our ship, on their way home. I didn't know that Mekashe was one of them."

"He's in the military." She groaned inwardly. "I was eloquent about how I hated the military, too. He never said a word."

Her father didn't answer. He noticed that nobody came near them, nobody spoke to them. Even the families of the other ambassadors kept well away, glancing toward them uneasily.

"The emperor's greeting all three of those new ambassadors. But you're the first human ambassador ever to come here. Why is he ignoring you?" Jasmine asked haughtily. "It's not right!"

"If you value your life, and mine, be quiet," her father said curtly.

She gaped at her father. It began to occur to her that they might have been lepers for the way the other guests were treating them. The emperor never looked their way once. Neither did Mekashe, who stood at attention and never glanced at Jasmine.

Her heart fell. Something was wrong. Something was very wrong. She stood on tiptoe to whisper to her father.

"What's happening here?" she asked under her breath.

He couldn't even tell her. And the cold treatment they were receiving was having an effect on him.

It was a humiliation that he'd never suffered before in his life.

Finally, the emperor nodded to the other ambassadors, turned and started out the door. Mekashe shot orders to his men, turned and marched them out after the emperor.

"He's not even going to speak to you?" Jasmine said angrily.

"Jasmine…!"

"How rude! How very…!"

"Jasmine!"

She shut up. Her father was looking at her with fierce anger. She was nonplussed. He'd never been so harsh with her.

A minute later, a steward came to them. He didn't bow or make any other acknowledgment.

"Your belongings have been carefully packed and are waiting aboard the starcruiser at the spaceport," he told Ambassador Dupont coldly. "Your passage is already arranged. Transport awaits you outside the building."

He didn't even nod. He turned on his heel and walked away.

Jasmine was so shocked that she forgot to be indignant as her father took her hand and pulled her with him to the steps.

CHAPTER NINE

THEY WERE SETTLED in their stateroom aboard the Terravegan-bound starliner before Jasmine could collect herself enough to ask what was going on.

"I've been recalled," Ambassador Dupont said as they sat in the living room. "My appointment has been rescinded."

"But why?" she asked, still crying. "Mekashe didn't even look at me! The emperor didn't speak to us. I don't understand!"

"Jasmine…"

She dabbed at her eyes. Then she looked at her father with horror. "You told me to be quiet, when we were going into the building. I said some things about the doglike aliens… Was that why?"

"Of course not," he began.

"You're not telling the truth," she said, reading it in his tired face. "It was, wasn't it? I offended the emperor because I was indiscreet about his guests and I made that comment about the cat statues. Mekashe warned me that he took offense easily." Her face reddened. "Well, what a stupid, silly attitude! Imagine sending an ambassador home because his daughter insulted some dumb alien race and didn't like cat statues! And Mekashe didn't even defend me, did he?" she raged. "He just let me go without a word!"

"Mekashe is obligated to do what he's told by the emperor," her father said.

"Like a perfect soldier," she said furiously. "I thought he cared about me! I thought he wanted a life with me! Well, if he's that petty, if his race is that petty, I don't want to be part of them!"

He knew that she was trying to make the best of a bad situation. He couldn't tell her about Mekashe, about his true form. He couldn't tell her that her screams and insults toward the Cehn-Tahr aboard the starcruiser had brought them to this. He didn't dare reveal to her that the Mekashe she'd grown to know was actually something quite different. He was bound by law not to reveal the Cehn-Tahr's true form. In any case, knowing Mekashe's true form would hurt her even more. With her morbid fear of cats, she couldn't have had a life with Mekashe.

She noticed her father's reticence, finally, and looked at him. He was devastated. That was when she realized just how bad things were going to be. He'd lost his job. Worse than that, he'd lost a position that had been the first of its kind. He would be the first and last human ambassador to the Cehn-Tahr. All that because she'd spoken out of turn, and not even about the Cehn-Tahr themselves, for heaven's sake! She'd been only mildly insulting about a creature at the reception! And, well, there were those comments about the cat statues. If they were religious objects, it wasn't surprising that she'd caused offense.

She went close to him, worried. "Daddy, I'm so sorry," she said softly. "I know how much this job meant to you. But it will be all right. I mean, your bosses can contact the emperor, can't they, and explain that it was my fault." She brightened. "Then it will be all right, and you can come back." She grimaced. "I won't come with you, of course. I might offend someone else and cause more trouble. I can get a job."

Her tone was bitter. She'd cared so much for Mekashe, and he hadn't even looked at her. Probably, he'd just been having a bit of fun with her before he went back home to his military job with his cat statues.

Religious objects. She frowned. Did they actually worship cats?

She started to ask her father, but he'd slumped down into a chair and closed his eyes.

"I haven't slept well for a long time," he said gently. "I think I'll try to nap, if you don't mind."

"Of course I don't." She bent and kissed the top of his head. "I'll just watch the news in my room."

He heard her footsteps die away. He fell asleep from sheer exhaustion. At least the worst was over, he thought.

JASMINE WENT FROM station to station on the Tri-D vid, restlessly, but nothing interested her. She turned off the vid and pulled out the little virtual Nagaashe that she'd bought that wonderful day with Mekashe when they'd visited Dacerius in the holoroom.

Tears streamed down her cheeks. She'd never loved anyone so much. It had been agony to part from him, even overnight. Now she'd part from him for a lifetime.

He was in the military. To have achieved such a high position at his age—he had to be in his early thirties—meant that he'd been a soldier for a long time. He hadn't told her. No wonder. She'd been so blunt about her distaste for anything military. Why would he have told her?

That attitude, and her fear of cats, had been a hurdle he must have felt they couldn't overcome. But he might have tried, except for the emperor's cold shoulder. She couldn't believe that such a tiny thing—her brash words—had been responsible for getting her father fired. She'd never have thought the Cehn-Tahr were so petty. She knew their society was rigid in its beliefs, but that was ridiculous.

Her father said the cat statues were religious objects. No wonder they were everywhere on Memcache. She'd noticed that Mekashe was uncomfortable when she screamed at the virtual galot at his villa. She groaned inwardly. She'd made a complete fool of herself, cost her father the position of his dreams, set diplomatic relations back a hundred years, lost Mekashe…

She walked to the wall and touched a button, opening the view to space. Stars in their various colors flew by as the starliner headed back toward Terravega. This would be a quick trip, too. This ship was the fastest in the fleet. Their passage had been arranged and paid for by the diplomatic service. Apparently, they were anxious to get the Duponts home before they could make things worse. Before Jasmine could make things worse.

She heard a faint purring sound and looked down. The little Nagaashe was looking up at her with pretty blue eyes.

She reached down and coaxed it into her cupped hands. She lifted it to her face and felt it purr as it rubbed its head against her cheek. It wasn't until then that she realized she was crying.

"I've ruined everything," she whispered. "Everything!"

The little creature just purred softly, the sound comforting in the silence of her cabin.

THEY WERE MET at the spaceport by a delegation, headed by Councilman Vickers, the presidential adviser who'd championed Professor Dupont's appointment by the president for the position, against many protests.

"I'm so sorry," Professor Dupont said heavily.

Vickers glanced from him to Jasmine, who was visibly subdued. "So are we," he said quietly. "It was a magnificent opportunity for us, to have ties to the Cehn-Tahr Empire. It would have been a boost to our economy to open trade with the hundred and ten worlds they embrace. Many exotic products would have found their way to our shops, including some medicines that would have delighted the medical sector."

"Yes." Dupont was lost for words.

Jasmine started to speak, but Vickers gave her a look of such distaste that she shut her mouth and flushed.

"We'll speak later," he told her father. "For now, get some rest while I try to save as many political heads as I can—mine included."

"I had great hopes," Dupont choked out.

"So did we all."

The delegation left them at the spaceport. Jasmine felt worse by the minute when she began to realize the trouble she'd made not only for her father, but for her planet.

"It's not all so bad," she tried to comfort him on the way back to the house they still owned. "I mean, you can always go back to teaching."

He didn't look at her. "Do you think so?" he asked in a subdued tone.

"Of course. It will be all right," she added softly. "Really, it will."

IT WASN'T. THE Tri-D news was full of the ambassador's expulsion from Memcache the very next day.
His failure was punctuated by a statement from the
ambassadorial service that the wrong person had obviously been chosen for such an important position.
It should have been a career politician, they stated,
as they'd said when Councilman Vickers insisted on
appointing an academic to the job and convinced the
president to go along. Vickers had lost his position,
along with all the councilmen who'd approved Professor Dupont's appointment.

On and on it went. Day by day, Professor Dupont
grew more despondent. He'd stopped going out at
all, having been subjected to verbal abuse almost everywhere he went. He'd tried to take Jasmine to the
opera, to cheer her up, when they'd been stopped at
the door by two angry women with ties to the embassy.

Jasmine was in tears when they came home. She
went to her room and refused to leave it.

Things got worse. Her father tried to get his old
teaching job back, only to be told that considering
his notoriety at the moment, the university felt that
it would place them in an untenable position. They
had the good name of their institution to consider,
was their final word.

IN THE WEEKS that followed, every attempt he made
to find a teaching job was thwarted by the ongoing

publicity. It never stopped. The public outrage was horrendous. Imagine, one commentator said, having one person destroy all hopes of a new era in interplanetary relations. And all because his daughter couldn't keep her mouth shut.

Professor Dupont had tried to shield Jasmine from what people were saying, but he couldn't do it. She felt the guilt like an invading disease. Especially when her father's small savings were used up and they faced the loss of their home.

"I'll get a job," she said firmly.

He just looked at her, morose and sad and quiet. His pride was shattered. His future was gone. He had no desire to do anything.

She got a copy of the digital want ads and started looking for a suitable position. Only to realize that she didn't know how to do anything. She had no skills, no education past secondary school, and unskilled labor was limited to supervising robotic workers. She couldn't even do that, having no robotic training.

DEPRESSED, WORRIED AND dejected, she went back home after a terrible dead end of job seeking and found medics and law enforcement in the front yard.

She saw them bringing out a still form in an ambu-tube, covered in white fabric, with blood coming through where the head would be.

"Daddy!" she screamed.

One of the law-enforcement officials caught her

before she could get to the ambutube. "It's too late," he said in a gruff tone. "He's gone."

"When? How?"

"He killed himself," came the quiet reply.

He was saying something else, but Jasmine couldn't really hear it. She fainted.

MEKASHE WENT ABOUT his duties with a heavy heart. He held no animosity toward Tresar or the emperor, especially now that he knew how impossible it would have been for him to have a life with Jasmine.

Still, the feelings he had for her were stubborn. He couldn't close his eyes without seeing her beautiful face, hearing her laugh, watching her explore the places he'd taken her with the joy and fascination of a young child. She colored his dreams, haunted him waking and sleeping.

Tresar noticed his sadness and apologized once again for the misery his reaction to Jasmine's outburst had caused.

Mekashe put a big hand on his shoulder and managed a smile for his friend. *"Karamesh,"* he said simply. Fate.

Tresar nodded after a minute. *"Karamesh."*

THE EMPEROR ALSO noticed Mekashe's preoccupation. He looked as if he never slept. His mischievous personality had gone forever. He was solemn, quiet, devoted to duty and his men, but the job became his life.

Tnurat called him into his office at the Dectat one afternoon. To Mekashe's surprise, Rhemun was sitting in a chair beside the desk where the emperor was seated.

"If we had one other officer present, I would expect to be court-martialed," Mekashe said with a faint flash of green humor in his eyes.

"Nothing so dire." The emperor chuckled. "No, it is another matter entirely. Now that Rhemun has two small children, his mate has become overanxious about having him in command of a warship."

Mekashe smiled. "Dr. Mallory has a point," he replied with a glance at Rhemun.

The commander of the Holconcom stood up to greet his best friend. "She does," Rhemun replied. "Kipling is now an adolescent, and he and Dtimun's son, Komak, are finding many things to occupy them that my mate is unable to prevent. The boy is the pride of my house, but he needs a strong hand. Edris is too soft with him."

"Not to mention that your daughter is without equal at finding dangerous things to explore," Mekashe mused.

The emperor chuckled. "Indeed. My granddaughter uncovered a store of nag-tassles in a bag stored in a closet at the Fortress," he said, meaning the home he had once shared with Lady Caneese, his mate. It was now occupied by Dtimun, Madeline and their sons. "It has been there for a century or more, undisturbed."

"Until Larisse pushed a button and ignited the lot," Rhemun said, shaking his head. "It took two hours of bathing to neutralize the smell. And I fear your son's closet," he told the emperor, "will never be the same again, despite the hazard crew's best efforts."

"It was simple enough to reconstruct the closet," came the amused reply. "I think Larisse has the makings of a scientist, like her grandmother. My mate is unsurpassed in biochemistry."

"I must agree," Rhemun said. "She and Madeline Ruszel are working on some secret project that they will not share with any of us."

"Most likely a new form of anesthetic," the emperor said. "Rognan is helping them by combing the forest for rare herbs."

"At least he can still fly," Rhemun mused, "even if one leg is less than functional."

The emperor nodded. "Meg-Ravens are fascinating to observe. Rognan has been with me since Dtimun was born, over two and a half centuries ago." He got to his feet. "But I digress. I asked you here," he told Mekashe, "because Rhemun would very much like to trade places with you."

For a few seconds, Mekashe thought of wild things like sensor nets, like the ones humans had believed that the Cehn-Tahr of the Holconcom had employed to keep their true form secret from the humans with whom they served. Actually, the shape-shifting ability was due to the genetic tampering of millennia ago, along with the use of microcyborgs to stabilize their humanoid forms.

"Not literally." Rhemun chuckled as he saw his friend's expression.

"How sad," Mekashe teased. "I would like a child. Two would be magnificent."

"Bond with someone and make your own" was the quick reply, just as quickly regretted. Rhemun grimaced and started to apologize, but Mekashe just shook his head and smiled.

"What he means," the emperor interrupted, "is that he would like to return to the kehmatemer. Which would leave his position as commander of the Holconcom to you, as next in line in Clan status. How would you feel about that?"

Mekashe took a deep breath. "Two weeks ago, I would have resisted with all my heart," he confessed. "However, now I think an assignment aboard a warship suits my mood. And since I already know the officers and men, it will be like a homecoming."

Rhemun beamed. "I thought you might approve."

The emperor smiled, as well. "I think it will be good for you," he told Mekashe. He drew in a breath. "I deeply regret the result of my anger," he added heavily. "I did not foresee the firestorm of hatred that would follow Professor Dupont and his daughter back to Terravega."

Mekashe knew what he meant. He'd seen the vids, raging about the loss of a valuable diplomatic station. In fact, it had disturbed him so greatly to think of those gentle people suffering such anger that he'd stopped watching the news at all.

"They were both sensitive, in many ways. Jasmine was very young. And very spoiled," he added reluctantly.

"Life will be hard for her, without her father," the emperor agreed.

"Without her father?" Mekashe exclaimed.

The emperor's face was lined with his regrets. "Professor Dupont committed suicide. The pressure was more than he could bear, especially when he was unable to return to an academic career because of his notoriety."

Mekashe closed his eyes and groaned inwardly. That kind, gentle man, who'd loved music and books. It had never occurred to him that the humans would be so cruel. And poor Jasmine, alone, completely alone, with no other family to console her.

He felt a hand on his shoulder. The emperor searched his eyes. "You did not know."

"No," Mekashe said. "I stopped watching news vids some time ago." He paused. "I became close to Jasmine's father. We played chess almost every day. He was a good, kind person. I will mourn him."

The emperor's hand fell away and he turned. "As I grow older, I begin to see many faults in myself. More than I imagined. The humans are vicious with their own kind. If I had been less judgmental, less rigid, perhaps there might have been another way to save face without destroying a family."

Mekashe didn't reply. He stared at his highly polished black boots. "It has been our way for centuries," he said finally. "The offense was legitimate."

The emperor turned. "Your young friend had only seen eighteen summers," he told Mekashe.

The other alien was shocked. He'd never considered age. It hadn't occurred to him to ask how old she was. She seemed mature at times, and almost juvenile at others. But to him, whose life span had already covered more than two and a half centuries, the contrast was alarming.

"I had no idea," he said after a minute.

"Compared to us, with our lives measured in centuries, she was a child," the emperor said sadly. "Children make outbursts. They say things without understanding the effect they have. If the ambassador himself had said such things, perhaps I would have been justified. But this punishment was unjust. And I regret it most fervently."

Neither of his relatives knew quite what to say. That he was upset was quite obvious, and that was rare. The emperor was widely known for his lack of facial expression when he wanted to conceal his true feelings.

"I have had consultation with the Dectat," he said after a minute, turning to them. "We are debating other methods of dealing with offenses by aliens on Memcache. Less drastic ones. It is too late for Professor Dupont. But it may ensure that another diplomat does not suffer the same fate."

"That is gracious of you," Mekashe said.

"Quite gracious," Rhemun seconded.

The emperor took a breath and forced a smile. "So," he said to Mekashe. "When would you like to assume command of the Holconcom?"

Mekashe and Rhemun traded smiles. "As soon as possible, I would think," Mekashe said.

"As soon as possible," Rhemun agreed.

IT TOOK WEEKS to deal with her father's loss, with the funeral, with the horrible aftermath of the publicity that had led him to take his own life. She turned nineteen in the interim and hardly noticed the addition of an extra year—in fact, she didn't even celebrate it. She had barely scraped up enough credits for a meager funeral. Oddly, there had been a stranger at the facility who asked to see the body before it was cremated to take a tissue sample. She asked the director if he was a government official. The director only said that it was routine these days, but he didn't meet her eyes as he said it.

The funeral was badly attended. Jasmine and two friends from school and her mother's best friend were the only attendees. Professor Dupont's colleagues stayed away, perhaps concerned that the taint of his disgrace might rub off on them. It only made Jasmine more bitter, if that was possible. The happy, thoughtless girl had become a cold, angry woman. The loss of her only parent was devastating.

SHE GAVE A harsh interview to a single member of the Tri-D press and told the reporter without reservation that she held all the news media accountable for her father's suicide. They had blood on their hands that would never wash away, she added bitterly. Their constant harping on his disgrace, their ongoing commentary, had made it impossible for him to find work, leaving him despondent and destitute. He was unable to show his face in public without being verbally assaulted anywhere he went.

And how would the reporter like that? she added viciously. How would he like being harassed and harangued on the nightly news for weeks, with no relief from the hounding publicity?

He had no answer. When he gave the story online, he didn't cut one single word of her diatribe. In fact, he seemed to agree with her. It was after that when she discovered that she could go outside without having people yell at her about her father's disgrace.

The only concession she'd made was not to mention the Cehn-Tahr or the part they had played in her father's destruction. The emperor had great power and his reach was far, even into the Tri-Galaxy Council. Enraging him would accomplish nothing, except to make her life even harder. Nevertheless, she blamed him for her father's death. She blamed all the Cehn-Tahr, with their rigid culture that punished words.

Her father's suicide was a turning point for her, in many ways. The publicity went away. Another story sent the newspeople rushing after a disgraced theatrical figure who had given his child up for adoption after his wife's death. He was treated as badly as poor Professor Dupont had been. Jasmine felt sorry for him and hoped that he wouldn't take the same path.

SHE CONSIDERED A PROFESSION, because there was nothing left of her father's small estate. She grimaced as she surveyed her expensive wardrobe, which had eaten up the advance the embassy had given him for expenses. She'd bought pretty things to wear for Mekashe. For Mekashe, who'd betrayed her, who'd turned his back on her, who hadn't even looked at her that last day at the reception.

She blamed the Cehn-Tahr for all her misery. There had been a tentative offer from a politician on behalf of the Cehn-Tahr government, the offer of a scholarship. She'd turned away, after telling him that she would cheerfully starve to death before she would accept a single credit from the government that had sent her father home to die.

She'd wanted badly to follow in her late mother's footsteps and become a physician. But she had no money for the training that she would require. It was expensive. There were grants, certainly, but when she stood the preliminary tests, her scores were not high enough to merit scholarships. She had a diploma from secondary school, but her focus had been on fun and fashion, not on any difficult subjects like chemistry or physics or even languages, which would have helped her get into college.

She could go into the military and they would provide the necessary training, all expenses paid, and she would have a place to live. But she had issues with the Terravegan military authority. There were still rumors about the three-strikes law that turned military personnel into lab rats after three infractions of military law. A pirate named Percy Blount had exposed a black-ops team that was trying to apprehend Dr. Edris Mallory, Rhemun's mate, when she'd fled the Holconcom after an altercation with Rhemun before they bonded. The publicity had caused a great stir and many people lost jobs in the medical sector. But Jasmine heard gossip that some physicians in the military were still required to grow clones covertly for replacement organs for the high levels of society, even though this was outlawed. She'd also heard that the three-strikes provision was still in effect to gain live human material for experimentation in bioweapons labs. It was distasteful.

On the other hand, she had very few options. One was to get a job, any job, just until she could decide what to do next. She'd tried everything, but so far with no success. She got out the latest virtual ads, resigned to further disappointment, and went through them.

There was actually one prospect, although it was a distant one. A researcher needed someone who could take dictation and use a computer to manage and arrange her notes. It would mean some travel, and the woman was quite specific about the sort of help she wanted. Someone poised, used to social situations, intelligent, quick-witted and used to working odd hours.

That wasn't quite Jasmine, but she felt she could adapt. And there was nothing else available. So she shot a virtual query to the researcher, who agreed to meet her in the spaceport at Hayes Corner on Terravega the next day.

JASMINE WAS SITTING in the spaceport, waiting with desperate hope for her potential employer, when she felt eyes on her.

She looked up, and a tall, powerfully built Rojok in a black military uniform was looking down at her. He had very long straight blond hair, dusky skin and slit eyes. With a start, she recognized him from the reception on Memcache. That was Chacon, the president of the Rojok government.

She stood up. "Sir," she said politely.

He smiled. "Jasmine Dupont?"

"Yes, sir."

"An odd place to find you," he remarked.

She drew in a breath. "I'm waiting for a potential employer, a researcher who needs someone to write notes," she said miserably as she sat back down. "It was the only thing I could find."

"I had heard that you were interested in a career with the military, studying medicine," he said after a minute.

"Well, yes," she said hesitantly, wondering how he'd heard something that she was certain hadn't been spoken aloud. "But there are some things…" She hesitated to criticize her government. "I'm not sure that our military is where I belong," she finished with a long sigh.

"Then how would you feel about my military?" he asked.

Her lips fell open. "Your…military?"

"The Cehn-Tahr have a tradition—the Cularian medical specialist aboard their flagship is always a human female." He chuckled. "I have been amazed at the acceptance of this odd placement, both among the government and the military itself. So it occurred to me that a pilot project would be worth the trouble. I would like to have you trained as a Cularian specialist and assign you to the flagship of our own military authority."

Her heart lifted. She couldn't believe her good fortune. "Sir, I would be… It would be an honor… I never dreamed…!" She was babbling. She couldn't even manage a sentence.

He smiled. "Then you would consider it?"

"Yes! Oh yes!"

"I will arrange this with my adjutant, and have him contact you with the required visas and credentials. We have the finest military academy in the three galaxies on Enmehkmehk, my home planet. I think it will invigorate my command to have a human female in charge of sick bay, as you humans refer to it."

She was stunned. She just smiled. "Thank you, sir. Thank you very much! I'll study hard. I won't let you down, ever."

"I know that already." He looked up. Another military officer was beckoning to him. "Lieumek, my second in command," he said, indicating the other Rojok. "He'll contact you in a day or so."

"Thank you again. But don't you need my address…?"

He waved that away. "Lieumek can find anyone." He chuckled. "I will see you again, Jasmine Dupont."

He made her a brief bow and walked away, leaving her wide-eyed and shell-shocked.

The crackle of her communicator ring brought

her out of her stupor. She touched the crystal and a heavyset woman's face appeared. "Miss Dupont?"

"Yes."

"I'm Dr. Madge Norton. I deeply regret to tell you that my niece pleaded to come with me on my next expedition, and I no longer have a position to offer you. I'm very sorry."

"Dr. Norton, no worries," Jasmine told her. "Actually, I've just accepted a position that I never dreamed would be available. So it worked out well for both of us, it seems."

"Indeed." The other woman smiled. "I wish you good fortune."

"The same to you."

The image faded. Jasmine got to her feet and walked out to the curb to hire transport back to the small apartment she'd wrangled from the meager savings her mother had left her, which hadn't been entailed for her father's debts. She still couldn't believe her good fortune. It was the first happiness she'd felt since she and her late father had departed from Memcache. At least now she had the promise of work, and in a field she knew she was going to love. She couldn't believe her good luck. It was such a wonderful coincidence that Chacon had come to Terravega and chanced to meet her in the airport. She fixed herself a cup of hot chocolate and sat down to drink it.

CHACON TOUCHED A control on his desk in the office aboard his flagship. The emperor's face appeared a minute later.

"She accepted," he told Tnurat.

The older alien smiled. "I am in your debt," he said. "I have been racked with guilt over her father's death. This, at least, will make things easier for her. I can easily afford her expenses…"

"Not necessary, sir," the Rojok replied. "We have scholarships, and she will certainly qualify. Our military will cover her other expenses and her training. It will be interesting to see how this works out. A human female aboard a Rojok warship." He chuckled. "I begin to see why you Cehn-Tahr value your warwomen so much. As a species, they are fascinating."

"I must agree. You will keep me informed of her progress? Her life has been one of ease and wealth. It will be difficult for her to adjust."

"She will have all the assistance she needs," Chacon said. "Lyceria and I will make sure of it."

"How is my daughter?"

Chacon's eyes twinkled. "Very close to her delivery date. We are both nervous."

Tnurat chuckled. "We all are, when the first child arrives. You will both cope." He sighed. "Another grandchild. You give me a greater gift than you know."

"It is a gift for me, as well," Chacon replied gently.

"I have been alone, apart, for many decades. The joy Lyceria has brought to my life is indescribable. And now a child. It is more than I ever dreamed of. I was not certain about a pregnancy. We are both Cularian species, but different in some ways. However, her physician assures us that there will be no difficulties with the delivery. She has done quite well up to now."

"Your child will be unique," Tnurat said. "Just as my other grandchildren are. There has never been a Cehn-Tahr mother of a Rojok child. You will make history. Again." The older alien chuckled.

"I must confess that I sometimes miss the conflict of years past," he said. "When Dtimun and I fought great battles first together and then against each other. He was a most worthy opponent across a space battleground."

"My son would certainly echo that feeling," Tnurat replied. "I must go and tell Caneese the news. Not to mention Dtimun and Madeline. We are all excited about the addition to our Clan."

"No more than I am. I will be in touch again as soon as labor begins."

"I will anticipate that."

Tnurat broke the connection and sat back in his chair, his face sad and quiet. Jasmine sat heavily on his conscience. Mekashe's grief was an almost-tangible thing. If Tnurat could make the child's life even a little easier, it would help him bear the guilt he felt. He was grateful to Chacon for suggesting a solution to Jasmine's problems after he'd voiced his regrets that she wouldn't accept help from him. The Rojok soldier had felt a great sympathy for the child whose unruly tongue had brought her family to grief. When his investigation showed that the child was facing a life of poverty, and further queries turned up an interest in medicine and the military, it gave Chacon a solid idea.

Jasmine hadn't wanted to go into the Terravegan military because she knew too much from her mother about the things that went on in the medical sector. Tnurat had tried to offer a scholarship, but it became quickly apparent that Jasmine hated the Cehn-Tahr and wanted nothing from them. Chacon's offer had been accepted at once, and happily. It made Tnurat feel just a little better.

He went home to tell his family about Chacon's good news. The other news, about Jasmine, as well as a covert mission he'd authorized to obtain biological samples from Professor Dupont's body, was something he didn't intend to share. There would be time to speak of it later, much later, when the bulk of Mekashe's grief had eased. And when Tnurat's conscience healed, just a little more.

CHAPTER TEN

ROJOK CULTURE WAS fascinating to Jasmine. She, who had never been exposed to aliens before her trip to Memcache, was fascinated by the genetically enhanced military. Their appearance, very humanoid, was joined to a rousing sense of humor and a reputation for excellence that made even the Terravegan military envious.

Chacon had headed the armed forces as their field marshal in the time before the wars ended. Now there were regional conflicts and uprisings in the outer colonies, so the military had to be maintained. But there was far less stress than in the old days.

Lieumek took her to a large pavilion in the heart of the Rojok capital city, Corelkek. The name was a tongue twister that tripped her up on its first pronunciation, but Lieumek only laughed.

"It is difficult even for us to pronounce," he assured her as he led her to the first of many offices where she was granted a dormitory placement, proof of scholarships and her initial military academy assignment where she would live as she studied. "I hesitate to tell you that learning to speak our language will be a priority. At least, you will not be required to speak the ancient tongue," he added with a chuckle. "That, even I have trouble speaking. It is used in only the most ceremonial occasion. We have few of those."

"Your culture is fascinating," she said, looking around at the muted desert colors that permeated even the inside of the building. Many of the structures were built of some crystal that radiated either heat or cold. The systems were actually part of the stone used in construction. Not only that, the population lived in neat, compact houses whose major component seemed to be gardens under domes, like the huge complexes on Terravega.

"The construction is elegant," she continued. "And the heating and cooling systems…! I've never encountered anything like them."

"Even our rivals, the Cehn-Tahr, have no such quarries on their home planet," Lieumek said with something like disdain. "They build with stone, which retains heat and cold, but they do not have access to lesarkium. That is the amber-colored stone you see in our architecture."

She shook her head. "Magnificent," she said under her breath.

Lieumek beamed.

So did the official who put his virtual stamp on Jasmine's documents while listening to the pretty little human enthuse about Enmehkmehk. He even smiled, when he looked like a person who never did.

"I hope that you will enjoy your time with us," the official said, and actually stood.

Jasmine smiled at him warmly. "Thank you very much. I've never enjoyed anything so much. I look forward to learning your language."

The official rolled his eyes. "It is an impossible language," he said honestly. "But if you study hard, you will master it." He leaned forward. "After all, I did," he added with a chuckle.

She grinned at him, thanked him and left with Lieumek, who looked as if he'd tried to swallow a melon whole.

She looked up at him when they were outside in the warm sunshine, her eyebrows raised in a question.

"That was Holmek," he told her, still stunned. "I have never seen him smile in all the years I've dealt with him. And it was widely rumored that he had an innate prejudice for humans." He laughed. "I must tell Chacon. He will be amused."

"Chacon is very nice," she said.

"He is. Unless you are facing him across a battlefield, as his enemies can attest," he told her with a proud smile. "Come. I will escort you to the training camp." He saw her worry. "Do not be concerned. The officers have all been briefed, and they are looking forward to the experience. Many of them have an ongoing rivalry with the Cehn-Tahr. Knowledge that we will have a warwoman of our own, on our flagship, has given them a great sense of pride. Also," he added with a chuckle, "it will unsettle the Cehn-Tahr, something we all enjoy."

She beamed. She was going to like it here.

THAT WAS WHAT she thought, right up until she donned the black fatigues that were part and parcel of the military and crawled across a field against live chasat fire. She was dying in the unnatural heat. Rojoks had some reptilian DNA in their complicated physical makeup, and they loved the hot sun. Jasmine, who had spent her life in a climate that was carefully controlled, was aghast at living in a natural environment.

"Give up, human," one of the other inductees whispered with a grin, his slit eyes glittering with humor. "Admit that we are too tough for you!"

"In your dreams, mister," she shot back. She ground her teeth together and crawled faster. She wasn't going to let Chacon down. He'd given her this chance and, if it killed her, she was going to finish the course.

The heat beat down on her like a living thing. The close-fitting uniform was drenched. That was when something unexpected happened. It behaved as a built-in cooling system. Suddenly, instead of facing heatstroke, she was comfortable. Her expression reflected the surprise.

The other recruit noticed. "And you thought we

were given these thick uniforms for punishment, didn't you, human?" he teased.

She shot him a grin, which seemed to shock him. While he was absorbing the nonverbal retort, she put on a burst of speed and beat him to the finish line.

She noticed that his eyebrow ridges were raised as she was given her marks and dismissed. *So much for his taunting*, she thought.

CLASSES BEGAN THE next day for her medical training, in the afternoon. It seemed that she would spend mornings at the military range and afternoons in a classroom. Not a bad fit.

The students were placed at long tables, furnished with virtual pads, and the instructor came in and started to lecture.

He noticed Jasmine at the back of the class. His eyebrow ridges rose and he had a whimsical look for a few seconds, but it was quickly erased. He began to lecture in Standard, which all the other recruits understood. But there were a few hidden smiles. The classes were traditionally conducted in the Rojok tongue.

Jasmine, who was fascinated with the subject and listening intently, didn't know that she was being given a token of respect by the professor. He did seem to find her intense interest flattering.

SHE ENDURED HER first lab with a pale face and frequent bouts of nausea that, thank goodness, didn't send her running for the unisex restroom or searching for a bucket to throw up in. Dr. Amalok was somber and imposing. Jasmine was a little unnerved by him. He seemed to find the most vicious forms of life to lecture on and order dissections of.

The creatures she was given to identify in the lab were disgusting. They'd studied these in class, where Dr. Amalok had warmed to his subject and his eyes actually twinkled as he described how they attached themselves to a soldier's lower leg and destroyed nerve tissue and muscle with a deadly toxin.

To Jasmine, who'd never been exposed to indigenous life on other worlds, they were intimidating. She couldn't tell the difference between a tentacle and a toe, even with the virtual diagrams, much less find the creature's stomach, where she was supposed to obtain a tissue sample for cloning. But she learned quickly. She watched one of the other students begin his incision and copied him. He noticed and shot her a grin. She grinned back. The ordeal she'd expected was no ordeal at all.

She didn't ask why they were gathering samples for cloning. She knew that the Rojok were competent geneticists, and that they frequently cloned diseased persons of high position. They were able to reproduce not only the body, but the mind and memories, as well. They had no issues with clones, as

Terravegans had, and there was no prejudice here against them. It was one of many things she liked about their culture.

The attitude of the other students in her lab class was reflected in the rest of her classes, and in every military exercise in which she participated. Instead of prejudice and avoidance, her fellow recruits seemed to accept her as one of their own. As the weeks of training progressed, she became just another soldier trying to survive the complicated schedule. She even excelled on the forced marches, with infrequent attacks by "insurgents" from camouflage along the way. She learned defensive as well as offensive tactics. Often she thought, if only her father could see her now, covered in sand and slimy vines, her hair full of spider nets, her uniform stained and spotted! He wouldn't recognize this new Jasmine, who didn't flinch even at the sudden wave of virtual Nagaashe that attacked them in the simulations.

She still had her virtual Nagaashe, which lived with her in her quarters. It was a sad memory of the happiest time in her young life. Despite her anger and bitterness about what had happened to her father, the little serpent was a companion who helped fill her few leisure hours with delight.

As JASMINE LEARNED more defense tactics in military training and progressed to virtual surgeries in her medical training, she marveled at the differences in her life from the pampered young woman of yesterday to the fearless, competent soldier of today. The daily exercise had slowly turned her soft body into a hard weapon of war. She learned hand-to-hand killing techniques, along with chasat practice and use of tech to spy on the enemy. She learned the differences in Cularian species, their pharmacology and physiology, and how to administer drugs and perform surgical techniques. The classes, all of them, were like honey to a bear. She discovered a natural talent for medicine. She discovered an even-stronger one for combat, sometimes overcoming some of the tougher male students.

One of them was the Rojok who'd chided her on her first obstacle course. She took great pleasure in heaving him a little too far off the mat during hand-to-hand practice.

"Dupont, that was sloppy," the instructor said curtly. "Five kuskons off your record."

Kuskons were like demerits in the Terravegan military. She only smiled blithely. "Sorry, sir, my hand slipped," she added with a wicked grin at her ruffled opponent.

The Rojok instructor made a harrumphing sound and turned to a student who was trying unsuccessfully to throw his opponent. "No, no, Kraslok, not like that! Use his strength against him. Tollek, show him!"

"Ouch," the opponent she'd thrown whispered.

She chuckled under her breath. "Sorry," she whispered.

He laughed, too.

After class, he walked out beside her.

"Rusmok."

She glanced at him. "Sorry?"

"My name. Rusmok."

"Oh!" She stopped walking. "Jasmine Dupont," she said, looking up at him. It was a long way. She noticed that his hair was cut short. In the Rojok military, haircuts denoted rank. Chacon's hair was to his waist, which meant he had the highest rank in the military. Recruits had short hair. Even Jasmine was obliged to follow this rule, so her platinum hair curled around her small ears toward her beautiful face. Soft blue eyes looked up at her companion.

He smiled. "You have surprised us all," he said after a minute. "There were some complaints that a female was being forced into our ranks." He shrugged. "Mine was one of them. It is difficult to adjust to this change, when we have always been a male fighting force. However, you perform the exercises as well as any of us." He put a hand to his back and made a mock grimace. "Better than some," he added amusedly.

She laughed softly. "It surprised me, too," she said honestly. "I lived in a very sheltered environment. I had never even seen an alien when I went with my father…" Her voice trailed off. Grief almost over-whelmed her.

Rusmok turned and looked down at her. "We know of your father's tragedy," he said quietly. "The Cehn-Tahr are too fond of rules and too rigid in their social structure. We have been allies with them in-frequently, but over the centuries, our natural dispo-sition has been to decimate them on battlegrounds."

"I don't speak of what happened," she said after a minute. Her face hardened. "But there is no race in the three galaxies that I hate more than the Cehn-Tahr. I will never agree to treat one, not even if they court-martial me."

He chuckled. "I can assure you that our contact with the Cehn-Tahr these days is limited to saluting our president's bonded companion, Lyceria. She is Cehn-Tahr, but nothing like others of her race," he added. "You will see. She is kind and gentle. And very pregnant," he added with a grin. "The first Cehn-Tahr and Rojok child ever to be born in our culture."

"Lyceria is the Cehn-Tahr emperor's daughter, isn't she?" she asked.

"Yes. An exceptional person. We revere her."

They started walking again. "I read about her in one of the Tri-D virtual magazines," she said. "She was captured with the Holconcom and held at Ahk-mau…" She grimaced, glancing up. "Sorry." She knew that the infamous prison camp was something the Rojok were still having to live down. Its depravity was exposed after the Morcai Battalion's formation. In fact, the Morcai Battalion—half-human, half-Cehn-Tahr—had leveled Ahkmau after its escape, with some covert help from Chacon.

He waved away the apology. "Ahkmau is something we all have to live with in the military. None of us believed that something so disgusting could even exist until we were faced with the truth, after Mangus Lo's removal."

"He was your leader before Chacon," she recalled.

"Not quite. Mangus Lo's nephew, Chan Ho, succeeded him, but he was overthrown by Chacon and millions of veteran soldiers from other races—even Cehn-Tahr, surprisingly."

"It must have been quite a battle."

He smiled. "It was glorious," he said. "I was there, at the last battleground, when Chan Ho surrendered. The cheers were deafening. Chacon had planned to remain as military commander, but he was elected president by acclamation. Not a single dissenting vote." He glanced at her. "He was always revered by his soldiers. Even by his enemies. His tactics are taught at military academies across the three galaxies."

"He was very kind to me," she said. "He offered me this position. I had nothing left after my father died. I couldn't even get a job." Her face hardened.

"The Cehn-Tahr government offered me a scholarship. I refused."

He frowned. "An odd gesture."

"An odd people," she retorted.

"Agreed." He stopped just outside the commissary. "Your Terravegan government also has a military."

"And you wonder why I didn't agree to study there," she said, smiling. "Let's just say I'm not entirely confident that I could stay clear of the three-strikes law."

"Ah," he replied. "We all know of that. Patch exposed your medical authority. We found it intensely amusing, watching your politicians run from the Tri-D press."

She laughed. "I wasn't paying much attention to the news in those days. I was still at school." She frowned. "Who's Patch?"

"Percival Blount," he said. "He's called a pirate, but he heads what government exists on Benaski Port. He's human, but we consider him a good business partner."

"Benaski Port! I've heard of it."

"It is an infamous destination, full of vice and danger." He glanced at her and grinned. "When we go on maneuvers, it is a favorite place of ours for R & R. I will enjoy acquainting you with its depravity," he teased. "If you survive basic training," he added with a wicked grin.

"I'll survive," she said, and laughed. "I wouldn't want to miss the depravity," she added, tongue in cheek.

He chuckled softly.

"THIS IS NOT POSSIBLE," she panted, trying to climb a virtual wall in one of the holodens reserved for military training, with no success at all. She couldn't even get up a foot. Her hooks kept sliding off the stone. "They give us these—" she shook the two hooks at Rusmok, her climbing partner "—and expect us to scale that!" She pointed at the solid face of the wall.

"Observe," he said, ignoring the harangue.

He placed one in each hand and slid one, hook side down, along the wall and up until it encountered an invisible indentation and latched on. He followed with the other one. "You must feel for the depression and put the hook in it."

Her lips fell open as she followed his example. She laughed. "Incredible!" she exclaimed.

"Beat you to the top, Dupont," he drawled.

"You wish." She started up ahead of him. "Shouldn't have shown me how it's done, Rusmok," she called back down.

He laughed.

"STOP MONOPOLIZING OUR only human," one of two other recruits told Rusmok as they sat down beside them with their trays.

"It is she who monopolizes me," Rusmok replied haughtily, "because I am obviously superior to the rest of you."

Jasmine laughed wholeheartedly. "He's right," she confessed. "Nobody in the unit is half as obnoxious as he is. He sets a new standard for it, in fact!"

He glowered at her in mock anger. "Excuse me. Nobody in the entire unit is as completely obnoxious as I am."

"I stand corrected," she replied, and saluted him with her spoon.

"I am Delsox," one of the other recruits introduced himself. "That is Tollek."

"Pleased to meet you," she replied with a smile.

"Is it true that Chacon himself invited you to train with us?" Tollek, who was the youngest of the three, asked with awe in his voice.

"It is, indeed. I ran into him at the spaceport on Terravega while I was waiting on a job interview with an anthropologist."

"An anthro-what?" Rusmok asked.

"Someone who studies the physical history of humans. Bones and such," she amended when she realized they didn't understand.

Rusmok shivered. "We have no such field of study here. We are a superstitious people," he explained.

"Our dead are placed in great stone vaults which are only opened by outworlders, and then only to place new residents inside."

She stopped with her spoon of grelkosh—a sort of Rojok meat pie, very tasty—halfway to her mouth. "You don't, forgive me, cremate your dead?"

There were faint gasps. "No!" Tollek said huskily. "It is sacrilege. We believe that in the afterworld, our bodies are given new life. How can we have new life with no body?"

She blinked. It was a question she'd never entertained. Her father had been cremated. All Terravegans were, as a matter of course, because there was so little available land. Pressure domes contained the population and space was always at a premium.

"What do your people believe?" Rusmok wondered. "Do you believe in a life beyond death?"

She stared at him. "Well, I'm not sure," she confessed, a little ashamed. "Daddy was a philosopher. He read the classics, from the time of Dolmar the Great—a human who helped colonize Terravega. That was two thousand years ago. He said that we died and nobody knew what happened then. Of course, we have religious people who do believe in an afterworld. The Allfaith subscribers think we go to a place of eternal green fields and flowing clean streams of water."

Rusmok chuckled, along with his classmates. "We believe the afterlife is a glorious desert with many life-forms and endless places to stalk and hunt game."

She'd run into this obsession with hunting before. It seemed to be a staple of Rojok society. Stalking techniques were taught here alongside battle tactics.

"I think I might like hunting," she remarked.

There were huge smiles.

"I'm taking a group out at week's end to hunt sandsabers," Rusmok told her. "If you would like to come, you would be welcome."

"True," Tollek said at once. "Delsox and I are also going."

"Will I need to bring a weapon?" she asked.

"We don't use chasats on hunts." Rusmok chuckled. "We use teralek and miskol."

She pursed her lips. "Okay, my meager Rojok isn't adequate to translate that."

"Nets and spears," Rusmok said with a grin. "It is a test of courage as much as a hunt. And before you ask, we eat the sandsaber and send the teeth and claws to researchers to use in concocting new medicines to combat disease in our young."

"Also, we tan the hides and give them to the poor for winter, which is harsh even on Enmehkmehk."

Obviously, someone had told them that she didn't like killing animals and that she was a vegan. She wondered who. She hadn't liked those things, true, but her attitudes had adjusted to the realities of life on Enmehkmehk.

"There is snow." Tollek sighed and smiled.

"Snow?" she asked. "What is snow?"

They all had arched eyebrows.

Rusmok laughed. "Frozen water that falls from the skies in great huge white flakes. It covers the ground and makes marching challenging. We learn to fight in it, because many conflicts come about on worlds where snow is eternal."

She sighed. "So much to learn," she said. She looked up. "You know, I was a vegetarian before I started training here. Impossible to continue it in a place where nothing is served that doesn't contain meat." She chuckled.

"We are carnivores," Rusmok said easily.

"I noticed," she teased. She sighed. "Well, when in Rome…"

"What is Rome?" they wanted to know.

She opened her eyes wide. "Why, I don't really know," she said. "The reference is one that I've heard used all my life, but nobody knows where it came from. Basically, it means you adapt to the place where you live."

"A sound piece of advice." Rusmok glanced at her. "You aren't squeamish? Hunting sandsabers is messy. And bloody."

"Nothing is bloodier than Dr. Amalok's dissections," she said with a mock shiver. "He sets a new standard for it, in fact."

"And his lectures." Tollek groaned. "He never

seems to lose enthusiasm for the most dangerous life-forms."

"Something even graduate officers refer to." Rusmok sighed. "He is a legend at the academy."

"I love his lectures," she said, drawing stunned attention from her companions. "I've never even encountered alien life-forms before. It's all new and fascinating to me."

"I had noticed her rapt attention in class," Tollek said with amusement.

"Dr. Amalok noticed, too," Rusmok mused. "Have you noticed that he seems to lecture directly to her in class these days?"

"That's because most of the rest of the class is asleep." Delsox chuckled.

"I just hate the labs." She sighed, finishing her meal. She put down her spoon. "Don't you people eat dessert?" she wondered aloud.

They stared at her.

"Dessert," she emphasized. "I haven't had dessert since I left Terravega."

"We have deserts all around our capital," Rusmok began.

"Not deserts," she emphasized. "Dessert. It's a pastry or a pudding," she explained. "Sweets. Pies with whipped cream. Cakes. Puddings with tapioca or vanilla or chocolate." She was going dreamy at just the memory.

"Empty but fattening calories," Rusmok murmured, finishing his own meal. "Useless to a soldier."

"They're not useless," she moaned. "I lie awake nights, dreaming of empty but fattening calories. Oh, what I wouldn't do for a cookie!"

"A what?"

"A cookie! Wait." She pulled out her virtual device, used for calculations in most of her classes but also attuned to the galactic Nexus. "Here." She showed them a picture of cookies on a plate.

"More useless but fattening calories," Rusmok teased.

She actually groaned. "It's hopeless. You don't know what you're missing. You truly don't."

"In which case, why should we miss it?" Tollek asked.

She put up the virtual device and rested her elbows on the table, cupping her pretty face in her palms. "I wish I could cook." She sighed. "I'd try to make my own."

"You can buy—what did you call them, cookies?—when we get to Benaski Port on our first R & R," Rusmok said comfortingly. "It will give you something to anticipate."

She brightened. "I forgot! Well! If I have cookies to look forward to, I can survive anything."

"Eat too many, and you will never scale the holo-wall again, and our instructor will fail you," Rusmok chided.

"I can always find an antidote. After all, I'm a doctor. Well, almost," she corrected. She looked from one of them to the other. "If one of you would like to break something, I'll prove it to you. I already have my wrist scanner." She pulled up her sleeve to reveal the minicomp which was embedded in the soft skin of her wrist. It was standard procedure for medical students in all military, something borrowed from the Terravegan military, which had initiated it decades ago.

"Wait until our days off." Tollek chuckled. "You will have work on the sandsaber hunt, I can assure you."

"It is true," Delsox added. "Someone always falls off an embankment or gets too close to the claws and teeth. There are many injuries."

"I used to be deathly afraid of cats," Jasmine remarked as she sipped the teskor that passed for human java, in a thick mug. It had a form of light caffeine that made it essential to military personnel, whose maneuvers were often unexpected and interrupted sleep.

"Truly?" Rusmok asked.

She nodded. "When I first came here, they administered an unusual drug that rid me of any phobias. I didn't know such a thing existed. I expected years of therapy by psychoanalysis."

Rusmok smiled. "We have many medical techniques that are unknown to outworlders. We rarely share them."

"This was a very good one. I would hate to miss the hunt," she added.

"You will not throw up at the sight of so much blood and gore?" Tollek teased.

"I would never disgrace my unit by such an unprofessional and juvenile display," she promised him.

WHICH MADE IT doubly embarrassing that the first thing she did, at the very first kill of the day, was to throw up profusely all over her own shoes.

The men rolled over laughing. Tears actually fell from their slit eyes, especially when she started swearing in Rojok at her own weakness.

"It happens to all of us," Rusmok said sympathetically as she got to her feet and mopped her mouth with a synthesized towelette from her pack.

"I was sure it wouldn't happen to me," she groaned.

"Your first hunt was expected to be somewhat traumatic," he returned. "You will adjust." He handed her another spear to go with her net. "Tollek killed the first. You are certain to kill the next."

She gave him a doubting look.

"You will see."

THEY WAITED WHILE the designated skinner went to work, deftly reducing the carcass to its component parts. A kombar, or teleporting device, was used to whisk the components back to the appropriate department in the capital city.

Then they were off to the next sandsaber.

Jasmine fell in behind the others, treading over the rocky terrain as the sun beat down on her blond head. She liked the feeling of comradeship that she got, being part of the team.

Hunting wasn't the ordeal she'd expected it to be. And despite her nausea, excitement was rapidly claiming her. Stalking game was invigorating. Once again, she was amused at the difference between the old Jasmine and the new.

FAR AWAY, NEAR the rim, the Holconcom was getting ready for an assault on a dissident camp, on Salash, an outer planet where Rojok colonists were under attack by pirates. Stores of Helium three were coveted by colonists and Cehn-Tahr alike. The pirates stole it and sold it on the black market, to renegades like themselves holding out on Tri-Galaxy Council planets throughout the galaxies.

Although the Cehn-Tahr's treaty with the Nagaashe on Akaashe provided them with plenty of Helium three for their reactors on Memcache, the colonists equally required the rare element for their own reactors. It was too far and perilous to try to transport it from Memcache all the way to the rim. So the Holconcom was ordered to deal with the pirates.

"Here we go again," Holt Stern, the flagship Morcai's astrogator groaned as they made orbit. "You'd think these guys would give up eventually. Everybody hunts them, even Rojoks."

Mekashe smiled faintly. "Surely, you aren't tiring of the hunt, Stern?" he teased.

"Me, sir? Never!" the former captain of the SSC warship Bellatrix assured him. "It's just the trip here. Tedious, to say the least, even at our speeds with the lightsteds thrown."

"True. I, too, tire of the travel," Mekashe confided.

"As do we all," his exec, Btnu, added. "But the conflict is what we train for."

"Mustn't let our expensive education go to waste, right, sir?" Stern chuckled.

"Absolutely," Mekashe agreed. "Btnu, organize the landing party."

"Yes, sir."

As Btnu left to get the unit together, and assign transport, Mekashe looked vacantly at the viewscreen. Rojoks did, indeed, love a hunt. So did Cehn-Tahr. He recalled that Jasmine had hated hunting, been afraid of cats, hated the military, had contempt for other races. It was a painful memory.

He wondered what her life was like now, on Terravega, after the death of her father. He was forbidden to touch her mind, to inquire about her circumstances, even to ask anyone about her. The taboo was unbreakable.

Just as well, he told himself over and over. There was no place in his life for her now. And she would never be able to accept him as he was. Nor could she deal with combat in any form. Just the thought of Jasmine in a battle of any sort was amusing. The elegant, sophisticated woman he'd known would flinch at getting her clothing soiled.

"Ready to go, sir." Btnu's voice came over the comm.

"On my way," Mekashe replied tersely. "Stern, you have the conn. Please don't break the ship in my absence," he added, the first faint bit of humor coming from him since his assignment to command the Holconcom.

Stern chuckled. "I won't break her, sir. But I might bend her. Just a little."

Mekashe flashed him a green smile on his way off the bridge.

CHAPTER ELEVEN

JASMINE WAS SLOGGING her way through the nastiest
swamp she'd ever seen in her life. It was the unit's
first combat training assignment, fighting insurgents on Lagana, in the Dibella system. She recalled
vaguely that the Holconcom had fought an epic battle here with Rojoks during the reign of Mangus Lo.

"Dupont, keep up!" the officer in charge called
to her.

"Yes, Dupont, keep up," Rusmok chided as he
passed her. "Or no Benaski Port R & R for you!"

"We'll see about that!" she retorted, and doubled
her efforts to wade through the mel-leaches that already covered her boots and trousers. She groaned
and, avoiding detection by the officer in charge,
pulled out a small stunning device from her medical
wrist unit and stunned the creatures. They dropped
off at once. She grinned to herself as she replaced
the device.

"Five kuskons off your record, Dupont, for un-
lawful use of tech." The instructor's voice bit into
her ear.

"Yes, sir." She sighed. "Sorry, sir."

"Reprobate," Rusmok chided as she caught up to him. "You already have more kuskons than the rest of us combined."

"I hate mel-leaches," she muttered. "And our unit leader must have eyes in the back of his head!"

He leaned to her ear. "He's a telepath," he whispered with a laugh in his voice. "Nobody can keep anything from him."

"Just my luck." She shook her head, noticing that the mel-leaches were once again crawling up her legs. "Can't we collect these things and stew them?" she asked facetiously.

"An admirable thought, Dupont. Proceed. We will expect you to cook it, as well, when we finish here," the unit leader told her smugly.

Rusmok made a face. "They induce unconsciousness," he told her.

"Not in small doses, Rusmok," the leader replied. "In fact, they have a rather intoxicating effect. We will all learn from Dupont's example. I love mel-leaches. In fact, I keep them as pets."

She sighed. "Figures," she muttered under her breath.

Fortunately for her, the leader pretended not to hear her.

"Come! Move faster! A true Rojok soldier is always eager to do battle, to prove his courage and commitment to the service! Swamps are wonderful! Mel-leaches are delightful! How fortunate for us that we are tested by such a beautiful environment!"

As he spoke, tangling vines reached out and tried to curl around Jasmine's leg, and six mel-leaches reached her throat and tried to latch on to the soft flesh. With a sigh of resignation she brushed them off and removed the vines, which secreted a white toxic substance. It fell on one of the mel-leaches and it promptly dropped to the ground.

An idea was born. She tore two of the vines in half and applied them to the other mel-leaches with a huge smile.

"Now, that is proper curiosity turned to advantage," the instructor said, halting the group. "Notice what Dupont has just done," he told them. "She has discovered that the toxin in the attacking vines can be used to dislodge the mel-leaches. Use this new knowledge!"

The other recruits followed suit, raising a cheer to Jasmine under their collective breaths. She burst out laughing, not caring if she got more black marks for it.

"I owe you a synthale for that," Rusmok told her. "A far better use for the foul creatures than a stew."

She chuckled. "I'll hold you to that."

THEY WERE HALFWAY through the mission when a surprise attack by a party of insurgents, led by an Altairian, exploded around them. Firing insurgents burst out of the swamp.

Jasmine was shocked into immobility for a few seconds, before she regained her senses and rolled onto the swampy ground, pulling her chasat on the way down.

She shot at the first pair of boots she saw, recognizable as non-Rojok issue. A shout of pain was followed by a hard thud. Another recruit finished the insurgent off. Jasmine got to her feet, continuing low to the ground, and started looking around automatically for wounded.

Months of intensive training in the holo simulators, added to the constant reinforcement of her diagnostic and surgical skills, had hardened her to the gore of battle. Her only focus was on the patients, on relieving suffering and saving lives. She learned to overlook the horrible images, drawn from life in the simulators, that were imprinted on her subconscious as she progressed in her studies.

She treated two minor wounds and quickly moved on. There was one other Cularian specialist in the unit, a male, but he'd gone forward to treat a more serious wound. Jasmine fell behind as she searched for other wounded. She found a dead soldier from her unit and performed the simple, mandated ritual for the passing of a fellow recruit. She hadn't known the Rojok well, but unit became family as they trained together. She was sorry for his loss.

It took a minute for her to realize that she hadn't seen Rusmok since the attack began. He was probably up with the unit leader, who was calling out terse instructions as insurgents were captured. She peered through the thick vegetation, but she didn't see her friend.

"Tollek," she called to another friend, "have you seen Rusmok?"

He grimaced. "No, Dupont, I haven't. I thought he was with our leader."

"So did I, but he isn't."

Tollek sighed. "There were several casualties that we passed on the way here. We didn't have time to look closely…"

"I'll run back and check," she said, turning.

She kept her chasat at her waist, her hand on it, as she searched through the insurgent bodies. There were five, all beyond saving. But no Rusmok. Perhaps he'd been somewhere near the leader, and she just hadn't seen him, she rationalized. There was so much confusion that it would be easy to overlook someone.

He was the first friend she'd made on Enmehkmehk. He'd been first chiding, and then encouraging. They spent a lot of time together on liberty, going from gaming station to bar. They found many things in common. There was no romantic aspect to it. Rusmok was suffering from unrequited love for a female who'd thrown him over when he announced his intention to go into the military. He still mourned her. While Jasmine had never gotten over Mekashe and was uncertain that she ever would. She blamed him for turning his back on her. But the memories were pervasive. It was unfortunate.

Her heart dropped. Her thoughts scattered. She walked into a small clearing and there was Rusmok.

Her heart fell to her feet. He was lying on his back, gasping for breath. As she grew closer, she saw that two chasat holes were burned into his chest.

She ran to him and dropped to her knees at his side, fighting tears. "No! No, no, no!" she whispered as she pulled out her wrist scanner and started to diagnose his injuries. She reached over to put a diagnostic sensor in place.

But his big six-fingered hand covered hers where it rested on his heaving chest.

"Too late, Dupont," he whispered with a wan smile. "I should have…ducked."

Tears were boiling down her cheeks. "It's not the new weapons," she said, fighting the horror she felt. She caught her breath. "Not the ones that do catastrophic damage. These are just chasat burns. Your lungs are punctured…but…not…irreversibly…!"

While she was speaking, she was working. She initiated a repair on the first lung, sealed off the damage until she had time to finish reducing the wound. Her hands, steady and competent, went on to the second injury, the lesser of the two.

"Too late," he said in a drained tone.

"It most certainly is not! Don't you dare give up!" she raged. "Don't you dare!"

He was trying not to laugh. He failed. Even through the pain, her indomitable spirit amused him, even as her fear for him touched him. He gave up trying to speak and let her work.

A few minutes later, he was breathing more easily. The pain was severe, and her pain medication was limited to what her wrist unit could carry. But he would live. She sat back on her heels, oblivious to the diminishing signs of conflict around them.

"I don't believe this," she muttered.

"What?" he asked in a strained tone.

"You'd let yourself be shot to get out of buying me that synthale you owe me?" she returned.

The unit leader, standing behind her, let out an involuntary laugh before he could stop himself. The other recruits slowly fell in around him, most of them grinning. She went back to work on Rusmok while the unit leader called in a medevac for Rusmok and the other wounded, and a prisoner transport for the insurgents they'd captured.

Jasmine didn't realize then what she'd done. Much later, it was related to her by someone outside the military that her blatant concern for an alien not even of her species had convinced her superiors that she was everything Chacon hoped she would be. Her coolness under fire, her competence even as a novice medic, earned her high marks from both her military and medical instructors.

And Rusmok bought her that synthale. In fact, he bought her two.

RHEMUN'S LITTLE GIRL followed Mekashe around the villa, trying to match her small steps to his stride. He chuckled as he noticed her behind him.

"We will make a soldier of you yet," he told her.

She grinned up at him. "Want to be a soldier," she agreed.

"Not yet," Rhemun said firmly. "First you learn to eat your skemache, then you join the military."

She made a face at him, and then spoiled the mock anger by running into his arms to be picked up.

Rhemun nuzzled his cheek against hers. "Torment," he chided.

"Where is Kipling?" she asked.

"Gone to school with Komak."

"Want to go to school."

"Not yet."

She sighed. "I can eat my skemache now," she said in such a resigned tone that both adults laughed.

While she played in the grassy yard, Rhemun and Mekashe sipped ale in the cool of the steps. Both of them were off duty for two days, a holiday of sorts. It was rare for both of them to be at leisure at the same time. Especially for Mekashe, whose duty as commander of the Holconcom took him to far distant parts of the galaxy from time to time.

"Edris will be sorry that she missed you," Rhemun said. "She and Madeline went on a shopping trip to the moon bazaar."

"She never seems to age," Mekashe said. He stared into his tall stone glass, lost in reverie.

"You still dwell on the ambassador's daughter," Rhemun said quietly.

Mekashe sighed and let out a hollow laugh. "It has been five years," he said. "One would think that the passing of time would diminish the attraction. That has not been the case."

Rhemun studied his friend covertly. The other Cehn-Tahr had aged visibly. The hard-faced military man across from him no longer resembled his Kahn-Bo partner who was full of mischief and always kidding. Mekashe had become like Dtimun, who formerly led the Holconcom, battle-hardened and authoritative.

But even with that coldness, the Cehn-Tahr and humans aboard the Morcai still revered their new commander. Not one of them had asked to transfer to other duty since his appointment. Rhemun recalled wryly that every human aboard ship had tried to transfer back to the Terravegan military soon after Rhemun's appointment. He'd made enemies of everyone aboard with his long-standing prejudices against humans. He'd finally overcome those and won the respect of his men. But Mekashe had never had to struggle with his command. The men welcomed him like a member of the family.

"You still have Tellas serving as Cularian medicine specialist aboard the Morcai," Rhemun commented.

Mekashe shrugged. "It has been difficult to find a human female willing to serve with us," he said simply. "We have petitioned the Terravegans, but to no avail." He gave his friend a wry smile. "I think the medical authority on Trimerius holds us responsible for the revelation of their so-called three-strikes provision and the illegal black-ops medical experimentation that we reported to the three galaxies from Benaski Port."

"That was my responsibility," Rhemun recalled. "I would do it again in a second. Edris was in danger of becoming a laboratory experiment after I sent her running from the Morcai." He sighed. "I was horrible to the humans in the Holconcom. They forgave me, but it was a black mark that I could never erase. At least you had no prejudices to stand between you and the crew when you took command."

Mekashe smiled. "They were like family. They still are. I missed the Morcai when I was appointed captain of the Imperial Guard."

"You were next in line for that task, as I was next in line for command of the Holconcom when Dtimun was revealed publicly to be the emperor's son."

"Clan is all," his friend replied.

"As it ever was, and ever shall be," Rhemun agreed. "I do regret the loss of a warwoman aboard the Morcai," he added. "It was a mark of distinction for us. One which the Rojoks have now appropriated."

"The Rojoks have a warwoman?" Mekashe asked, chuckling. "With their prejudices against females in the military? Not to mention," he added, "their distaste for humans, from whom they must have taken the idea!"

"I hear that it was Chacon's idea," came the amused reply. "He is still quite fond of Madeline Ruszel."

Mekashe shook his head. "Where did they ever find a Rojok female who was willing to undertake such a task? Is she a physician?"

"Yes. A Cularian specialist. We can discover nothing more about her. Not even the emperor has been able to learn who she is. A very well-kept secret."

"Chacon surely knows."

"He will not reveal anything, not even to his mate, the emperor's daughter." Rhemun chuckled. "But the best gossip in the fleet, gleaned from an outcast Rojok who has ties to the military on Enmehkmehk, is that she is human."

"A human female, among Rojoks." Mekashe made an odd sound. "She must be unique. I do not remember ever hearing of a human female setting foot on Enmehkmehk."

"Nor I."

"How sad, that the Rojoks are stealing our idea and making it their own." Mekashe pursed his lips. "Perhaps we should ask the emperor to use his influence with the Tri-Galaxy Council to find us another human warwoman. Lawson would listen to him, even if the medical authority there ignores us."

"I will make it a point to ask him," Rhemun promised.

JASMINE AND RUSMOK were assigned duty aboard different vessels when they graduated from the military academy. It was a sad leave-taking, after all their time together.

"Don't get shot," she cautioned him. "I won't be there to save you."

He grinned. "If I do get shot, I will have them find you and bring you to treat me, wherever I am."

"Deal." She sighed. "Well, we're real soldiers now."

"With real weapons and real duties," he agreed. "I hear that Chacon and his mate invited you to their home for a traditional Rojok banquet, with a guest of your choice."

She nodded. She made a face. "I wish you were going to be here to go with me," she confessed. "I'm a misfit. I don't really have any other friends. Nobody here wants to put up with me," she joked.

"Ask Tollek," he advised with a smile. "He likes you."

"I like him, too." She shrugged. "But there's only one Rusmok." She laughed, but she was fighting tears.

"Do not do that," he cautioned immediately.

"Excuse me?"

"Weep," he said. "If you do, I will, and my reputation as a warrior will suffer irreparable damage. I assure you."

She drew in a steadying breath and ground down hard on the pins in her throat. She forced a smile. "I'll control my impulses," she promised. "Hey. There's always R & R. I'll try to make sure I get it when you do. If we can find a mutual bar."

"Benaski Port," he said with a chuckle. "All our ships dock there for liberty." He leaned forward. "Stop getting kuskons, so that you have the opportunity to get liberty."

She sighed. "You won't be around, so I'll stay out of trouble, I guess."

"A sound idea. Farewell, Jasmine Dupont," he said softly. "I will miss you."

She felt as if her throat was full of thorns, but she smiled. "I will miss you, too. Farewell."

He picked up his kit and walked away. He didn't

look back. Neither did she. It would have embarrassed her to burst into tears and have the other soldiers see her do it.

CHACON'S HOUSE WAS elegant and spacious, like the villa Jasmine had visited in the holoroom with Mekashe. She wondered if Chacon's mate, Lyceria, hadn't helped with that design, since it was very reminiscent of Cehn-Tahr architecture.

Lyceria, heavy with pregnancy, met her at the door in a flowing blue garment with gold trim.

"Welcome," she said gently.

"Thank you for inviting me. It truly is an honor. This is my friend Tollek," she added, introducing the starstruck soldier beside her.

"Your Highness," he said, and made her a sweeping bow.

Jasmine wondered if she should follow suit. Lyceria laughed softly. "You do not bow," she told Jasmine. "Only on Memcache. Not here. We are not so formal. My mate is reprimanding some high official in his office. Fortunately, there is a sound panel between us so that the foul language will not travel this far," she added wickedly. "He has an amazing vocabulary."

"I know a few other soldiers who do, as well." Jasmine laughed.

"Please, come in." She led them into the living area, where sumptuous couches and cushioned chairs were scattered on a stone floor that radiated heat, because winter had arrived on Enmehkmehk and snow was falling softly outside.

She offered them seats and had a valet bring warm drinks.

"We were fortunate to have a passing vessel bring sea shrimps from the Vegan colonies," Lyceria said. "So seafood is on the menu, along with native breads and fruits."

"What a treat," Jasmine exclaimed. "I'm fond of all the local meats, but seafood is rare in our mess hall."

"Considering the embargo that existed until recently on Vegan products, I imagine the military budget would not stand it," Lyceria said, smiling. "Are you happy here?"

"Happier than I've been in a long time," came the soft reply. "I was surprised that your mate offered me the chance to train here. And more surprised that I was accepted so easily by the other soldiers. A human female among Rojok males. I expected it to be very difficult."

"You won them over quite easily," Lyceria said. "They admire courage and stubbornness more than most other traits. You never gave up on the hardest obstacle courses, although you'd never been exposed to such rough treatment. The men respected you for it."

"I led a sheltered life," Jasmine said quietly. "Too

sheltered. After my mother died, my father was so afraid of losing me that he became overprotective."

"It was that way with my father, after my younger brother was killed on Terramer, and I was captured and tortured by Mangus Lo at Ahkmau," Lyceria said, her voice tinged with sadness. "Chacon saved me. I kept contact with him all through the war, despite my parents' fears that I would be jailed for treason. He was the light of my life from my first sight of him."

"He is an exceptional military leader," Jasmine said. "The men speak of him in whispers. They respect no one more."

"No one except my brother," Lyceria said with a wicked smile. "When he led the Holconcom, his exploits were the stuff of legends. I think he misses command. But his mate is happier having him off the battlefield, especially with their sons so young."

"His mate is human," Jasmine recalled.

"Very," Lyceria said. She laughed out loud. "If you could have seen them on Benaski Port together! Madeline was very pregnant, as I am now, and Dtimun had threatened to lock her in a room for being disrespectful. She said that she could climb out of windows, so let him try it." She shook her head in a very human manner. "She and my brother were adversaries for three years, until they were forced to work together to save my mate. Chacon's own security force was trying to kidnap him, so that Chan Ho could reopen

Ahkmau and begin the reign of terror all over again. They saved him. It is why he and Dtimun and Madeline are so close."

"I believe that he saved them first," came a deep, amused voice from behind them.

Chacon moved into view, still in his military uniform, which he wore to most social functions. He touched his mate's cheek gently. "Although I confess that saving you was my focus. Their liberation was a secondary benefit."

She smiled back, catching his hand. "For which we all still give thanks. You know Jasmine Dupont," she added, nodding toward her.

Jasmine stood and saluted him respectfully, as did Tollek.

"It is good to see you," he said.

"This is my friend Tollek," she added, indicating the soldier beside her. "We survived boot camp—excuse me, recruit passage—together."

"Along with your friend Rusmok," Chacon added surprisingly. "It was difficult not to interfere, when you were assigned to different ships," he added as he dropped down beside his mate. "The two of you were inseparable. But the good of the military comes first."

"Indeed it does, sir. Although Rusmok and I have high hopes of reuniting in the not-too-distant future at Benaski Port to wreck a few bars. In disguise. So that we aren't connected with the Rojok military, of course…" She flushed red at her own boldness.

But Chacon wasn't offended. He roared.

"I have it on good authority that Dr. Madeline Ruszel wrecked several bars while she was attached to the Holconcom," he replied. "In fact, when Dtimun called her out for it, she said that an insult from a rival unit about him was responsible. Never have I seen two less likely mates for each other."

"Nor I," Lyceria added. "But it has been a grand affair."

"Their children are unique. As ours is expected to be," he added with a smile at his mate.

He turned back to Jasmine. "How do you like your new assignment?" he asked.

"It's an honor, sir," she replied. "The sole Cularian specialist on the flagship of the Rojok fleet. I never dreamed of such an appointment. Honestly, I expected to do duty on Enmehkmehk at the infirmary."

"You did not," he chided with a smile. "I recall telling you when I made the offer of training that your ultimate assignment would be such."

"Yes, sir, but I expected that to be after I'd proven myself," she began.

"You proved yourself in combat, when you refused to give up on a fatally wounded fellow recruit," he replied. "The entire unit sent a petition to my office, asking for a commendation for you. Which I was inclined to give. However, I did not want to single you out for possible harassment at so early a stage of your training." He leaned forward with a rueful smile. "You will learn that Rojoks are extremely competitive. Especially in the early stages of training. By singling you out, I would have exposed you to some rather brutal retaliation."

"I'm very flattered that the men thought so highly of me," Jasmine responded. She smiled. "There's a saying among humans, that it's the thought that really counts, as much as the action."

"So I have heard."

A tiny bell rang and Lyceria smiled as she got to her feet. "I believe that our meal is now ready. Come. Vegan seafood is a delicacy not to be missed!"

IT WAS A pleasant meal, far from the ordeal Jasmine had expected it to be. A visit to the home of the president of the Rojok government would intimidate most soldiers. But it was like being at home, long ago. An odd feeling, considering her resentment for Cehn-Tahr, after the agony her father's dismissal had caused.

But then, Lyceria was hardly to blame for something the emperor did, she reminded herself. Mekashe, on the other hand, she would never stop blaming.

She noticed Lyceria's sudden worried glance, but it was quickly erased and followed by a question about Jasmine's medical scores, which had been impressive.

IT WASN'T UNTIL Jasmine was back in the barracks that she recalled something troubling. Lyceria was of the Royal Clan. And they were all telepaths. She hoped against hope that she hadn't given offense to that kind, gracious soul. It would have wounded her, when Lyceria—and Chacon—had been so kind.

She rolled over in bed and closed her eyes. Tomorrow would be her first day aboard the Kreskkom, the flagship of the Rojok fleet. She looked forward to it, even as she dreaded the new and overwhelming responsibility. Her training had been superb. Now it was time to repay it.

IN THE ABSENCE of Admiral Baklor, who was recuperating from surgery, the commanding officer was Captain Tregor, a veteran of many wars. He had as many campaign ribbons as Admiral Lawson of the Tri-Galaxy Fleet, and a temper about twice as bad.

He was railing out a subordinate for a sloppy drill when Jasmine walked onto the bridge and saluted.

He stopped his tirade and turned to her. He had long straight blond hair, not as long as Chacon's— it came only to his shoulders. His slit eyes studied her quietly in a hard, dusky face. He lifted his chin. "You are Dr. Dupont."

"Yes, sir," she said, still standing at attention.

"You were selected for this assignment by Chacon himself."

"Yes, sir, I was."

He made a rough sound in his throat. "We have never had a female aboard any ship in the fleet, much less a flagship," he scoffed. "Only Chacon would consider something so radical. Copying the Cehn-Tahr, with their famous warwomen!"

Jasmine, wisely, said nothing.

"Very well. If I must bend to innovation, I must," he said curtly. "We have a veteran physician in sick bay. He will be in charge. You will follow his orders as if they were mine, and you will do nothing without his permission. Do you understand?"

"Sir, yes, sir," she said formally.

He made another sound. He turned away. "Dismissed. Now, Lekkom, let us discuss how you may make amends for your inferior performance on the abandon-ship drill!" He spoke to the intimidated officer standing at rigid attention in front of him.

JASMINE PURSED HER lips and let out a faint breath after she left the bridge. She hadn't expected it to be easy. The captain was an older Rojok. Change came hard to veteran officers. But if she kept her head down, she might survive.

She stowed her gear in the berth to which she was assigned and reported to Dr. Meklor in sick bay.

"Dr. Jasmine Dupont, reporting for duty, sir," she said formally, and with a rigid salute.

Dr. Meklor glanced at her with twinkling eyes.

"Our warwoman," he said. "I gather that the captain had several bites of you to top off his breakfast?" he teased.

She was surprised by the question and not at all sure how to respond.

He waved a six-fingered hand. "I'm harmless," he assured her. "Although the captain is not. He has six decorations for courage under fire and he has a reputation for eating recruits raw. You will adjust to him in time. Meanwhile, let me acquaint you with our glowing technology and superior java brewer. This infirmary runs on java, just as I'm told your Tri-Galaxy medical authority on Trimerius does, covertly, of course."

She couldn't repress a smile. He reminded her strongly of her unit leader in basic training, the one who'd teased her about mel-leaches.

To her surprise, the doctor turned and chuckled. "Ah, so you trained under my brother," he said, nodding at her expression, revealing that he had the same telepathic capabilities as his brother. "He loves swamps and predators and insects. I had to survive basic training under him, just as you did. When I graduated, I put a bucket of mel-leaches in his bed and disabled the lights."

She burst out laughing.

"Yes—" he nodded "—I do have a vindictive personality. It comes in handy aboard this vessel." He gave her a wicked smile. "The captain can never be certain if his sheets are safe to sleep in."

She was going to like it here, she decided. Despite the captain.

THEIR FIRST AWAY mission was the rescue of a party of Jebob archaeologists from an erupting volcano.

"Idiots," the captain muttered at the briefing, which Jasmine attended with the doctor. "There were seismic patterns for weeks, indicating magma flow. They sat on their common sense and continued digging. Now you see the result. We must put a landing party down and risk the lives of our own people to save theirs!"

Nobody argued.

"Dupont, this is your hour," he told her with a sarcastic smile. "Several of the Jebob have injuries. You will accompany the landing party and treat them."

"Yes, sir," she said.

He looked for any sign of reluctance and found none.

"Very well," he said. "Report every hour, unless the land beneath you becomes molten and swallows you," he said, waving a hand. "In which case, there are many recruits awaiting assignment back at the academy," he added nastily.

Jasmine bit her tongue. Dr. Meklor grinned at the captain. "In which case, you will be allowed to explain the demise of our warwoman to President

Chacon," he told the ruffled older Rojok. "I shall enjoy the spectacle," he added with a blithe smile. "Permission to leave, sir?"

"Dismissed," the captain snarled. His dusky red face was even redder with temper.

Jasmine put a hand over her mouth to keep from laughing as they made it into the corridor. She was almost bursting with humor.

"Pompous ass," the doctor said haughtily. "His mate beats him nightly, I hear, and he takes it out on the crew. You be careful," he said, waving a finger at her. "If you allow yourself to be killed, I will be on the rough side of Chacon's temper along with the captain. I assure you, I will dig up your body and jump up and down on it if you subject me to such treatment."

She couldn't hold back the laughter. "Sir, you are…"

"Incorrigible? I am indeed. Three court-martials, two competency hearings and a legal review, and they still cannot find a way to get rid of me." He grinned. "It is a reputation of which I am most proud!"

She shook her head. "Sir, I promise never to tick you off. Ever."

"A wise decision!"

CHAPTER TWELVE

THE LANDING WAS TRICKY, but their pilot managed it. The ground was rumbling. Jebob archaeologists welcomed their rescuers with overwhelming delight.

"We become so engrossed in our discoveries that we pay attention to nothing else," the elder of the group told the Rojok landing party. His purple eyes found Jasmine and he hesitated. "A human? Among Rojoks?" he exclaimed. "How extraordinary!"

"I'm a Cularian specialist, sir," she said with a smile. "I'm here to treat the injured."

"Extraordinary," he repeated. "Yes, well, they are here, in the dome." He grimaced as he glanced at the volcano, which was belching fire. "At least we did not face a pyroclastic flow," he murmured, "or we should all have died before we could send the distress call."

"We must be quick, nevertheless," the ranking officer said. "Earthquakes are no less dangerous, and these present deep crevasses."

"Yes, indeed. We have at least two broken limbs, and three of our members were badly burned when the first eruption occurred in the darkness," he told Jasmine.

"Not to worry, sir," she said gently. "I can take care of them."

He left her to it. She worked her way through the burn victims, whose injuries were more urgent, to the sedated members of the party who had broken bones. Those were mended, as well. The banks of her wrist scanner were almost empty when she finished. She had extra ampoules in her waist kit, but she hadn't had to use those.

"They're all stabilized," she told the officer. "I could use an ambutube for the worst of the burn victims, but he'll make it back to the ship without danger. I've sedated him as well, to deal with the pain. Once aboard, the doctor and I can do skin grafts to treat the burns."

"Excellent work, Dupont," the officer said with a smile. "Load them up," he told the rest of the party.

It was a tight squeeze, but they managed to get everyone on the ship, which they boarded minutes before the volcano below erupted with new vigor and completely wiped out the camp where the archaeological group had worked.

"We even managed to save their samples and documentation," Jasmine told the doctor. She shook her head. "I suppose we all get lost in our work from time to time."

The doctor chuckled. "Remind me to tell you about

the time I was treating an Altairian for a burbvine inflammation when a meteorite hit a few hundred meters behind me and buried us both." He glanced at her. "I'll save that for another day."

She grinned. "I'll look forward to it, sir."

JASMINE GREW QUICKLY into her role as Cularian specialist aboard the flagship Kreskkom. The captain was promoted to admiral and went to command a lesser squadron out near the rim. Gossip was that he'd finally rubbed Chacon the wrong way with his advice on a new treaty. Jasmine wasn't sorry to see him go. Admiral Baklor had come aboard soon after Jasmine's assignment, and she liked him. He was a no-nonsense military leader with a flair for command. No sense of humor, sadly, but he was fair and his men respected him.

Jasmine and Rusmok were able to get at least two liberties together on Benaski Port, where they traded tales of bravery and drank a lot.

When she was on her own, aboard ship, Jasmine kept to herself. Neutering drugs were used not only by the humans, but by Rojoks as well to keep fraternization to a minimum in the close confines of ships in space. A relationship gone wrong could lead to turmoil and issues of morale that worsened. It was a wise precaution. Besides, she had no inclination to set up housekeeping with any Rojok, not even Rusmok, whom she adored.

Her stubborn mind would keep going back to Me-kashe and those wonderful days aboard the starliner on the way to Memcache. Life had been sweeter than honey, exciting, wonderful. She grieved for him. Over the years, the bitterness had receded very little. She understood that he was obligated to the emperor, that he had to fall in line with his employer's position. But it didn't negate the sting of his betrayal. She'd done nothing to justify such a harsh punishment from the Cehn-Tahr government.

She'd mentioned that to Rusmok during one of their liberties. He'd agreed that what she'd said seemed very mild to cost her father his position. The Cehn-Tahr were rigid in their behaviors, he added, but not that rigid. Perhaps the minor alien diplomat she'd insulted had been a personal friend or something.

He'd added another thing offhand that niggled at her brain. He'd said that while Rojoks used genetic engineering to modify their strengths, they hadn't been as drastically changed as the Cehn-Tahr had. It puzzled her, that comment. She'd started to question him when his shipmate had signaled that they were ready to lift, and the conversation had been lost in hurried farewells.

What had he meant, that the Cehn-Tahr were changed? They looked as human as Jasmine, except for the eyes. He might have meant some internal changes, organic ones. Probably that was it.

But in the long run, it made no difference. Jasmine held a bitter resentment for the Cehn-Tahr. She refused to go on any away missions that would require her to treat or even interact with Cehn-Tahr, risking court-martial for her stance. Luckily for her, the admiral hated Cehn-Tahr no less than she did, and he overlooked her attitude. Fortunately, there were relatively few missions that even brought the Rojok fleet into contact with any Cehn-Tahr unit.

IT WAS LATE AUTUMN, as Enmehkmehk designated the season of falling leaves, when the Kreskkom was sent as part of a joint task force to put down a vicious attempt at conquest of a member planet of the Tri-Galaxy Council. A combined force of renegade Rojoks and humans, with an Altairian general, had planned to grab rich mineral wealth on Terramer, known as the Peace Planet in honor of settlements made by many member governments.

The assault was on a mountainous island continent with rich stores of emerillium, a mineral used in power cores by many worlds, among them the Rojok. Jasmine was included in the away team, along with two Cularian interns, because there were Rojok field personnel involved in defense of the compound.

She made sure that the drug banks in her wrist scanner were filled and that its software was updated and calibrated before she strapped on her chasat and her extra medical supplies and darted into the lander.

"There will be Cehn-Tahr on this mission," Tollek teased. He'd been assigned to the flagship only a few standard weeks earlier. Jasmine was fond of him, so she took the teasing in stride.

"If they step in front of chasat fire, they can call for their own medics," she quipped.

"There will be an interplanetary incident, in such case." Tollek chuckled. "The Cehn-Tahr force is Holconcom."

One of the younger recruits glanced worriedly at Tollek. "Is that true?"

"Never mind. I will make sure that they do not eat you. At least, until I am positive that you are dead," he promised the younger alien, and chuckled.

But the other member of the unit wasn't smiling. He looked genuinely concerned. "I was a child on Merabak when the Holconcom came, at the end of the Great Galaxy War," he said uneasily. "I have never seen such carnage. None of the bodies were recognizable."

"You exaggerate." Another soldier laughed. "The Holconcom are nothing more than a commando unit."

"Have you ever seen them fight, Deksos?" was Tollek's somber reply.

"Well, no," the alien confessed. "But gossip always makes things seem worse than they are."

"The Holconcom is the most feared battle group in the three galaxies, and I assure you that their reputation is not exaggerated," said the young recruit.

"For a time, when the humans among them were first settled aboard the Morcai, the commander forbade his men to fight as they always had, for fear of terrorizing the humans. But this new commander puts no such restraint on them. He does this, we are told, with the emperor's blessing. It is how they maintain order among their extended colonies. And it serves to demoralize their enemies."

"Who commands them now?" Tollek asked curiously.

"We know nothing about him. They never allow the names or ranks of their crew to be publicized. We only know that he is Alamantimichar."

"The Royal Clan?" Tollek asked, surprised.

"All their military and political positions are Clan based. The emperor himself was the first leader of the Holconcom. He was succeeded by his son, and then his grandson. Their new commander certainly has Clan status, or he would not lead them." Deksos hesitated. "Gossip says that he was a recruit when the Holconcom was captured by our people and taken to Ahkmau. He has been a member of the group since its inception."

"He was at Ahkmau?" Tollek said heavily. "He must hate us."

Deksos laughed. "It is said that he hates everyone," he replied. "Except his men. And they would die for him."

"He must be a superb leader, to command such respect even from humans."

"This one would hate him on sight," Deksos teased Jasmine, who had been hanging on every word. "She has no use for Cehn-Tahr."

"Except as subjects for vivisection," she returned, tongue in cheek.

They both laughed.

"I hope they have their own medics," she said as the ship began its descent. "Because no matter what, I'm not working on any Cehn-Tahr!"

"If they dispute this, we will simply tell them that you are a funny-looking Rojok, Dupont," Tollek said with a grin.

She laughed, as she was meant to. She did hope that the rescue would be simple, without any complications like the sort that often arose as the result of a combined command.

THERE WERE MANY WOUNDED, but Jasmine's main concern was the equivalent of a four-star general in the Terravegan Strategic Space Command, an officer named Lanak. He had been a member of Chacon's personal staff before he was given command of the defense unit here on Terramer. There were few officers whom Chacon valued more.

He was in pretty bad shape. While she waited for an ambutube, Jasmine set about treating the worst of his injuries. His stomach and esophagus had sustained damage which would have proved fatal if he'd had to wait much longer for help. It was going to be touch and go, because she suspected internal bleeding. Her sensors were less than efficient in the electrical storm that was raging around them. *Odd storm, too*, she thought distractedly, because it came without rain. Just lightning and thunder, and lots of strikes near their hastily erected triage camp.

"How about my ambutube?" Jasmine asked a passing corpsman.

He was running. He didn't break stride. "Sorry, ma'am, but we've got complications! There are four insurgent ships incoming, and our transport just went up in smoke!"

"What?" she exclaimed.

She keyed her communicator ring. "Sir," she began. "I've got a badly wounded, high-level patient…!"

"We're going to do all we… Look out!"

There was an explosion, and then static. Jasmine looked up. In the distance, there was a blue-hued fireball where their ship had been sitting.

"Was that our ship?" Tollek exclaimed.

"Yes!" the corpsman panted, returning in a two-man skimmer. "The Jebob landing ship is gone, crew and all. There's one last transport, but it's for troops only, and we have orders to rendezvous with it in five standard minutes! Run!"

"But my patient…!" Jasmine shot at them.

"We'll send help," Tollek promised. "Let's go!" He waved the corpsman onward.

Jasmine stood by her patient, shell-shocked, as she watched her unit tear away toward the last of the landing ships, where an officer was motioning frantically for them to hurry.

She looked down at the unconscious, barely stabilized Rojok general. "Now what?" she asked herself dully.

THERE WAS ONE attempt to contact her. She recognized the admiral's adjutant, but he was quickly cut off and his garbled speech replaced by intermittent static with only one or two recognizable words.

As if to punctuate the dire situation, she looked up and saw an odd-shaped copper ship—no, a landing skimmer—putting down near her. It bore no markings, as SSC or Rojok vessels did. Not even its color gave it away. It wasn't blue, so it couldn't be a Jebob or Altairian lander.

While she watched, it put down and a slit opened in the hull. Three humans and two Cehn-Tahr in red uniforms poured out of it, weapons in hand.

There was a skirl of Cehn-Tahr. Jasmine's jaw tautened. The uniforms were impossible to mistake. That was a Holconcom lander.

Even as she thought it, the Cehn-Tahr in charge waved an arm in her direction, and a big, husky blond human came loping toward her with another human right behind him.

"Do you require assistance?" the human asked in a kind, gravelly voice.

"No, sir, I do not," she said, glaring past him at the two Cehn-Tahr who were apparently the ranking officers. "I'm waiting for a Rojok transport to pick us up."

The blond man's eyebrows arched. "A human?"

"Dr. Jasmine Dupont," she said coldly.

His expression went from pleasant to ice-cold in seconds. So did that of the second human. "Your patient?" he asked.

"General Lanak," she replied, surprised by the hostility. "He was a member of Chacon's personal staff before he was assigned to duty with the admiral's flagship."

There was a buzz of conversation coming from the older human's ear. He hesitated, listened and then replied in Cehn-Tahr.

"You speak that language?" Jasmine asked curtly.

"We all speak it," he replied. "We're citizens of the Cehn-Tahr Empire. I've just been informed that a squadron of attack ships is inbound. You need to come with us…"

"I will not," she said icily. "I'd rather die than set foot in a Cehn-Tahr vessel!"

"That would be your choice. But I advise you not to make it for your patient," he added, nodding toward the unconscious Rojok. "Chacon will hold you directly responsible if General Lanak dies. And I will be pleased to quote you verbatim if I'm called to testify at your court-martial."

She felt ruffled, but she wasn't confident enough to keep arguing. If no relief ship was coming, the general would die. His injuries required more treatment than she could give with a medi-scanner. Her pride was smarting. This human was very unpleasant and frankly hostile. Her remarks about the Cehn-Tahr seemed to have set him off.

"I don't want…!" she began.

There was a curt command in the human's ear, in a deep and harsh tone.

"Yes, sir," the human said at once. He turned back to Jasmine. His dark eyes were cold. "The commander says that if you don't want to come with us, we aren't to force you."

"How kind of him," she said sarcastically.

He didn't blink. "Back in my day, a doctor's primary obligation was the saving of life. Any life. Apparently they don't teach ethics in medical school these days. Sit on your pride, Doctor, and I use the title loosely. Your patient will pay for it with his life." He turned on his heel. "Jones, round up the others and see if you can find me some Vegan touch serum for that little one over there." He indicated a small child with a deep gash in his arm, stoic and uncomplaining nevertheless.

"Yes, sir, Doc. I'll carry the little boy aboard."

"Thanks, son."

"You're a doctor?" she asked.

"Strick Hahnson, human life sciences," he returned. "If you'll excuse me, I have patients to get aboard."

He turned without another word and stalked off, leaving Jasmine alone with her stiff attitude and a dying patient.

SCANT MINUTES LATER, the lander was loaded and ready to lift.

None of the crew came near Jasmine. She realized belatedly that they had every intention of taking off without her.

She panicked as she realized finally what she was doing. She was condemning an innocent man to death.

"Doctor..." She searched for his name in her memory. "Dr. Hahnson," she recalled, wondering why the name sounded so familiar. "We're coming with you. Do you have an ambutube...?"

Hahnson didn't answer her. He sent two corpsmen over to carry the patient into the lander and place him gently on a bunk. Jasmine climbed in behind them. She noticed that not only the doctor was glaring at her, the other humans and the two Cehn-Tahr were glaring, as well.

She averted her eyes. Well, she had no more consideration for them than they had for her. She sat down beside her patient and checked his vitals while the pilot sped up into the atmosphere with the small craft.

IN THE DISTANCE, she saw the Cehn-Tahr flagship Morcai. It was saucer shaped, copper hued, enormous. Inside, when they boarded, she was surprised at the width of the corridors. Several men could have stood side by side with arms outstretched without touching either side of the glowing walls.

The temperature was chilly, much cooler than a Rojok ship, and she noticed that personnel ran from post to post. All of them.

She would have asked questions, but nobody spoke to her. The corpsmen had an ambutube waiting at the airlock. Her patient was placed gently inside and the controls activated that would place him in stasis with the necessary drugs to help his body heal.

She started to thank Hahnson, but he'd already gone. The other human who'd come off the lander with him escorted Jasmine to sick bay. Rather, to the Cularian sick bay, where a medic named Tellas was caring for several Jebob and an Altairian who looked as if they'd suffered traumatic burns.

Tellas looked up, but he didn't speak. He went right back to his work.

"This is Tellas," the human told Jasmine. "I'm

Jones, Ensign Jones. I'm part of the commander's personal bodyguard. You already met Dr. Hahnson."

The human wasn't as hostile as the others had been. She managed a smile. "Yes."

"Your patient has been placed in the back of the infirmary, there," Tellas said, indicating the berth with a jerk of his head. "Your temporary quarters are adjacent to it. The cabin has a synthesizer to provide you with whatever meals you prefer. Linen for the bed is in the closet in your bathroom."

Tellas walked off before she could question him further.

"Everyone's so friendly," she said blithely.

Jones stared at her. "Begging your pardon, ma'am, but your name rings around here like a gong. Everybody knows who you are and what... Well, never mind. It would probably be best if you stay in your quarters when you aren't with your patient. Just to keep things calm."

"I didn't have any intention of wandering the corridors looking for a fight, Ensign," she replied coolly. She frowned. "I know I've heard Dr. Hahnson's name before, somewhere."

"He was at Ahkmau with us," Jones said quietly. "The Rojoks knew we'd hidden the commander and they wanted him, badly. We wouldn't give him up. Dr. Hahnson was tortured in front of the whole camp to try and make us tell. He never gave an inch. They cut off his hands..." He swallowed, hard. The memory was difficult. "He died to keep the commander safe."

"But he's here…"

"The commander cloned him for Dr. Ruszel and Captain Stern," Jones continued. "They were grieving. Also, it kept them from mutiny when the commander hijacked them from Admiral Lawson, along with the rest of the crew from the SSC ship Bellatrix. Captain Stern commanded it, before it was destroyed by the Rojoks. Dr. Ruszel and Dr. Hahnson served with Stern for ten years before we all ended up over here."

That was where she'd heard the name. Hahnson was an inspiration to doctors everywhere. He was almost a legend.

"Even the rank-and-file Rojoks know about Ahkmau," she said.

"They should," Jones mused. "It was Chacon who helped the Holconcom escape. He didn't do it on purpose, but it sort of worked out that way. We owe him a lot."

"So do I," she said without elaborating. Her blue eyes narrowed. "Can I ask why it's being suggested that I stay in my quarters?"

"We have statues of Cashto everywhere."

She frowned. "Of whom?"

"Cashto. He's the major Cehn-Tahr deity. They revere him."

"What does that have to do with my being con-fined?"

"He is, he was, a galot, ma'am. The giant cats of Eridanus Three?" he added when she looked blank.

"Cat statues," she remarked offhandedly.

He went a little rigid. "Holy relics, ma'am," he corrected.

She just stared at him for a minute before her attention went back to her patient. "Tellas—he's your Cularian expert?"

"Yes, ma'am. He's been here since before Dr. Mallory and the former commander, Rhemun, were bonded. He was her second in command."

She was tempted to ask who the commander was now, but she really didn't care, and it didn't matter.

"Thanks, Jones," she said.

"Yes, ma'am."

He went out and left her to her patient.

TELLAS WAS BACK and forth, caring for two Jebob patients, one of them very young, who'd been wounded in the firefight. He was efficient, very thorough. He had a kind bedside manner.

Jasmine had a small book reader in her pocket, but it didn't seem to work. She had to ask Tellas how to connect it to the ship's systems.

"That isn't allowed. Sorry. Regulations," he said shortly.

"You mean I can't use my personal reader to look at my notes while I'm aboard?" she asked, aghast.

"Regulations," he repeated. He turned and left the cubicle.

She muttered under her breath as she took the vitals of her patient and renewed the treatment that was healing his internal injuries. At least she'd been able to find and close the small arterial flow that had been hampering his recovery.

"Can you at least tell me when a Rojok ship is due to pick us up?" she asked Tellas an hour later when he came back through.

"That doesn't fall under my jurisdiction, Doctor," he replied. "You might ask Jones. He's command staff."

And he was gone again.

Jasmine walked into the corridor to see if she could catch a glimpse of Jones. She didn't recognize any of the other crew. There seemed to be as many humans as Cehn-Tahr. One of the humans had jet-black curly hair and black eyes. He paused by the medical bay.

"You're the Rojok Cularian expert," he said.

"Yes," she said.

"The commander would like a word with you."

Finally, she thought, she'd be able to get some answers. "Lead on," she said.

He took off at a fast pace. She was barely able to keep up. She noticed as they went along that she was attracting a lot of attention, and none of it seemed very pleasant.

"I don't have a contagious disease," she muttered, glaring back at a passing crewman.

"No, ma'am, but you do have a distinctly unpleasant reputation," he said shortly. "We all know who you are."

"Then you also know that my father was fired from his job and sent home to Terravega to die," she said bitterly. "The emperor was responsible for his death."

The crewman, an officer, she realized belatedly, stopped at the door to a cubicle and turned to her. "You insulted one of our own," he said coldly. "Not only insulted. Humiliated. The Cehn-Tahr are our family."

"I complained about all the cat statues," she said shortly. "That's all I did! My father was punished for it, instead of me. He was sent home in disgrace."

"The penalty was death," he returned, stunning her. "The emperor made a very rare exception for you and your father, allowing you to leave Memcache without the ultimate penalty. That caused him some problems in the Dectat. Such insults are not tolerated."

She didn't understand. But while she was trying to form a question, her companion touched a panel.

"The Rojok physician is here, sir."

"Send her, Stern," came the curt reply.

The officer stood back and nodded toward the door. Then he left. She realized belatedly that her companion had been Captain Holt Stern.

SHE TOUCHED THE panel and the door slid open. She walked through, into what would have been called an office on a Rojok ship. It contained a desk and a huge viewscreen, which the officer was facing. Behind him, on the desk, was a mass of equipment that read star charts and connected him to communications panels all over the vessel.

He was tall, even for a Cehn-Tahr. He had long, curly hair down to his waist in back. She'd heard that some of the Cehn-Tahr followed Rojok tradition for command rank—denoting high rank by length of hair. This officer's hair was almost as long as Chacon's. He was powerfully built. His uniform, bloodred, stretched tight over his muscular frame.

"I'm Dr. Jasmine Dupont," she said shortly. "You wanted to see me?"

He turned. His eyes were dark brown with anger. His face, despite its hard lines and rigid composure, was all too familiar.

"Mekashe!" she exclaimed, shocked.

His chin lifted. "Commander Mekashe," he corrected icily. "Here, tradition rules."

She drew herself to attention. "Sir," she said, drawling the word.

"Your Rojok unit met heavy resistance as it lifted.

Only one ship made it through the insurgent's block-ade, and it took severe damage. It will require one solar week for another to be dispatched to retrieve you and your patient."

"A week," she said irritably.

"I assure you that your desire to leave this vessel is no less than mine to have you off it," he snapped back.

She was surprised by his cold demeanor. This wasn't the man she remembered from the starliner. He was as rigid as Chacon, a warrior. The last time she'd seen him, he was captain of the Imperial Guard. Obviously, he'd moved up the chain of command.

"One of my men will inform you as soon as the rendezvous is arranged. That is all."

She shifted restlessly. "I would like to know…"

"Dismissed, madam!"

She saluted automatically. "Yes, sir."

She turned and left, shaking inside. She was shocked to find her former companion heading the most ruthless commando unit in explored space. She was more shocked to realize that he was as hostile as the rest of his crew. Several days in this environ-ment, and she might wish she'd smuggled some of Rusmok's synthale on board with her.

CHAPTER THIRTEEN

JASMINE HADN'T EXPECTED to find her companions as
hostile as she'd been to them. She thought her anger
was justified. She blamed the Cehn-Tahr for her father's death, for her sad state afterward. But apparently, they blamed her for something more than just
distaste for their religious objects. She had no idea
what they thought she'd done. Had someone been
spreading malicious gossip about her?

The obvious person to blame would have been
Mekashe, but he'd hardly been a gossiping sort of
person when she knew him. The Rojoks had acquaintances among the Cehn-Tahr, so perhaps they'd re-
layed her contempt for them at some point, and that
had caused them to have hard feelings toward her.

On the other hand, she'd never felt more like an
invading disease. She did keep to her quarters, because it was so uncomfortable to even walk out into
the corridor. There were glares and murmured con-
versations that stopped when she was within earshot.

Dr. Hahnson was particularly cool to her. She didn't
see him often, but he did lab work for Tellas when

the Morcai's Cularian expert was overwhelmed. He brought back some lab results. He and Tellas got along well. They were friendly. But when Hahnson glanced at Jasmine, the smile faded at once.

"Sir, have you heard when our transport is going to get here?" she asked Hahnson.

"No, I have not. The commander will notify you when it arrives."

"I haven't killed anyone," she said haughtily.

He turned and looked at her. "Your contempt for us is quite well-known," he said. "Especially your opinion of the Cehn-Tahr. What a shame that you weren't with us at Ahkmau, when human and Cehn-Tahr marched off together to the ovens to spare our commander's life. They are a noble, kind people. They're our family."

"I made an unwise comment about cat statues and I insulted a minor alien race," she said, exasperated. "What does that have to do with anything that happened to my father?"

He gaped at her. "You think your father's position was terminated, that the Terravegan government was humiliated, because of that? You think the emperor would be so petty?"

She was losing ground. She didn't know how to respond, what to say. She'd spent the past five years holding a grudge over her father's treatment, supposing it to result from a minor remark she'd made. Now she wasn't so sure.

"You really are clueless, Doctor," he said. He turned and left the cubicle.

SHE WAS CHANGING a smartbandage on her patient when she heard voices in the next cubicle.

She finished, cleaned her hands and walked to the door. Mekashe was bending over a small boy who'd suffered second-degree burns. On a Jebob child, they were harder to treat, because of the megaradiation and its effect on his complicated genetic structure.

Mekashe's voice was soft, deep, quiet. There was a smile in it as he spoke to the little boy, obviously in the child's own tongue.

The little boy laughed, his purple eyes radiant. He reached up a hand and touched Mekashe's face and said something.

Mekashe laughed and replied.

"Now go to sleep," Tellas told the child. He put a laserdot into the boy's neck with a smile and watched him drop off.

"Sorry, sir, you're overstaying your welcome," Tellas chided.

Mekashe laughed softly. "As I often do. Uskus is a sweet child. I grieve for him. To lose both parents at such an age is a sorrow."

"You lost yours when you were not so much older than Uskus," Tellas said quietly.

"Yes, but I had Clan. He has none. I have Jennings searching for any distant relative who might be will-

ing to take him. There are rumors of an uncle…"
He turned abruptly and saw Jasmine standing there.
"Yes, Doctor?" he asked coldly.

"I was…" She swallowed. "I wondered if you'd
heard anything more about our transport. Sir."

"If I had, you would have been informed, madam,"
he returned. He turned back to Tellas. "Keep me informed. If he needs any special medicines, I can obtain them through central supply."

"I will. Thank you."

Mekashe left without a backward glance. Jasmine
glanced at the sleeping child and turned away. She'd
wanted children so desperately. It seemed like a lifetime ago, now. She went back to her patient.

THREE DAYS LATER, the commander sent for her again.

"Your transport is four solar days' distance," he
told her. "Barring problems, you will be reunited
with your command shortly."

"I thank you for your hospitality, sir," she said
icily. "I feel so welcome here."

"I think Hahnson would have offered you quarters in the brig, had I permitted it," he shot back.
"His bonded mate was Cehn-Tahr. He has as much
reason to resent you as I do."

"What are you talking about?" she asked, exasperated. "For heaven's sake, I was insulting about the
cat statues, yes, I admit it. I made a facetious remark
about a four-legged race…!"

"And you think that prompted your father's problems?" he asked, almost a purr in his tone.

"Your emperor killed my father!" she snapped. "He killed him, as surely as if he'd…!"

She broke off and jumped back as Mekashe, his temper mastering him, suddenly shifted into his true form.

Jasmine gaped at him, horrified. The creature she'd seen in the gym of the starliner, it hadn't been a creature at all. It had been a Cehn-Tahr! And she'd never known! Her father must have known, but he didn't tell her!

Mekashe bared his fangs. He moved toward her stealthily, huge and menacing, his black mane flowing down his back. "We were creatures, you said. Monsters. We should have been caged, kept away from civilized beings. We should have been put down, like the animals we were!"

She backed up another step. Mekashe had loved her. She'd called his race monsters. She realized all at once just what she'd done to provoke the emperor. Such an insult was more than any head of government could have tolerated.

"Don't you want to scream?" he purred icily.

She couldn't even manage words. The horror she felt was reflected in her face, but it wasn't the horror he thought he understood. It wasn't fear of him that caused it. It was anguish over what she'd done. She'd killed her father. She'd spent years blaming the emperor, blaming the Cehn-Tahr, insulting them at every turn. And it had been her fault, not theirs at all.

"My father," she choked out. "He knew!"

He managed to control his anger and shifted back into the humanoid form she'd first seen when they met. "Yes," he said coldly. "He knew. But he was bound by secrecy not to reveal it to you. We do not share such things with outworlders."

He turned away from her. "The offense was worse because you were overheard by others in the gym, one of them a Rojok. Such an insult could not be ignored."

She stared at him with anguish in her face. Only now did she begin to see what an impossibly spoiled brat she'd been, so selfish and thoughtless that she had no feeling at all for other people. And she'd thought her offense was minor. That she'd done nothing wrong.

She closed her eyes and shivered. She'd destroyed lives.

An intercom sounded. "Yes?" Mekashe asked harshly.

There was a spate of Cehn-Tahr, which he answered. He glanced at Jasmine.

"You have a patient to attend, madam," he said shortly. "I will contact your transport personally and see if I can expedite your recovery. Dismissed."

She swallowed, hard. "Yes, sir."

She was too sick even to salute him. She turned

and walked back to her cubicle like a sleepwalker. When she got inside, she threw herself onto her bunk and wept as if her heart would break.

HAHNSON BRAVED MEKASHE'S temper two days later.

"Something to report?" Mekashe asked.

Hahnson grimaced. "It's Dr. Dupont," he said reluctantly. "She hasn't been out of her cubicle in two days. She checks on her patient and goes right back inside. She hasn't eaten or slept or interacted with any of us."

Mekashe drew in a breath. "I lost my temper and shifted in front of her," he said harshly. "I suppose she is still getting over the shock of being aboard a ship full of monsters."

His tone was bitter. Hahnson sighed. "I don't think it's that. The one time I did get a glimpse of her... Well, I think she's been crying. A lot."

That was news. Mekashe was surprised. The human doctor had been quite vocal about putting blame on everyone except herself for her father's banishment. It must have come as a surprise to learn what her true offense had been.

It had caused him no end of anguish to see her reaction to his comrade's Cehn-Tahr form. He'd had such hopes. But then, they would have come to nothing, in any case. Cehn-Tahr with modified genetics, as his were, could never mate with humans. It was hopeless, as his feelings for her had been hopeless.

Whatever those feelings were even now, he didn't dare entertain them.

Still, her anguish disturbed him enough to have Hahnson send her to his office.

THE SOFT BUZZ at her cabin door brought her temporarily out of her misery. She dabbed at her red eyes and opened it, keeping her eyes down. "Yes?" she asked in a subdued tone.

"The commander would like to see you," Hahnson said. He wasn't antagonistic, for the first time since she'd boarded the Morcai.

"Very well," she said in a tone without inflection.

She jogged down the corridor in a daze, unaware of the faintly concerned looks she was getting from the humans. Some of them felt guilty for their treatment of her. Gossip ran wild aboard a ship in space, there being little else except routine to occupy the crew. Jasmine's self-imposed isolation had disturbed them. Apparently, she wasn't as bad as they'd first thought. Despite her preference for Rojoks.

She touched a panel on the commander's door and was allowed inside.

"You sent for me, sir?" she asked formally and without meeting his eyes. If she had, she'd have seen deep blue concern in them, not the brown anger of recent days.

"You have isolated yourself."

She didn't reply.

He moved around the desk. He saw her tense and leaned back against his desk, his eyes narrow on what he could see of her lowered face.

"Among my people, there is a word that reflects our belief in the order of things in the universe," he said. "*Karamesh*. In your tongue, it translates as 'fate.' We believe that our lives are written before our birth. If this is the case, and there is hardly any room in the military for philosophy, then your father's end was preordained. Nothing you did would have changed what happened to him. Although I must tell you that I deeply regret the manner of his passing. He was a good man."

"He was, and a better father than I deserved." She laughed hollowly, her face still lowered. "For five years, I blamed you, blamed the emperor, blamed the Cehn-Tahr people. And all along, I was responsible for everything that happened to my father. I don't know…how to live with it," she said gruffly, fighting more tears.

He folded his arms across his broad chest. "Since I was an adolescent, the military has been my life," he began quietly. "Over two hundred years before you were born, I was ordering good soldiers to their deaths in pursuit of military objectives. That responsibility sits heavily on my conscience. But I live with it, because I must. You will have to learn to live with your burden."

She looked up then, shocked. "Two…hundred

years…" she faltered, because he still looked no older than a human in his early thirties.

"Because you have a medic's credentials, I can tell you this," he continued. "Many Clans accepted advanced genetic modification in the early days of the empire. The emperor's clan, Alamantimichar, was the recipient of the most advanced. The genetic tampering resulted in the mutated form you saw in the gym aboard the starliner. We are no longer completely humanoid. It is our shame that we became 'monsters,'" he added, watching her eyelids flinch as she registered her own harsh words, "because of the modifications. We share traits with the great galot race of Eridanus Three. We revere Cashto, the first of the great cats that we drew our genetics from—the statues you saw at my villa in the holoroom were of him. They are religious objects, although we exact no punishment for other races' opinions of them."

She was still trying to process his age. Over two hundred years.

"Our emperor is over four hundred years old," he said, reading the thought in her mind. "Experts think he may share the life span of the great cats, which runs to many centuries."

"Will you live so long?" she asked huskily.

He shrugged. "I share his bloodline, so it is possible."

His bloodline. Alamantimichar. The Royal Clan. She closed her eyes and shivered. "They said that two members of that Clan were aboard the starliner and I never realized that one of them was you." She looked up, anguished. "The things I said…!"

He turned away and went behind the desk, as if to distance himself from her pain. "I had hopes, at the time, that were ungrounded in reality," he said after a minute. "Genetically modified Cehn-Tahr cannot mate with humans. It would be instantly fatal."

She recalled hearing that gossip from the Rojoks with whom she served.

"Yes," he said, reading the thought. "The Rojoks have been allies and enemies for millennia. They know more about us than most other races."

It suddenly dawned on her that he'd read her mind. She was stunned.

"I read what lies on the surface only," he corrected. "We are not permitted to look deeply into the thoughts of others. We consider it bad manners."

She had known so little about him, for all her imaginings. They'd spoken of a life together, of children. Impossible dreams.

"But your emperor's son is bonded to a human," she said.

"That is true. But a classified experiment permitted that bonding, and the birth of two children. The sample was consumed in the experiment. It has never been replicated."

"The former commander of the Holconcom…"

"Yes. Rhemun. My best friend. He bonded with

the former Cularian specialist aboard the Morcai,
Dr. Edris Mallory. But Rhemun's father went to war
with the empire to prevent genetic modification of
his child. Rhemun has only classified tech as the
basis of his great strength. Mine is genetic."

She still couldn't grasp it. "But you were able to
touch me."

"Hahnson used nanobytes and dravelzium to
permit that," he said heavily. "It was permissible
only because there was no giving or acceptance of a
gift, the precursor to courtship." His face hardened.
"Once the mating cycle begins, a Cehn-Tahr will kill
any male who comes near the object of his pursuit.
There is a saying that nothing in the three galaxies is
as dangerous as a Cehn-Tahr male who is hunting."

She drew in a long breath. "I see."

"The differences between us would have made
anything other than friendship impossible," he said
with faint bitterness. "So it was just as well that you
hated us. Perhaps it made your path a little easier,
after the loss of your father."

She bit her lower lip. She couldn't quite contain
the grief. *I mourned you*, she thought miserably.

"As I mourned you," he replied roughly.

She looked up into the solemn blue of his eyes
and fought tears.

He averted his gaze to the computer bank on his
desk. "Your patient is mending well. By the time
your transport arrives, he will be conscious."

"Yes."

"I wish you well, Dr. Dupont," he said after a minute.

"I wish you...the same."

"Dismissed."

"Yes, sir." She saluted him and turned away. It hurt too much to look at him.

TWO SOLAR DAYS LATER, she had her patient awake and aware as he was transported over to the waiting Rojok vessel.

Jasmine hated the very thought of leaving the Morcai. Of course, there was no hope of a future with Mekashe. She knew that. But it didn't stop her from aching just for a sight of him, just to hear his deep voice in sick bay as he spoke to the orphaned alien child there. For the rest of her life, she would never see him again. It tormented her.

She realized that the physical differences would make bonding with him impossible. There could never be a child. Even if she were allowed to serve with him, it would be daily anguish, because of unfulfilled hopes, dead dreams. That didn't stop her from wishing that she didn't have to leave.

She had to get herself together. This would serve no purpose. She had a patient whose welfare she was responsible for. She had duties of her own, aboard the Rojok flagship. She had to leave. There was no other way.

She heard, or thought she heard, a strange voice in her head, assuring her that everything would be all right. Now she was hearing things. She opened her kit and looked at the small ball that contained her virtual Nagaashe, the physical memory of a happy time in her life. Not that the little creature could have spoken to her. She kept it close, treasured it, never took it out of her kit because she was so afraid of losing it. She could get another, but it wouldn't have the memories attached to this one. It was precious because she was with Mekashe when she'd bought it. Mekashe, who would pass out of her life now like a bright shadow, barely seen, barely touched. She fought tears once again. All she did lately was cry. She had to get herself together. This was no way to behave. She was an officer and a physician. She had to consider her duty. That was all she had left.

HAHNSON TAPPED AT her cubicle.

She opened it, her tragic face causing him to grimace.

"The Rojok transport just docked with us," he said, and not unkindly. "Tellas will float your patient down to the airlock for you, while you get your things together."

"Thanks," she replied, starting to turn away.

"I know how it feels," he blurted out.

She turned back, her eyebrows lifted in a question.

"I bonded with an outcast female Cehn-Tahr, at

the end of the Great Galaxy War," he said quietly. "She was my...whole life. Our one attempt at mating almost cost me my life. While I was recovering, she took her life. The knowledge that we couldn't have any sort of a relationship was too much for her." His teeth ground together. "I never got over her."

She studied his broad, hard face. "You're a clone," she began.

"Yes." He managed a smile. "But the cloning technique the Cehn-Tahr use employs advanced tech that can even re-create memories. I am everything that my original was. In a detailed scan, physical and psychological, you couldn't find a speck of difference between the man I was and the clone I am."

"The Rojoks can do the same," she said. "I've seen it used, in rare cases where important people were reconstructed."

"They're still debating whether the soul goes with the transference. For my part, I'd guess that it does. I have the same feelings for Holt Stern and Madeline Ruszel that my original had. We were a team for ten years before we ended up in the Holconcom. We're still close, although Maddie lives the life of a royal now."

She drew in a long breath. "I'm sorry for your pain."

"I'm sorry for yours," he replied. "None of us was kind to you, when you came aboard. I apologize for that."

"Don't," she replied. She smiled. "I was a total idiot. I spent years blaming everybody but myself for what happened. It's been hard, realizing that the real culprit was me." She sighed. "I would have walked through fire for Mekashe," she added huskily. "I had no idea, until one of the Rojoks told me, that humans and genetically enhanced Cehn-Tahr are incompatible. I had such dreams..." She stopped, laughing hollowly.

"So did I," he confessed. "I guess we take what we can get in life, and live on memories."

"Mine are sweet," she confessed.

He smiled. "So are mine. Farewell, Doctor. Maybe we'll meet again one day."

"Unlikely. But I'm glad we part in a happier way than we began."

"Me, too."

JASMINE'S PATIENT WAS graved through the airlock into the Rojok ship. Jasmine hesitated a little, hoping for one last glance at Mekashe. But he was nowhere in sight as she jogged down the wide corridor with her kit, on her way to follow her patient aboard the Rojok vessel.

She was almost to the airlock when the ship was suddenly jarred as if giant fists had slammed into it. The artificial gravity warped and she hit the overhead with a thud. Simultaneously she heard Mekashe's deep voice over the intership comm giving orders.

On the viewscreen along the corridor, she watched as the Rojok ship suddenly sped away. The Morcai dashed in a different direction so quickly that the stars became a white blur with the speed.

Artificial gravity reasserted itself and Jasmine hit the deck with a thump.

"What happened?" she asked a passing crewman.

"Unknown," he said, still rushing. "They're running diagnostics. We were in a disputed area, near the Terramer system to rendezvous with the Rojok ship. It might have been an attack."

He ran ahead. She went back to sick bay. Hahnson was on the comms, asking questions and apparently getting no answers.

"Nobody knows what's going on," he told her. "Sorry about your ride, but the Rojok ship cleared off and so did we. Until we know what happened, it would have been dangerous to stick around. They'll arrange another rendezvous."

"Of course." She leaned against the bulkhead to get her breath. "Gravity is a painful thing," she murmured with a hand to her bruised back.

He chuckled. "You should serve aboard one of the old Terravegan fleet ships, the ones we had before they gave us the Bellatrix that Stern commanded. Gravity was iffy at best, especially during any confrontations with the enemy."

"I guess I've missed some adventures."

"Believe me, you have no idea," he said with a grin.

Tellas came into the cubicle. "We have some minor injuries, nothing major. They're saying it was a gravity wave," he added in a disbelieving tone. "But there was nothing on the scanners."

"Sometimes they don't show up," Hahnson said. "And, forgive me," he said to Jasmine, "but our friends the Rojoks have been known to use jamming tech when we're at close quarters. Both governments are still very closemouthed about their equipment. Despite the better relations, we don't share well."

"All too true," Tellas said. He glanced at Jasmine. "Doctor, if you have the time, my assistant is down with Altairian flu and I'm a bit short staffed."

"No problem," she said easily. "I might as well work for my supper."

Tellas frowned. "Excuse me?"

"Colloquial terminology," she said. "I might as well be useful."

"Ah. I see. Then if you'll follow me?"

She jogged along behind him to the Cularian sector.

MEKASHE ANNOUNCED, IN STANDARD, that they were moving to Memcache for spacedock repairs. Apparently, a major piece of equipment had been damaged.

Jasmine was sad about that. Her last memory of

the home planet of the Cehn-Tahr was an unhappy one. But then, she'd hardly be expected to go down to the surface. Surely, the Rojok fleet would send a ship for her soon.

IT DIDN'T WORK out quite that way. They ported at Memcache and the ship had an unexpected visit from a very unexpected person. The emperor himself came aboard with Rhemun at the head of his Imperial bodyguard.

The corridor was lined with humans and Cehn-Tahr, all standing at rigid attention. Even though Jasmine wasn't attached to the ship, or its command structure, she stood at attention, as well. Her one memory of the Cehn-Tahr emperor had been from a distance. But as he approached, she saw that he was very tall, as tall as Mekashe, with a thick head of white hair and a chest full of medals. He wore a Cehn-Tahr military uniform, but it was obvious that he was far and away more than a soldier.

"Sir," Mekashe said formally, bowing. "We are honored by your presence."

The others bowed, as well.

The emperor nodded. "I have not been aboard the Morcai in some time. Not since we rushed to Ruszel's rescue on Akaashe," he said with a smile in his voice. "We miss you in the kehmatemer," he added to Mekashe.

"Not much," Rhemun murmured drily.

The emperor chuckled. "You only say that because your mate is happy to have you on Memcache rather than in constant danger in the Holconcom."

"That is true," Rhemun mused, still standing at rigid attention.

The emperor turned unexpectedly and looked straight at Jasmine, who cringed inwardly as she recalled her terrible behavior and its tragic consequences in the past.

But he didn't seem angry. He approached her, his head cocked as he studied her curiously. "Dr. Dupont," he said gently. "My mate is a seer. She has the gift of prophecy. She has requested your presence on Memcache, if you are willing."

"The empress? Sir, I…" She swallowed, still standing at attention. "It would be an honor, sir."

"Mekashe can bring you down," he said, turning his attention to the Morcai's commander, who looked vaguely surprised.

"Yes, sir," Mekashe said, as it was obviously an order.

"Good. We will expect you this evening, as we reckon time here."

"My transport," she began.

The emperor waved a hand. "Chacon can send another to Memcache. It is no great issue. Your temporary replacement is caring for your patient aboard the Rojok flagship. He reports that his recovery is well under way."

"Thank you, sir."

She was stunned. It seemed that the emperor had already spoken to both Chacon and the commander of the Rojok flagship, in advance of this meeting. But she didn't say a word. She still stood at rigid attention, like the rest of the crew.

"Stern, you and Hahnson come with him," the emperor added, speaking to the officer with the wavy black hair whom Jasmine had only seen once or twice: Captain Stern.

"Yes, sir," Stern said. His black eyes twinkled. "Time to think up a few more good lies about our battle prowess to impress you with."

Hahnson laughed. So did the emperor, whose eyes were a howling green. He turned back to Jasmine.

"We will expect you, then," he told her. He turned away, returning the salutes as Mekashe walked him and the kehmatemer to the vator tube.

"Do we wear uniforms, or what?" Jasmine asked Hahnson, concerned.

"Yes. But it's informal," he replied.

"The emperor isn't what you think, Doctor," Stern seconded. "He's very down-to-earth. He started out as a farm worker. He was a soldier for decades, before he formed the Holconcom and led it on missions of conquest. He hasn't lost that touch. We revere him, of course. But he's pretty good at being just one of the guys." He chuckled.

"Thanks," she said. She grimaced. "I've been a real pain. Sorry about that."

"We've all had experiences that hardened us," Stern replied quietly. "That's life. We learn from them."

"Enough said," Hahnson agreed. "I'd better get to my sector and finish up the waiting room."

"I'm helping Tellas," Jasmine said. "I guess I'd better go, too."

"See you later," Stern told them both and jogged away.

"The emperor isn't anything like I thought he was," Jasmine told Hahnson as they ran down the corridor to the medical sector.

"He's surprisingly human," Hahnson replied with a grin. "I guess it comes from being around Maddie Ruszel so much. You'll meet her, and Dtimun, as well. They have two sons."

"Their children must be unique," she said.

"They are. Rhemun and Dr. Mallory have two children as well, except that one of theirs is female. Princess Lyceria was the first girl child born into the Royal Clan in centuries. Rhemun's was only the second. Girls are rare."

"I've met the princess. She fascinates me."

"She would have been there, too. But she's nearly ready to deliver, and Chacon won't risk moving her away from Enmehkmehk." He chuckled. "They say he's pacing around like a madman, worried to death, just as he was before the birth of their son." He shook his head. "How the mighty fall."

She smiled. "It sounds kind of nice. He seems to love her very much."

"And that's a story you'll hear, too," he said. "He risked his life and his career to save her life when she was taken to Ahkmau. In fact, in a way, the Morcai Battalion owes its existence to him."

"I'd love to hear that story."

"You'll hear that one, and more, tonight."

"I'm looking forward to it." She sighed. "I'm just glad that the emperor doesn't hold grudges."

"He's tolerant, when he wants to be. Still fearsome, at times, when dealing with insurgents."

"That's what emperors are supposed to be, right?"

He nodded. "I think so."

They arrived at the medical sector. Jasmine smiled at Hahnson and went to the Cularian cubicles to help Tellas with the backlog. She felt happier than she had in years.

The only thing that saddened her was knowing that she and Mekashe could never have a life together. Probably he'd adjusted to the reality, because he'd known for years. But she'd only just learned many things, including the impossibility of any relationship with him. Secretly, all those years, she'd never stopped loving him. She'd hated him for what she thought was his betrayal, but the love persisted.

Now she had a barren future ahead. But at least she had a purposeful job, one that defined her existence. It was cold comfort. But she did have that.

CHAPTER FOURTEEN

JASMINE HAD NEVER seen so much green, even during her first visit to Memcache. The skimmer flew over the capital city and out toward a line of distant mountains. The emperor had sent a skiff to bear Mekashe, Stern, Hahnson and Jasmine to the Fortress, the place the Imperial family called home.

The forests were just like those she'd seen in the holoroom with Mekashe, all those years ago. They looked like massive bamboo forests, with beautiful villas tucked into them, most made of some bright, hard stone that she'd also seen in the holoroom.

"It looks like marble," she commented, only then remembering that she'd said that in the holoroom with Mekashe, long ago.

"It's similar," Hahnson replied. "It's an igneous stone, but it conducts electricity. It's used in construction because it retains heat and cold when they're introduced to it."

"The Rojoks mine a stone which they use in construction, some amber igneous sort of rock. It radiates heat or cold as needed," she said.

"I forgot that you'd lived on Enmehkmehk," Stern said, chuckling. "What was it like, being the only human on the planet?"

"Fascinating," she replied. "I took a lot of heat at first, because I was such a wimp. But I toughened up pretty quickly when one of my fellow recruits, Rusmok, started chiding me." She smiled. "He's been my best friend ever since."

"Aha," Stern said. "A romantic interest?" he teased.

"No," she said, aware of Mekashe's narrow glance. "He has his heart set on a female who hates the military." She sighed. "But he lives on hope. We meet on Benaski Port on liberty, when we can, to catch up on news. He's second in command on one of the big battle cruisers now. He may make captain in a year or so. I'm very proud of him."

"Maddie Ruszel is like that about Chacon." Stern chuckled. "He saved her life a couple of times, and she saved his. Dtimun was a little jealous, but he got over it after Komak was born."

"He sort of got over it," Hahnson mused. "Chacon is a powerful rival. Or he would be, if he wasn't head over heels in love with Lyceria."

"A truly beautiful woman," Stern said, sighing.

"And kind," Hahnson added. "Which is more important."

"Is that the Fortress?" Jasmine asked suddenly, as a huge gray stone structure began to fill the viewscreen. She leaned forward to look out. "It's magnificent! And look at the gardens!"

There were flowers everywhere. In the late afternoon, with the planet's two moons just becoming visible and the sun casting red-and-gold clouds as it began to go low in the sky, it was like a fairy setting.

"It's so beautiful," she said breathlessly.

Mekashe was looking at her with eyes full of pain. He averted them before she could see. So long ago, he'd dreamed of bringing her here, having her as part of his family, his Clan. And it was impossible. Impossible.

"The Imperial family spends some time in the capital. There's a building that serves as governmental, religious and residential home. But this province is where they prefer to live," Hahnson said. "Dtimun and Maddie live here at the Fortress. The emperor and empress have a huge residence of their own over the mountains. Rhemun has a villa not too far away, where he and Edris live with their children."

The skimmer put down on the large stone-paved area adjacent to the Fortress. A woman with long red-gold hair was standing there with two children. She was accompanied by a tall Cehn-Tahr woman with long silver hair down to her waist.

"We're truly honored," Hahnson remarked. "That's the empress herself, standing with Maddie and Komak and Clint!"

"Gosh." Jasmine was totally surprised. She was

certain that they were there to see the others, not herself. Still, it really was an honor.

SHE WAS VERY nervous as she exited the ship and approached the waiting group with her comrades. She was still wearing the uniform of the Rojok Republic, a black one with mesag marks on the sleeves denoting her rank. Her blond hair, which had been long and elegant, was now collar length, a visible symbol of her status as an officer. She was beautiful, despite her military trappings, something that was noted by both women in the greeting party.

"You are Jasmine, yes?" the empress asked gently. "I am Caneese."

"Lady Caneese," Jasmine said, bowing. "It's an honor, Your Highness."

"Just Caneese." The alien woman laughed softly. "Here is home, or at least our second home," she amended with a smile toward the other woman, who laughed. "Protocols are put aside when we are with family. Hahnson, Stern, Mekashe. I greet you."

They bowed. Mekashe approached and she touched his cheek and laid her forehead against his. Jasmine didn't know, but this was a greeting only used with family.

"You look well," Caneese told him.

He smiled. "So do you, Your Highness."

"The children keep me young," she said. "And this is Madeline Ruszel. Lady Maltiche, when she is formally addressed, away from here." She indicated the woman with long red-gold hair that showed only a few threads of silver.

Madeline laughed. "But since we're not away from here, I'm just Maddie," she said with a mischievous glance at the empress, and she moved forward to hug Jasmine warmly. "Welcome to the Fortress, Jasmine."

"Thank you," Jasmine said, smiling. "These are your sons?" she asked, brightening.

"Yes. That's Komak," she said, nodding to the eldest, who grinned at Jasmine with a very human smile. "And that's Clint. He was named for my father," she added as she indicated the younger boy, who was almost as tall as Komak, with the same dark hair and laughing green eyes. Except that his hair was black and Komak's had red highlights.

"I'm happy to meet you both," Jasmine told them.

"You're in the Rojok military?" Komak enthused. "Gosh, that uniform is totally solar," he added. "You're a doctor, too, like Mom?"

"I am," Jasmine replied, smiling. "I serve aboard the Kreskkom, the flagship of the Rojok fleet."

"Wow," the younger boy said, impressed. "Just like Mom used to, aboard the Morcai."

"And Edris." Madeline chuckled. "She'll be over soon. Kipling had a test with his tutor, so she's waiting for his grade. He's very smart."

"We're very smart, too," Komak murmured wickedly.

"Too smart!" his mother returned, with a glance. "How could you trap Larisse in the Nagaashe grotto?"

"She loved it!" Komak replied smugly. "She and the mother Nagaashe had a whole conversation about how they like snow."

Madeline rolled her eyes. "Just the same…"

"I won't do it again," Komak promised. "Honest."

"Children!" Madeline groaned. "I had an easier time in combat on Ondar!"

"Do you serve with a forward unit, like Mom did?" Komak wanted to know.

Jasmine nodded. "Yes, I do. We learn combat techniques in basic, and we have ongoing training under fire, even when we're in port on Enmehk-mehk."

"Chacon and Aunt Lyceria come to visit all the time with their son, Lomek, except right now," Komak said, "on account of the baby. We get to see as soon as it's born. Mom's set up the…!"

"Komak!" his mother warned gruffly. Because her son was about to mention the holon, which was top secret tech and not mentioned in company.

"Sorry." He grimaced. "I mean, on the multi-scanners, Mom," he added quickly.

She shook her head. "You'll be the death of me!"

"No, I won't, and years from now, we'll wreck bars together!" he replied with a mischievous grin.

She rolled her eyes. "Komak…!"

"You and your brother should go and play now.

But we'll expect you for dinner. And you'll dress for it," the empress said with twinkling green eyes.

They groaned, but they hugged her and their mother and ran off, laughing.

"Come in," Caneese invited. "We have been looking forward to the company."

"It gives us an excuse to get out of the lab," Madeline said, tongue in cheek, smiling at her mate's mother.

"Indeed. Oh, Rognan, I forgot…" She indicated a huge bird who was hobbling toward them, hampered by his damaged leg. He had black feathers and golden eyes and he went right up to Jasmine.

She stood very still, not knowing what to expect. She'd never seen a bird so big.

"You…are Jasmine," the bird said in passable Standard. "Welcome."

Jasmine's intake of breath was audible. "You speak Standard!" she exclaimed.

"Yes." He bowed his head. "I speak many tongues. She—" he indicated Madeline "—speaks my own."

"Not as well as Komak does, but after a fashion." She laughed, stroking the bird's head. "Where's Kanthor…? Never mind," she added as a huge black galot appeared out of nowhere at the bird's side.

Five years ago, Jasmine would have screamed and gone running out the door. But her fear of cats had long passed, and she surveyed the newcomer with utter fascination. He was as tall as Mekashe if he'd been standing erect. He had green eyes and white fangs. He padded up to her stealthily, as if trying to provoke her into running.

She stood very still and just looked at him. Behind her, Mekashe was grinding his teeth together, expecting a very different response from her.

She smiled. "You're a galot," she said, searching his eyes, which were almost on a level with hers. "You're magnificent," she added, studying him.

"And you are gracious."

She caught her breath. He'd spoken. She'd never known that the great cats had speech, or that they were sentient.

"Yes, you are surprised," the galot continued, and he laughed. "We do not share our culture with outworlders. Only with family."

It took a minute for that to sink in. She fought tears. She bowed to him.

Mekashe's quick breath was audible. She'd shocked him, apparently. But her concentration was on the huge cat, who seemed far more like a person than an animal. She knew from what Mekashe had told her that the Cehn-Tahr revered the galots, from whom their transforming DNA had been obtained. She could see why they were held in such great respect. She'd never known these things about the species. Her past behavior still shamed her, now more than ever.

The big cat moved closer. "We cannot relive the past," he said softly, his voice much like a cat hissing, but the words quite well enunciated. "We must go forward. We do not prey on those who offend us. We wait and hope for their understanding."

She bit her lip. Strong emotion buffeted her. "As we grow older, we grow in wisdom. And we learn from our mistakes. But I am grievously sorry to have offended as much as I did."

The big cat lifted a huge paw to her shoulder. "You were a cub," he said. "Cubs are not held responsible for their mischief. If you had offended as much as you fear, you would never have been offered such a position with the Rojoks." He chuckled. "There was collusion."

She was all at sea. "I don't understand."

"You will." He brought down his paw. "Welcome."

She reached out a hand and instantly drew it back, for fear of committing another offense. "Sorry," she said, flushing.

"I will not be offended if you stroke me," he said. "I learned to tolerate it from that one's mate long ago." He indicated Madeline.

"In that case," Jasmine said, and she extended her hand to smooth over the beautifully soft fur of his head. She smiled and sighed. "You honor me."

"Ah," he said suddenly, and turned. "You have other visitors, as well." He glanced back at her. "You have no fear of serpents…?"

"I have a virtual Nagaashe who lives with me,"

she said, and flushed when she noted Mekashe's sudden start. He knew where she'd gotten it.

"So." Kanthor made a sound.

Two giant white serpents appeared beside him, along with a smaller one.

"These are our friends," Kanthor told her as he and Rognan moved aside to let the serpents closer. "They wanted to meet you."

She was fascinated. The serpents towered over her. They had blue eyes, like her little virtual one, and rounded instead of slit pupils. They swayed and began to purr.

"How magnificent," she murmured. She bowed to them, as she had to Kanthor.

They bowed back and hummed. In her mind she heard soft laughter. There was another burst of purring and they vanished as quickly as they'd appeared.

"Oh my," Jasmine said, stunned.

"Enough shocks for one day, I think," the empress said, laughing. "Come inside. My mate and my son will be here soon, as will Rhemun and Edris and their children. We have much to discuss."

JASMINE WAS STILL reeling from her recent revelations when they entered the enormous living area. There was an open fireplace where virtual logs burned with a blue flame. She knew from the past how the Cehn-Tahr revered trees and knew that wood would never be used in such a fashion.

"I forgot that I had told you that," Mekashe said softly.

She turned to him. "I remember a lot that you told me," she said, and her eyes were sad.

He turned away. The pain was terrible.

Caneese looked from one of them to the other, but she wasn't sad. She was smiling secretly. Madeline caught that smile and echoed it. They were sitting on a major experiment that might have great benefits for these two in the near future. But it was too soon to speak of it openly.

ROGNAN AND KANTHOR accompanied them into the house, but moved to the patio where Rognan ate a fruit that looked much like a Terravegan apple and Kanthor lapped milk from an enormous earthen bowl.

"How things have changed," Madeline mentioned, indicating the two. "When I first came here, they were bitter enemies."

Caneese laughed. "I recall when Komak was born and Dtimun tried to make them leave the room. They defied him."

"I told him they were family. They are," Madeline said. She studied Jasmine. "When we have time, I want to know all the new advances in med tech. It's been a while since I was on active duty."

Jasmine smiled. "There have been some major changes."

"I keep up with them on the Nexus," Madeline said. "But firsthand reports are better."

A household worker brought a tray with refreshments, including coffee.

Jasmine caught her breath. "Java!" she exclaimed. "Real java! I haven't had it in so long…! Rusmok managed to get two cups of it for our last liberty. He wouldn't tell me how he managed it, but we were on Benaski Port. You can get almost anything there. Even java!"

Madeline sipped her own, noting Caneese's pained expression. "They don't understand this human compulsion to consume caffeine," she told Jasmine teasingly. "They drink herbal tea that's caffeine free. But I have to have my java jolt. I have it shipped in from the Terravegan colonies."

"Admiral Lawson has it shipped in," Caneese corrected mischievously, "and you have Dtimun wheedle it out of him. It is illegal in the Terravegan military," she added for Jasmine's benefit.

Madeline chuckled. "I got in trouble for brewing it in my medical bay," she confessed. "The commander used to hold it over my head whenever I did something he didn't like. The former commander," she added, smiling at Mekashe, who grinned at her.

"That was when Dtimun commanded the Holconcom," Mekashe volunteered. "Long ago."

"Not so long," came an amused deep voice from the doorway.

They all turned. Dtimun entered, smiling. He touched Madeline's cheek and laid his forehead against hers, then repeated the action with his mother.

"Where is Tnurat?" Caneese asked.

"Trying to restrain himself from choking the president of the Dectat." Dtimun sighed. "I wanted to assist him, but he said that one member of the family, at least, should keep a cool head. He will be along momentarily." He approached Jasmine and smiled. "Dr. Dupont," he greeted. "Chacon speaks highly of you, as does my sister."

"They've both been very gracious to me," she said, smiling. She bowed. "It's an honor to meet you, sir. You're legendary among the Rojok."

He chuckled. "Chacon and I have had some interesting encounters over the years as enemies. However, our friendship goes back to the Great Galaxy War, when we studied together at the military academy on Dacerius."

"He spoke of that, as well," she said.

"Rhemun and Edris will be here shortly," Dtimun added. "Kipling is being spoken to very sternly about his marks." He glanced at his mate with sparkling green eyes. "It appears that our sons have been helping him evade his study hour in the evening."

"Again," Madeline groaned.

Jasmine was listening with fascination. She'd been in awe of the Royal Clan for years, even through her resentments. It had never occurred to her that they were like any other family, with the same problems and concerns.

Dtimun glanced at Mekashe. "I believe you expressed an interest in the new pavilion we erected near the religious compound. Dr. Dupont might find it enlightening."

Mekashe hesitated.

Madeline cleared her throat. Dtimun and Mekashe read her mind. Mekashe sighed.

"Very well, Lady Maltiche. If you are certain…?"

"Most certain," she replied. She opened her wrist scanner and performed a function with the minicomp. Seconds later she beckoned to Jasmine. "Two ccs in the artery at the base of the neck," she told her with a mischievous smile.

Jasmine frowned. "I don't understand."

"You will," Madeline said.

The others waved them away.

Mekashe led the way outside, opening the door for Jasmine before they wandered into the bamboo forest toward a group of stone buildings in the near distance.

"What is this?" she asked him, indicating the discs she carried in her palm.

"Dravelzium," he said shortly.

She frowned. "I remember. It's used to sedate large animals."

He turned to her. "Also to prevent mating behaviors in susceptible Cehn-Tahr," he interrupted gruffly. He opened the collar of his uniform. "If you please."

She hesitated just briefly before she pulled out a laserdot and put the dosage into the artery. "I don't understand why it would be necessary," she said stiffly. "You don't have those sort of feelings for me. Not after what I did and said."

He drew in a breath as the drug took effect. He fastened his collar. "Emotions are less easily controlled than you might imagine, even after such difficulties."

She looked up into his somber blue eyes. She sighed. "I was so stupid."

"You were, as Kanthor told you earlier, a cub," he said. "Cubs cannot be held to the same standard as adults."

Her face was sad. "I destroyed my father's career and cost him his life because I was spoiled and thoughtless," she said. "I'd give anything to go back and relive those days on the starliner."

He moved a step closer. He touched her soft, flushed cheek with the tips of his fingers. "I should never have taken you with me to see my cousin in the gym," he replied. "It was reckless. I knew that he abhorred the humanoid form we must effect in company of other races."

She winced at the memory. "We were so close," she said. "I know what you must have thought when

I behaved as I did." She lowered her eyes. "I can't imagine the pain. I behaved like a spoiled child. At least, now I understand why things happened the way they did when we got to Memcache."

"The emperor had deep regrets about your father," Mekashe said. "Our laws are absolute, although many have been changed in the past few years. Until Madeline bonded with Dtimun, it was forbidden for a Cehn-Tahr to mate with any other species."

"Yes, well, that law was probably one of the better ones," she said heavily. "It would have caused many tragic deaths."

He nodded solemnly. He studied her lovely face. "You humans are so fragile," he said softly. He smiled sadly. "I had dreams. Not until after your father was sent home was I allowed to know the truth, and then I had it from Hahnson. We are not allowed to discuss intimate subjects among ourselves, rarely even with Clan intimates."

"Dr. Hahnson has had a tragic life," she said.

He nodded. "He never recovered from the loss of his mate."

"He seems like a kind person."

"He is. Although he, and many of the crew, harbored resentment for you when you first came on board the Morcai." He chuckled softly. "The humans in the Holconcom think of themselves as Cehn-Tahr."

"I deserved what I got," she confessed.

"As I said, you were a child." His face hardened. "Compared to me, a very small child."

She searched his solemn blue eyes. "The memories were sweet. Even when I hated everyone, I couldn't stop remembering." She lowered her face. "I grieved for a long time."

"As did I." He smiled. "You kept the virtual Nagaashe," he commented.

She grimaced. "Well, yes. It was all I had of happier times, when we were close."

"I had the jeweled clip you wore in your hair, the night we went to the last concert aboard the starliner."

Her eyebrows arched. "That clip… I thought I'd lost it!"

He shook his head and his eyes made a faint green laugh. "In fact you did. I found it on the steps that led to the second deck. I would have returned it, but after I was required to report back to the emperor, I could not bring myself to do it. As you said, it was a reminder of happy times."

"Neither of us knew how hopeless things were." She sighed.

"No. But I think it would have made no difference. We were very much alike."

"Except that I was terrified of cats," she murmured drily.

He cocked his head. "A fear you seem to have discarded."

She nodded. "I had therapy when I first joined the Rojok military. They don't have cats as religious objects, but there's a form of sand cat that they're very fond of. They keep virtual pets of it. I lost my fear of cats soon after I enlisted."

"I should have been kinder to you, when you first came aboard the Morcai, but my resentments ate at me."

"So did mine." She touched the trunk of a nearby tree. "I was actively hostile. But after I learned the truth, people were kind. Especially Dr. Hahnson."

"He knows how it feels," he said simply.

"Yes, he does."

He started walking again.

"It's so beautiful here," she said. "I remembered the holoroom where you showed me your villa. It was lovely."

"We must make time to visit it, while we're in port."

She turned. "I would love that."

He drew in a breath. "We might take Rhemun and Edris with us, however," he said. "It would be unwise to venture too far alone together."

She searched his eyes. "You haven't given me anything. I haven't accepted anything," she added, recalling that gift-giving was a prelude to courtship.

He smiled sadly. "That would not matter, if I became careless with you." His eyes darkened slightly. "Even touching can initiate it, when strong emotions are involved. Thanks to Hahnson's drugs, I was able to touch you when we were aboard the starliner.

But the drugs become less effective with long use. Even with the dravelzium, it would be reckless to become too…involved with each other, physically. Once begun, the mating cycle is relentless and brutal. Past a certain point, control is lost. A Cehn-Tahr male, as I told you once, will kill any other male who comes close to the object of his interest."

She bit her lower lip and moved forward. "Cehn-Tahr women are lovely," she began.

"I have never been involved with any of them," he replied. "Nor have I wished to be. Only one female has ever moved me to thoughts of a shared life."

Her heart jumped. Of course, he might not mean her. But even as she processed the thought, she looked up at him and saw the helpless attraction in his face that found an echo in her own heart.

She felt the pain to the soles of her feet. "It's so hopeless," she said miserably.

He averted his eyes and fought for control. The dravelzium had a short life span. "Yes, it is. We should return to the others. It is unwise for us to remain here."

She turned and walked beside him, subdued. "It's probably a good thing that I'm stationed aboard a Rojok flagship and you're confined to the Morcai."

"I agree."

They walked in silence.

WHEN THEY RETURNED to the Fortress, a tall Cehn-Tahr in the blue uniform of the Imperial Guard was standing beside a small blonde human female. Beside them was a tall boy with long, curly blond hair and blue eyes. Next to him was a little girl with black curly hair, laughing.

Mekashe smiled. "Rhemun and Edris." He introduced them to his companion. "And their children, Kipling and Larisse. This is Dr. Jasmine Dupont."

"You're in the Rojok military!" Kipling said excitedly. "I'd love to hear some of your adventures, Doctor!"

She laughed. "I'd be delighted to tell you, although I don't do much actual fighting. I'm a doctor."

"So was Mom," Kipling said.

Edris groaned. "I flunked out of combat school with the lowest grade in academy history," she confessed. "I was better at being a doctor!" She laughed.

"I'm happy to meet all of you," Jasmine said, smiling. "I've heard a lot about you from Mekashe."

"Did he tell you that I can beat him with the Kahn-Bo?" Kipling asked excitedly. "Almost nobody else can!"

"Stop blowing your own horn, mister," Edris chided.

"Okay, Mom," he said. But he grinned and his eyes flashed green suddenly, the color of humor.

Jasmine's surprise was obvious.

"I look like my mom, but I have a lot of Dad's characteristics," Kipling said, revealing that he read Jasmine's thoughts.

"Amazing," Jasmine said, and she wasn't exaggerating.

"Too many, at times." Rhemun chuckled.

"Are you coming in now?" Lady Caneese said from the door. "Cook almost has the meal ready, and we must dress."

Jasmine ground her teeth together. "Oh dear..."

"We have a surprise." Lady Caneese chuckled. "Come with me, if you please."

Jasmine glanced at Mekashe, who still wore a faintly pained expression. She smiled at him, and then followed Lady Caneese inside.

"I'VE BEEN ASKED to pass something along," Hahnson said to Mekashe when they were briefly alone after they'd dressed in contemporary finery for the meal. "By the emperor."

"Oh?" Mekashe asked.

Hahnson looked around to make sure they weren't attracting too much attention. "Holon."

Mekashe frowned. "Excuse me?"

"Holon," Hahnson repeated. "You know what it's used for primarily, and why." He waited until Mekashe got the message.

The Cehn-Tahr's chiseled lips fell apart on an expulsion of breath. "But the other obstacles..."

"The primary one is the mating drive, which is alleviated by mating," Hahnson said. "The holon would allow a relationship that was almost normal. Of course, there couldn't be children."

"That would not matter," Mekashe said at once. "We both love them, but even that sacrifice would be preferable to a lifetime apart."

"I thought you'd say that," Hahnson said with a smile. "You would still have to bond, and there would be the issue of separation. But it's better than the alternative."

Mekashe felt his heart lift. "Far better. I had not even considered that it was a possibility."

"You'll have to talk her into it," Hahnson continued. "But the emperor has given you permission to share the holon tech with her."

"I'll ask her today."

Hahnson chuckled. "I think I can guess what she'll say."

Mekashe hoped that she would agree. It would be a sort of half life. But without her, his life had no meaning at all.

WHILE HE WAS pondering the possibilities, he heard her step on the winding stone staircase and looked up.

His heart stopped and ran wild. Jasmine was wearing a white gown with blue and gold accents. It reminded him very much of a gown she'd worn on board the starliner. Her hair was curled toward her lovely face. The gown clung to her exquisite figure.

Mekashe was so captivated that he didn't even notice the amused stares of his family around him.

Jasmine had eyes only for Mekashe. She came the rest of the way down and stopped in front of him.

"The empress had it woven for me," she stammered, nervous now. "I haven't worn anything feminine since... Well, not for a long time."

"You look enchanting," he said huskily.

She smiled softly. "You look devastating."

They stared at each other for several seconds.

"I have something to discuss with you later," he said.

"All right."

"But for now, we should join the others." He held out his arm. She put her hand on his forearm and let him lead her into the enormous dining room, where a table laden with all sorts of foods had already been set.

CHAPTER FIFTEEN

JASMINE SAT SANDWICHED between Mekashe and Madeline Ruszel. She and the doctor had a great deal in common. Madeline was an ongoing encyclopedia of medical research.

"Lady Caneese and I have been working on something revolutionary," she told Jasmine with twinkling green eyes. "In fact, we've just made a breakthrough. In a few months, we'll be ready to announce it. But we have a series of virtual trials to get through first."

"I'll look forward to hearing about it," Jasmine said. She smiled sadly. "I'll have to go back soon. My assistant is filling in for me aboard the flagship."

Madeline just nodded, but that twinkle was still in her eyes.

Mekashe was depressed when she said that. Did she want to leave? He felt less sure of the path ahead.

Jasmine, aware of his withdrawal, felt uneasy, too. She didn't know why he looked so demoralized.

"It will be all right," Lady Caneese said suddenly. She cocked her head and studied Jasmine. Then she smiled. "You will see."

She glanced at Mekashe, who was blocked by her mind. But she smiled at him, as well.

LATER, MEKASHE WALKED Jasmine out to a small glassed-in conservatory, where many flowering species of plants encircled a central bench that wound around the building.

"The Rojok military has been your home for five years," he began as they sat together.

"Yes. I had nowhere else to go, after…" She paused.

"My villa is very close to the Fortress," he continued. "There is a small clinic, devoted to Alamantimichar, our Royal Clan, where ailments are treated. They are always short staffed. We have many children in this sector who go to the clinic." He studied his highly polished black boots. "We have a secret device, called a holon. This tech is never discussed with outworlders. I have permission from the emperor to tell you about it."

She frowned. "Why?"

"You and I can never mate," he said heavily. "I would kill you. But the holon is very much like the tech used aboard the starliner, which permitted us to visit many virtual realities." He studied his boots again. "It is used primarily for bonded mates who are far apart from one another. It permits an intimacy which is indistinguishable from reality. If we used the holon, we could mate. We could bond and have an almost-normal life together, here on Memcache."

Her heart ran wild. She'd never considered that there might be any way that she and Mekashe could be together.

"You want to bond with me?" she asked, fascinated.

He turned and looked down into her eyes. "More than I want to continue breathing," he said roughly.

She swallowed. "It's like that with me, too," she confessed huskily as she searched his eyes. "I'd give anything to live with you."

"There could never be a child," he said sadly.

"I know." She forced a smile. "But there are worse things…"

His arms closed around her. He'd had Hahnson use dravelzium and the nanotech he'd employed once before. It made it possible for him to fold her close and kiss her with impassioned need. Despite the drugs, he had to keep a tight rein on his passion, to keep from hurting her.

She held on for dear life and kissed him back hungrily, five years of total abstinence feeding the anguished need.

When she thought that he wasn't going to be able to let go at all, there was a loud cough from the area surrounding them.

They both turned, still locked in each other's arms, with blank looks.

Madeline Ruszel smiled knowingly. "The empress thinks it might be wise if you rejoined us. In fact, so do I. Unfortunately, there are limits to the dravelzium. I have a rather intimate knowledge of its use," she added with a wicked look in her sparkling green eyes.

Mekashe chuckled. "Indeed," he said, reluctantly letting Jasmine move away. "We have heard many tales of your relationship with Dtimun in the Holconcom."

"Most of them were true," Madeline confessed. "We had a turbulent one. But it ended well, eventually, with some classified tech and a little DNA manipulation."

"The sample was consumed with use and never replicated, they say," Mekashe said sadly.

Madeline just smiled. "There's a nature vid that Jasmine might like to see. It's from Edris's tenure as a researcher on Eridanus Three."

"That's where the galots come from, isn't it?" Jasmine asked as they walked back toward the house. "I understood that they ate researchers."

Madeline laughed. "Indeed, they do. But Edris was befriended by Kanthor, who protected her and Kipling while they lived there. It's a long story, but treachery by Rhemun's houseman caused her to leave and Rhemun to think she died in a fire on the property, along with their son, Kipling. It was several years before a quirk of fate led him to the truth and he went looking for them."

"Edris seems very nice," Jasmine said.

"She is. We're protective of her, still. She's had a hard time in the military. From what we've heard about it, you and the Rojok military were a good fit."

"We are," she confessed. She shook her head. "I still don't understand how it happened. I was at the spaceport on Terravega, waiting for an interview, when Chacon happened to see me. He remembered me from that one day I spent on Memcache and offered me a scholarship." She flushed, as she recalled refusing one from the emperor, who had tried to help her even after she gave him grave offense.

"The emperor is not what you think," Mekashe said gently, reading her thoughts. "He deeply regretted the loss of your father."

"I know that now," she said sadly. "I've made some terrible mistakes in my life, but that…"

"You mustn't look back," Madeline said. "Only ahead. The future is going to be bright."

Mekashe looked down at Jasmine hungrily. "Indeed, it is."

They walked back into the Fortress. The emperor and Caneese were waiting for them.

"We understand that a bonding might be in the offing," the emperor said drily. "In which case, my mate would be happy to officiate."

"I would," Caneese added at once.

"But my assignment…" Jasmine began worriedly.

"Chacon has agreed to permit you to remain on the rolls as a reserve medic. He and Lyceria would love to come for the bonding, but their second child is due very soon and that is not possible," Caneese said. "But you can stay here with Madeline and Dtimun while we arrange the service. It will only take a standard day."

Jasmine was overwhelmed with joy. She looked up at Mekashe with her heart in her eyes.

He nodded. "That would be kind of you, Lady Caneese," he said huskily. "Very kind."

"Oh, yes!" Jasmine added. She sighed. If only her father could have been here. He'd loved Mekashe. She fought down sadness.

The emperor cleared his throat. "We have a bonding gift," he said abruptly. "Something we hope you will like."

"Something for me?" Jasmine asked, surprised. "Your Highness, I've given such offense…!"

"A child offends, but not with malice," he replied kindly, and his eyes were a warm golden color. "And such offenses are forgiven. Come."

THE EMPEROR AND empress led them down a long path through the heavily wooded area. Wind chimes stirred in the breeze. As they reached a clearing beside a small stream, Jasmine frowned. There was a house there. Incredibly, it looked like the one she and her father had shared on Terravega, so long ago.

She caught her breath. "It's just like my old home," she stammered, and fought tears. "Sir, I'm so grateful…!"

"This is not the surprise," he said gently. "Go inside, please. The rest of us will remain here."

She didn't understand why they wanted her to go in alone. It must be something personal.

She smiled and went forward to open the door. And there, in the lights that emanated from the walls, was her father with an open book in his hand and raised eyebrows. She gasped.

"Well, aren't you a sight for sore eyes!" he exclaimed, laughing. "Hello, child!"

She ran into his arms, sobbing, muttering things that were totally incoherent. "I don't understand," she said finally, raising her wet face. "How…?"

"I'll let the emperor explain that to you. But for all intents and purposes, I'm the exact person I used to be. I have all my memories—even the ones of your mother, God rest her soul. And the house and the property here is mine. The emperor thinks I may live for over two hundred years. I've had a few minor DNA adjustments," he added with a chuckle. "Where's Mekashe? I'm determined to beat him at chess at least once!"

The others filed in the door. Mekashe was as shocked as Jasmine seemed to be.

"Sir!" he exclaimed, and went forward to lock

forearms with the human. "It's so good to see you! I don't understand?" He turned to the emperor.

"You were curious about a sample that was taken before your father's passing ceremony on Terravega," the emperor said softly. "The sample was used to clone your father. I felt such guilt, for what happened to both of you. As a result of it, we changed certain laws pertaining to offenses committed by minors of other races. I wanted to make amends to you both. This was the only way that I could find…"

"Sir." Jasmine, in tears, hugged him. She didn't care if it broke every protocol in the book, which it probably did. "Thank you!"

He chuckled and embraced her. "You are most welcome. And now, we will leave you to visit."

He released her. She wiped her tears and beamed at him. "Sir, did Chacon really just happen to be in the spaceport that day?" she asked suspiciously.

He sighed. "Actually, knowing your circumstances as I did, and your distaste for the Terravegan medical corps and your reluctance to accept help from me, I asked him to intervene. He was happy to do it. Especially when he followed your training and saw how competent you were, both as a soldier and a medic. He thinks, as we do, that having a human female as a Cularian specialist aboard flagships is a magnificent idea. He intends to replace you. If you are willing to live on Memcache and work in the clinic near Mekashe's villa, that is," he added hesitantly.

She looked up at Mekashe. "I'd live in a shack on the beach and fish for my living if it was the only way I could be with him," she said huskily and watched emotions flash in many colors in his cat eyes. "I'd give up...anything!"

"As would I," Mekashe returned gruffly.

"You know," the empress interrupted, "since Edris bonded with Rhemun, there has been no female Cularian specialist aboard the Morcai." She pursed her lips and her eyes twinkled. "If you were bonded, the male crew members would be safe. And I understand that they already like Dr. Dupont."

The emperor laughed heartily. "This is true. What do you say, Jasmine? Would you like to serve with Mekashe in the Holconcom?"

Her breath caught. To be with him all the time, instead of here and only able to see him between missions, was a dream come true.

She didn't have to voice it. The emperor and Mekashe read her thoughts accurately.

"Done," the emperor said. "You both may have a standard week for, what do the humans call it, a bonding holiday? And then you report for duty."

"Thank you, sir," Mekashe said heartily. "For everything."

"Thank you very much," Jasmine seconded, bursting with joy.

The emperor and empress smiled and left them with Professor Dupont.

"And now, young man, about that chess match," the professor said drily and with a big smile.

THE BONDING CEREMONY was held at the Fortress. Mekashe wore his dress uniform, bloodred with gold piping. Jasmine wore a gown of sky blue, with gold trim, the colors of Alamantimichar. She had a small tiara with precious stones. She felt like an empress in her finery. But far more than clothing was her joy at being able to live with Mekashe, even in a convoluted fashion.

Are you nervous? he said mentally, and his voice was teasing. *There is no reason. You are among family and friends here.*

She was. Chacon and Lyceria had used the holon to be present at the bonding along with their son, Lomek, named for Chacon's father, who looked like Chacon except that he had his mother's elegant cat eyes. The Nagaashe parents and child were in attendance; as were Kanthor, the galot; and Rognan, the Meg-Raven; along with Madeline and Dtimun and their sons; Edris and Rhemun and their children; the emperor and several Cehn-Tahr whom Jasmine did not know.

There were flowers everywhere, in pots and arranged around the altar where a statue of Cashto had pride of place. Some of the plants were like orchids on Terravega. They grew from the branches of trees which surrounded the exterior patio where the bonding was held.

Above, the sky was an odd shade of blue, from the radiation that was used in the continent's reactors. The sunlight was subdued, but it was bright enough to highlight the stones in the tiara on Jasmine's head.

She was so nervous that she almost dropped the bouquet she was holding. It was secured in a sort of globe, living flowers with roots in solution, because the Cehn-Tahr never picked flowers. They revered any form of life, which was evident in the age of the trees and shrubs around them.

There are so many people, she thought back to Mekashe.

Family, he corrected warmly. *All Alamantimichar.*

She'd noticed that nobody was wearing sensor nets. The Cehn-Tahr were in their true forms, a testament to their trust of Jasmine. These forms were never shown to outworlders.

He laughed softly at her thoughts. *There is another here. He is family, so he had to be included. He is uncertain of his welcome. It is Tresar, whom you saw in his true form aboard the starliner...*

I don't hold grudges, she thought softly. *Especially not now.*

There was a smile in his deep voice. *That will please him. He has been distraught for me. He blamed himself.*

It was my fault, no one else's, she thought back. *But that's all in the past. We have such a future to look forward to!*

Yes. A bright one, if unorthodox.

She approached the altar where Mekashe was waiting. They joined hands and the empress invoked the blessing and the bonding words in the Holy Tongue, Old High Cehn-Tahr, which even few of the Royal Clan spoke.

Afterward, she translated into Standard for Jasmine's benefit. They were blessed and the ceremony was concluded.

"Where do we go now?" Jasmine asked.

"To my villa." Mekashe chuckled as they thanked the empress, received congratulations from the guests and finally sped off together in a skiff.

"I'm nervous. Do you mind?" she asked worriedly.

He chuckled. "I am also nervous. So, no, I do not mind."

She pressed close to his shoulder. "I only know about intimacy because of my medical training."

"I only know of intimacy through textdisks."

Her eyes opened wide as she stared at him. "You mean, you've never...?"

"I've never," he confessed.

She let out a sigh. "Well!"

He chuckled. "We are a pristine people. We mate for life. We never stray."

"I like that part." She hesitated. "So, do you think we'll know what to do?"

He laughed out loud. "I believe it comes naturally."

"Okay." And she grinned at him.

It DID, INDEED, come naturally. After a few minor fumbles, they consummated their bonding. Jasmine had hoped that it would be tender and long. Instead, it was brief and uncomfortable.

The first time was almost traumatic for her, even in a virtual setting, and despite Mekashe's fervent apologies as he explained the process afterward.

"This is a sad result of the DNA manipulation," he said regretfully as he comforted her in the aftermath. "We loathe what we have become because of it. This first time is always brutal, as it is in the great cats. We take no pleasure from it, because we are ashamed. The first mating is to prove fertility. It is usually fruitful. And I am dreadfully sorry."

She put her hand over his lips. "I'm not damaged," she said softly. "Only a little bruised. You told me how it would be, before we came in here. I wasn't afraid." She reached up to smooth her mouth over his. "And since we can't produce a child, although that saddens me, it means that we don't have to restrain ourselves from now on. At all."

"At all," he agreed. He rolled her over onto her back. "Heal the damage."

She did, using her wrist scanner. As she finished, there was a shock of pleasure in her mind so intense that she cried out.

"What...?" she exclaimed, shocked.

"I am making amends," he whispered. As he spoke, the pleasure came again, biting into her so fiercely that she wept, even as his body joined with hers in a slow, sweet melting of flesh with flesh.

"Making...amends," she managed, shaking violently with the increasing passion.

And she said nothing else, for a very long time.

THEY LAY TOGETHER, touching, tasting, in the lazy, sweet aftermath of such fulfillment that she thought she would die of it.

"We are far more compatible than I expected," he mused, drawing his mouth across her closed eyes.

She laughed softly. "Oh yes."

He stretched like a huge cat and rolled over toward her. In his true form, he looked very human, except for his size and the thick, curly mane that ran from his forehead almost to his waist in back. His nose was a little broader than a human's, and of course, he had cat eyes with slit pupils. But other than a strip of fur that ran down his backbone, he had no true cat characteristics.

She smoothed her hands over his muscular chest with its wedge of thick, curling black hair, contented.

"I can't believe this is virtual," she whispered. "It's so real!"

"This was why the holon was invented," he told her. "It permits bonded couples to enjoy each other even when they are many light-years' distance apart."

"I never dreamed that we'd end up like this," she said, pressing close to the virtual mate who was as warm and alive as the original. "Or that I'd have my father back. That was so generous of the emperor, especially after I'd given such offense."

"All of us mourned him," he said softly. "He was a good man. He still is," he added with a chuckle.

"Oh yes. And someday, he may even beat you at chess," she teased.

"Anything is possible."

She smoothed her hand over his thick, curling mane. "What about Dr. Hahnson?" she asked after a minute. "I mean, if you have the tech to copy a person, memories and all, couldn't they do that for his mate? Dr. Ruszel, Lady Maltiche, said that they still had cells from Dr. Hahnson's mate. They could bring her back, and the two of them could use the holon, just as we do."

"I believe the offer was made and refused," he said, stretching again. "Dr. Hahnson thinks that Lady Caneese and Lady Maltiche have made a break-through in their research that will affect Cehn-Tahr/human mating."

"Really?" she exclaimed, excited. "I wondered,

because they've been so secretive. And they smile a lot when they look at us and talk about it."

"They do," he agreed. "If their research does refine the process, it would allow us to have children. Hahnson says that he wants, how did he put it, all or nothing in such a case. He does not want his mate returned to him unless they can be together in every way." He smiled sadly. "Her suicide was traumatic for him, possibly even more so than his original's torturous death at Ahkmau, the Rojok prison camp. He feels that if she is brought back, even with the use of the holon, she may again become distraught and take her life a second time."

"So he's waiting, until they're sure they can actually mate and breed," she replied, nodding.

"Exactly."

"I had problems with him at first, aboard the Morcai." She laughed softly. "I was stiff and insulting." She glanced at him. "To everybody." She drew in a breath. "You'll never know how ashamed and guilt-ridden I was, when you shifted into your true form and I realized at last what I'd done aboard the star-liner, how much offense I'd given." She grimaced. "You cared for me, so much, and I said such horrible things…!"

He folded her close. "You were a child," he repeated, as he had many times before. "You reacted as a child would. But the fact that you were overheard, and the emperor did not know you, combined to produce a tragedy."

"It was my father who paid for my mistake," she said heavily. "Once I knew that it was my fault, I wanted to step out the airlock without a suit."

"We knew that. You were under constant surveillance until we reached Memcache. I could not bear to lose you, even when you offended me," he confided.

She pressed close into his arms and felt them envelop her against his warm, muscular body. "I grieved for you, for years. Even when I thought I was justified in hating the entire Cehn-Tahr race, I couldn't stop loving you. It's why I kept the virtual Nagaashe that we got from the holoroom that wonderful day on Dacerius."

"It is why I kept the jeweled comb that you thought you had lost on the starliner." He lifted his head and looked down at her with soft, golden eyes. "There was never another in my mind, in my heart."

"Or in mine."

He pursed his lips. "This Rojok you became close to," he began.

"Rusmok," she said. "We survived basic training together. We went on combat missions together. He's the best friend, really the only friend, I've ever had. But it was never a romantic thing. He's so much in love with this Rojok woman who hates the military." She looked up at him, tongue in cheek. "Gosh, isn't that like déjà vu?" she teased.

He scowled. "*Déjà* what?"

"Sorry. Idioms again. It means something that happens to you feels like it's happened before. But I guess what I really meant was that it's ironic, because that woman is just like me, when I first met you. I told you I hated the military." She sighed. "I didn't know anything about it, at the time. Now that I do, I feel even more guilty about all the stupid things I said."

He kissed her soft lips. "We cannot repeat the past. We must go forward and leave it behind, where it should be." He smiled against her mouth. "We have a bright, beautiful future in store for us. Starting with putting you in a Holconcom uniform," he added drily.

"Rusmok will have a stroke," she predicted, chuckling. She put her fingers over his lips when he started to speak. "He's my friend. So you have to tolerate him. I owe my life to him a couple of times."

He sighed. "Well, at least this bonding will keep me from killing him, as I might should there have been no possibility of intimacy between us. The savage behavior haunts us. It, like the first mating, are the result of tampering with natural things. The emperor saw, too late, the effects of the work his scientists did in transforming the Cehn-Tahr race so long ago. But the combination of galot and canolithe genes happened even before the emperor became the emperor. There was a civilization that predated this one, millennia ago. It was destroyed by the explosion of a miles-wide comet in the upper atmosphere. Only a handful of Cehn-Tahr survived, their genes corrupted even more by the resulting radiation."

"The Rojoks did genetic manipulation, as well," she pointed out.

"Yes, but their DNA tampering is far more recent," he replied. "We have had thousands of years to study and understand the results of our manipulation of natural processes. We have paid, and still pay, a high price for it."

She smoothed her hand over his strong jaw. "The most manipulation was used in the Royal Clan, Alamantimichar, wasn't it?"

"Yes." He smiled down at her. "And now you, as well, are Alamantimichar."

She sighed. "That's nice. Being part of a Clan, I mean. But I'll also enjoy being part of the Holconcom." She laughed. "Madeline's sons are very promilitary. So is Rhemun's son, Kipling."

"And his daughter, Larisse," he added on a chuckle. "She wants already to follow her brother into the military academy. That would have been an impossible dream only a decade ago. However, now that Madeline has a division of female troops in the Cehn-Tahr military, courtesy of the emperor, who made her a brigadier general, Larisse may one day even serve in the Holconcom."

"Exciting times," she said.

"Exciting."

She stretched lazily, watching his eyes darken slightly as they ran over her exquisite body.

"I love cats," she said.

He eased over her, chuckling. "Prove it."

She curled her arms around his neck. "I'd be delighted to," she whispered.

THE HOLCONCOM UNIFORM was similar to her old Rojok one, except that the new one was bloodred and there were no mesag marks on the sleeve.

"We don't have rank insignia, do we?" she asked Mekashe.

He chuckled. He touched a button on his communicator ring and pointed it at her sleeve. There were the rank marks of a Cehn-Tahr lieutenant commander equivalent.

"Goodness," she exclaimed, studying the marks.

"We never show them in public. Nor do we allow any vids or personal information about our soldiers to be publicized. The face of the commander is never shown to outworlders. In fact, my name is not known."

"Rojoks do exactly the opposite." She laughed.

"There will be some minor differences in protocol," he added. "Despite our relationship, you must salute me."

She pursed her lips. "All the time?"

"All the time that the holon is not in use," he whispered, wary of being overheard.

She laughed delightedly. "Okay." She stood at attention and gave him her best Rojok salute.

He groaned.

"Just kidding." She turned her fist the other way and struck her chest once, the Holconcom salute.

"Much better," he said drily. "Report to sick bay, Dr. Dupont," he added. "We lift soon."

She grinned. "I can't wait!"

She saluted again, was dismissed and jogged down the corridor to sick bay.

Holt Stern jogged alongside her. "Welcome to the Holconcom, Doctor," he said with flashing black eyes and a grin.

"Thanks, Captain," she returned.

"Good thing you're the Cularian specialist," he mused. "If I make you mad and break a leg, I could find it attached to my shoulder."

"Dead right, so don't do it," she shot back, chuckling. "I could raise your hair with stories about my exploits in the Rojok military."

"Save them for Madeline Ruszel's sons," he teased. "I understand that they, and Kipling, and Larisse, are harassing Madeline to have a party so you can be invited and they can corner you to get stories."

"I'd love to." She laughed "I love their sons. Komak and Clint are unique."

"They are. Clint is named for his grandfather, Madeline's father. You weren't told, but he's a colonel in the Paraguard."

"Wow! A military man. Is he like her?"

"Not so much. Her sense of humor is totally wild," he added with a grin. "She used to get in brawls with the First Fleet, over their insults about Dtimun. She threw one of them over a table and told him not to worry if she broke a bone—she was a doctor and she knew how to fix it."

"Good grief." She laughed out loud.

"And Edris can tell you some tales, too. Rhemun turned a pot of vegetable soup over her head when Madeline was pregnant with Komak."

Her gasp was audible.

"See what sort of Clan you married into?" he teased. "And that's just the tip of the iceberg, so to speak."

"What a great bunch of people," she exclaimed, and meant every word. "I can't wait to hear more of the stories."

"I'll make a point of telling them that," he said. "See you, ladybones," he added, and put on a burst of speed.

Stern, a clone of the original, had vast physical enhancements, a result of the Rojok tech that had produced him. She'd heard that he could fight any of the powerful Cehn-Tahr to a standstill. Besides that, he was nice.

Careful. She heard an amused voice in her mind. *Stern is off-limits. You belong to me now.*

I'm bonded to you now, she teased back mentally. *I'm not a possession.*

You are, he argued. *You possess me body and soul.*

That works both ways, Commander, she retorted.

Nice to know. Get busy, he said.

On my way to work, sir. She put on a burst of speed of her own.

CHAPTER SIXTEEN

SERVING ABOARD THE MORCAI was a little easier on the nerves than service on a Rojok vessel. There, officers were rigid about protocol and there was little frivolity. It was a different story with the Holconcom.

The humans aboard loved to gossip. They told Jasmine about an infamous incident with Rhemun, the last commander of the Holconcom. He and his men had rescued his future mate, Edris, from a potential tragedy on Benaski Port. There had been two little Parsifan girls that he also rescued and brought aboard, to take them to their last living relatives at a farming colony.

The children had a tragic past. They were afraid of Rhemun at first, but they discovered that he could tell stories. So every night he gathered the two children and told them traditional Cehn-Tahr fairy tales. One night, he heard noises outside the compartment. When he left the girls, he found half the command staff hiding in the shadows, listening, including Edris and Stern. When he burst out laughing, they confided that they were all products of Terravegan military nurseries and had never been told stories in their lives. They enjoyed story time as much as the children did.

Jasmine chuckled as they related the incident. There were others, like when the first commander, Dtimun, had a wound that he wouldn't let Madeline treat. She'd followed him out of the airlock when they docked and actually threw something after him, infuriated that he was bleeding and wouldn't let her repair the wound.

"This is really nothing like the Rojok military," she confided to Dr. Hahnson.

"Nothing is like the Rojok military," he chided. "But they're noble, honorable adversaries. I was with Dtimun when we fought them in the Great Galaxy War. Those conflicts were especially hard on Dtimun and Chacon, because they were best friends at the military academy on Dacerius when they were young."

"I owe Chacon a lot," she told him. "Not to mention the emperor. He's nothing like I pictured."

"He surprises people," he agreed.

"I love having my father back," she said, smiling. "It's so nice to contact him on the holon and talk. Mekashe plays chess with him on it. Daddy never wins, but he never seems to mind, either."

"Amazing tech they've developed at Kolmankash," he agreed. He pursed his lips and his eyes twinkled. "When we make port, we're all supposed to go to the Fortress for an announcement. It's going to be earthshaking."

She looked at him curiously. "Truly?"

"Truly. Wait and see."

"Tell me," she said. "Come on. Spill it."

"Not possible. The emperor would read my mind and I'll be mopping heads on the rim."

She laughed out loud. "That will never happen."

"Not so long as I keep my mouth shut, at least," he retorted.

SHE WONDERED ABOUT the announcement and hoped it might be the breakthrough that had been hinted about.

She didn't have long to wait. They ported at Mem-cache and a skimmer was assigned to take them directly to the Fortress. She and Mekashe were chauffeured there by themselves.

"Do you think it's what we've hoped for?" she asked.

"I don't know," he said softly. "But it would be the stuff of dreams, yes?"

"Yes." She searched his eyes hungrily. "I want a child so badly."

"So do I," he whispered.

She clung to his hand. "If only," she said softly. "Oh, if only!"

THE EMPRESS AND Madeline met them at the front door. They were both smiling.

"We did it," Madeline announced with a broad smile. "Virtual trials are over and we have a successful serum." She pursed her lips and looked at Jasmine. "Now all we need is a willing volunteer to be genetically enhanced..."

"Me!" Jasmine raised her hand.

Madeline grinned. "I was really hoping you'd say that."

"It is safe?" Mekashe worried, glancing at Jasmine.

"It is very safe," Lady Caneese assured him. "We would never risk her life if we weren't sure."

"Exactly," Madeline said. She didn't add that it was a serum that Komak had given them the basic formula for many years ago, when he revealed that he could travel in time. He brought back the original sample for Madeline, so that she could bond with Dtimun. But it couldn't be replicated until the Nagaashe signed a second treaty that allowed their biological samples to be used in production of the substance required. And it was extremely limited. Only in certain cases could it be used, Jasmine's being one of them.

Jasmine and Mekashe looked at each other with desperate hope. The two women facing them only smiled.

THERE WAS AN audience after the injection had been given, a laserdot into Jasmine's artery at the base of her neck.

"I don't really feel anything," she began. And then a warm flush worked its way over her body. She felt the change. Felt different. Felt other.

"Here." Madeline handed her a drasteel sphere. "See what you can do with it."

Jasmine was hesitant. But after a few seconds, she crushed the ball with her fingers into a misshapen mass. She just stared at it, stunned.

"And now the holon will no longer be required," Madeline whispered as she drew Jasmine to one side. "But a little dravelzium wouldn't hurt, just in case. I found that out the hard way myself." She grinned.

Jasmine hugged her, tears rolling down her cheeks. "I never dared to hope…" She drew back. "Can I have a child?" she asked quickly. "Is it possible?"

Madeline nodded. "The serum includes a small fix for the differences in genetic makeup and racial differences. I know that it works because I have two sons," she added, tongue in cheek.

"I'm just…speechless," Jasmine managed.

Mekashe joined them, the waiting impossible any longer when he saw tears on his mate's face.

"Is everything all right?" he asked worriedly.

Jasmine laughed. "Everything is fine!" she exclaimed. "We can have children!"

"Children." He caught his breath. "But we are different species."

"Not to worry," Madeline assured him. "Different species, but ultimately compatible." She indicated her two sons in the distance, both fighting Kipling in an impromptu Kahn-Bo match.

"I see your point." Mekashe sighed. "I am forever in your debt, Dr. Ruszel."

"So am I," Jasmine added. "And to the empress."

"I'll tell her," Madeline said. She cocked her head. "Don't you two want to test the serum? If I were you, I'd go home. You can come for dinner tomorrow. We'll have your dad and my father over, so they can get acquainted."

"That would be very nice," Jasmine said, but her eyes were locked into Mekashe's.

"Go home," Madeline repeated, waving them away. "I'll go entertain the troops by practicing the Holy Tongue to tell them luncheon is served. See you both tomorrow."

They called their thanks after her, waved to the others in the distance and made transportation history with their rush to Mekashe's villa.

"I DIDN'T BELIEVE it would ever be possible," Jasmine gasped after a passionate union that surpassed anything they'd shared in the holon. She was still shaking with delight in the turbulent aftermath. She ran her hands over Mekashe's muscular chest, fascinated with what had just happened.

"Nor did I," he confessed. He was still trying to get his breath and slow his wild heartbeat. He stretched and his powerful body shivered with re-membered pleasure.

She heard an odd, deep sound and put her hand in the center of his chest. The sound grew louder. It sounded like purring!

He rolled over, propping on one elbow as he bent to draw his face against hers. "Yes, the Cehn-Tahr purr when they mate," he whispered amusedly. "An-other closely guarded secret. Are you shocked?"

"I love it," she whispered back. She cuddled close and sighed. "I'm so happy."

"So am I." He scowled. "Jasmine, you might want to use your wrist scanner."

"Use my scanner...why?" she asked.

He put his big hand over her flat stomach and caught his breath. "I heard Dtimun speak of this. I confess that I never truly believed him. Until now. I can...feel the child!"

She gasped audibly. She fumbled her wrist scan-ner open, produced a sensor and laid it on her stom-ach. The results had her gasping as well, crying, almost hysterical as she pulled Mekashe close and kissed him until her mouth felt bruised.

"I'm pregnant!" she exclaimed. "I'm pregnant!"

He folded her close. Never in his long life had he

felt such tenderness for anyone. "Pregnant. We made a baby," he whispered, awed.

Her arms contracted around him. She'd never known such happiness in her whole life. Caught in the tender moment, frozen in time and space, she wished that the clock hands would never move, that this could last forever, this almost-liquid, tangible joy.

OF COURSE, IT didn't last, and they were wild to announce their good news. They called ahead, sharing the revelation with an excited Madeline Ruszel over the holon.

"Come for dinner tomorrow." Madeline repeated her earlier offer. "I'll tell you all about the future. Childbirth is the most fascinating, wonderful process ever known!"

"I'll look forward to it, Dr. Ruszel," Jasmine said, laughing.

"I'm just Maddie when I'm home," came the reply. "Tomorrow. Dinner. And congratulations from all of us. See you!"

Jasmine cuddled into Mekashe's strong arms and sighed. "I guess now we become good friends until I deliver," she said wistfully. "I read about it."

He pursed his lips. "The holon can be used for two avatars at the same time," he related with a wicked grin.

"Well, how innovative!" she exclaimed, and chuckled.

"Necessity drives invention," he replied. He touched her cheek with his fingers and then his forehead to hers. "I don't remember saying the words, although I've felt them for, oh, so long. But I love you."

"I know. I always knew. I love you, too."

His arms contracted. "Together, in the right way, and a child on the way. Can life confer a greater blessing?"

"An equal one," she corrected mischievously. "A family. A big family, made up of two compatible species."

"Absolutely true."

THE EMPEROR AND empress were ecstatic. So were the rest of the family. Sfilla came to the banquet with her son, Rhemun, and his mate, Edris, and their children. Dtimun and Madeline and their children joined the celebration.

Paraguard colonel Clinton Ruszel arrived after a long journey and was introduced to the couple, as well as to Jasmine's father. The two discovered many things in common, not the least of which was that Clinton Ruszel was a history nut. So was Clint, Madeline's younger son, who sequestered himself with the two adult men and drank in stories about the past of Terravega.

Komak and Kipling, and little Larisse, sat with Chacon and Lyceria and their son, Lomek, in the holon hookup to pump the Rojok warlord for his adventures rescuing the princess from Ahkmau, and helping, inadvertently, to form the Holconcom.

Mekashe and Jasmine sat with Dtimun and Madeline, and the emperor and empress.

"We seem to have compatible guests," the emperor mused. He glanced at Jasmine and Mekashe. "Your news delights me," he added softly. "I love my grandchildren. Each is unique, the product of millennia of evolution that brought us to this day." He grimaced. "Many times I have chided myself for allowing the genetic manipulation that changed us so drastically."

Mekashe just smiled. "We are the equals if not the superior of any fighting force we encounter," he said. "It allows us to win battles against the most formidable of insurgents."

"True," the emperor replied. "But it has caused many problems."

"Sir, now that we truly have the tech," Jasmine said to the emperor, "is there a chance that Dr. Hahnson will want his mate back? She could be cloned with the same tech that I enjoy even now."

"It is in discussion," the emperor said, smiling. "We are hopeful that Hahnson will permit it. He has grieved since the Great Galaxy War for her."

"He is a good man," Mekashe said solemnly. "The best of us all."

"In many ways, this is correct," the emperor replied. "I feel that…!"

He stopped abruptly because Jasmine slipped to the floor and lost the small meal she'd just eaten.

"I'm so…sorry!" she said, sobbing.

"Stop that. You're just pregnant, Cehn-Tahr style." Madeline chuckled, motioning to a house worker to clean up the mess. "Mekashe, we'd better put her to bed, just for a little while. It's all right," she reassured him as he swung Jasmine up into his arms and followed Madeline down the hall to a bedroom. "She'll be fine. I went through this. So did Edris."

"Yes, I did," Edris added, joining them. "The nausea is bad at first, but we have new medicines for it."

"We do. Nothing that will harm the baby," Madeline promised as she shot a drug into Jasmine's neck artery with a laserdot. "You'll be fine. But you should rest for a few minutes."

"Call if you need us," Edris added as she and Madeline went out and closed the door.

"Are you certain…?" Mekashe began.

Jasmine put her fingers against his chiseled mouth. "It's a growth spurt. I read about them." She stopped, stunned.

"What is it?" he asked, and then he, too, was very

still. His lips fell apart. "The child," he whispered in awe. "He speaks to me! How is this possible?"

"We'll ask Madeline," she said. She laughed. "How incredible! This isn't possible with human babies!"

"Another product of the DNA manipulation, perhaps," Mekashe said. He laughed. "But how delightful!"

"Oh yes!"

And for several minutes, they just listened, feeling the baby's emotions as if it were already out of the womb.

THEIR LITTLE BOY was born just a few months later, in a delivery that was quick and painless, presided over by both Madeline Ruszel and Edris Mallory.

"Have you thought of names?" Madeline asked as Jasmine held the baby in her arms and Mekashe touched his small head with its mass of thick black curls.

"Many," Mekashe confessed.

"Many, many," Jasmine added. She laughed, weary but joyful as she looked down at the small baby in her arms. "But we found one we like."

"Very much."

"What is it?" Madeline asked.

Mekashe pursed his lips and grinned. "We will announce it at the christening, with all of you and our guests present. And you will not be able to read my mind or hers to discover it," he teased, producing a white noise ball, one so powerful that it locked out even the emperor.

"Well!" Madeline exclaimed. But then she grinned.

THE CHRISTENING WAS attended by the entire family. Chacon and Lyceria came, with their brand-new son, Krusmok Maltiche Chacon. It turned out that Chacon was the Rojok commander's surname. No one, except Lyceria, knew his true first name. And she never divulged it.

Even Rusmok came, with Chacon's special permission. He was in line for promotion to commander of a new commando branch of the Rojok military. He had his own flagship and a brand-new human female who was their resident Cularian specialist. There were rumors, which Rusmok refused to dignify with an answer, that the new physician had Rusmok standing on his head.

The Cehn-Tahr priest performed the ceremony. When it was time to announce the name of the baby, the silence was profound.

"We have given our son these names," Mekashe announced. "He will be known as Malford Rhemun Rusmok Chacon Tnurat Mekashe. But we will call him Mal. For his human grandfather."

Malford Dupont had tears running down his cheeks as they made the announcement. Beside him, Chacon and Tnurat were beaming. Not to mention Rhemun,

Mekashe's best friend. Rusmok, in his dress military uniform, wiped something out of his eye that he said was an insect. There had never been an insect in the great facility in the capital city in its history.

AFTER THE CHRISTENING, there was a celebration at the Fortress.

Rusmok got to hold the child who would be his namesake. "He looks like his father," he pronounced with a smile at Mekashe. "But I think he will have lighter eyes than most Cehn-Tahr."

"I agree," Mekashe said. He cocked his head and studied the Rojok. "I have heard much about you."

Rusmok grinned. "And I have heard about you constantly for five years," he mused, laughing at Mekashe's surprise. "She hardly spoke of anyone else."

"Or he, of any female except Jasmine," Rhemun cut in. "Chacon says that you will have command of a new, deadlier operations group. Congratulations."

"We will one day be almost as famous as the Holconcom," Rusmok chided. "So be on your guard."

"We will never fight each other again," Mekashe said with a grin. He indicated Dtimun and Chacon, taking turns holding the new baby, who had a shock of blond hair like his famous father, along with the slit eyes. "They are too close to allow another conflict."

"There will always be uprisings and insurgents, sadly," Rusmok replied. He touched Jasmine's baby's soft hair. "Children are surprisingly interesting," he said, almost hypnotized by the baby. "I never was so close to one."

"They become addictive." Rhemun chuckled. "Which is why we have two."

"You should bond with someone and have babies of your own," Jasmine told Rusmok.

He shrugged. "Alas. The only female I want does not want me." His face hardened. "She has bonded. With an accountant." He made the word sound like the worst sort of curse word.

"I'm truly sorry," Jasmine said, because she knew that the Rojok, like the Cehn-Tahr, bonded for life.

"What do you Cehn-Tahr call it—*karamesh*?" he replied, using the word for *fate*.

"I suppose it was never meant to be."

"You'll find someone," Jasmine assured him. She smiled. "You're one of the kindest people I've ever known. Well, you were, until you landed me with that pirate who sold me a dresmok that had a depleted emerillium core and almost blew up the barracks when I used it!"

"It had depleted krelamok, not emerillium, and it was what you humans would call a 'stink bomb.'" He pursed his lips. "You got many kuskons for that one. It taught you not to be too trusting of merchants."

"I got him back," Jasmine said smugly.

Rusmok rolled his eyes. "She had two of our friends hijack a skimmer from the admiral's residence and park it in front of my barracks. They were kind enough to add a sample of my DNA to the steering mechanism. I was put in the brig for two days!"

"At least it didn't smell bad in there, did it?" she retorted.

Mekashe and Rhemun looked at each other. "Perhaps it is a very good thing that we don't have the two of them together in the Holconcom."

They laughed. So did Rusmok and Jasmine.

OF COURSE, THE BABY put limits on Jasmine for a short time. She had to stay at the villa and work at the local infirmary while Mal was little. But he grew at a surprising rate. Madeline Ruszel had told her about the accelerated growth of Cehn-Tahr children, but Jasmine hadn't believed her until she saw the results. A Cehn-Tahr child—even a hybrid one—grew at twice the rate of a human child.

"Very soon, you'll be back aboard the Morcai with me, and Mal will be in military school." Mekashe sighed. "Time goes quickly."

"Too quickly." She looked up at him and pursed her lips. "Not that I don't miss you. But another child might be nice. At the rate they grow, I won't be out of active duty for very long at all."

He chuckled at the wicked look she was giving him. "Suppose we discuss this, at length, later tonight?"

She sighed, smiling. "I think that's a great idea!"

She paused. "I think Mal might like to spend the night with his grandfather and learn to play chess."

"Nice idea," he agreed. He studied her beautiful face. "How convoluted our lives have been."

"Yes, but we ended up together after all the trials and tribulations."

"Life is strange," he mused.

She pressed close. "Strange and beautiful."

He drew her close with a sigh. "And endlessly satisfying."

A sentiment with which Jasmine agreed whole-heartedly. She closed her eyes and let herself dream of the long, sweet path ahead of them.

* * * * *

New York Times Bestselling Author

DIANA PALMER

**Can love find the space to take root on
the stunning Wyoming plains?**

Bring these Wyoming men home today!

"Palmer returns with a splendid Western contemporary
novel filled with passion, heartache and small-town life."
—*RT Book Reviews* on *Wyoming Brave* (Top Pick)

HQN™

www.HQNBooks.com

PHDPWMS17

Get 4 FREE REWARDS!

We'll send you 2 FREE Books plus 2 FREE Mystery Gifts.

FREE
Value Over
$20

Both the **Romance** and **Suspense** collections feature compelling novels written by many of today's best-selling authors.

YES! Please send me 2 FREE novels from the Essential Romance or Essential Suspense Collection and my 2 FREE gifts (gifts are worth about $10 retail). After receiving them, if I don't wish to receive any more books, I can return the shipping statement marked "cancel." If I don't cancel, I will receive 4 brand-new novels every month and be billed just $6.74 each in the U.S. or $7.24 each in Canada. That's a savings of at least 16% off the cover price. It's quite a bargain! Shipping and handling is just 50¢ per book in the U.S. and 75¢ per book in Canada*. I understand that accepting the 2 free books and gifts places me under no obligation to buy anything. I can always return a shipment and cancel at any time. The free books and gifts are mine to keep no matter what I decide.

Choose one: ☐ **Essential Romance**
(194/394 MDN GMY7)

☐ **Essential Suspense**
(191/391 MDN GMY7)

Name (please print)

Address   Apt. #

City   State/Province   Zip/Postal Code

Mail to the **Reader Service:**
IN U.S.A.: P.O. Box 1341, Buffalo, NY 14240-8531
IN CANADA: P.O. Box 603, Fort Erie, Ontario L2A 5X3

Want to try two free books from another series? Call 1-800-873-8635 or visit www.ReaderService.com.

*Terms and prices subject to change without notice. Prices do not include applicable taxes. Sales tax applicable in NY. Canadian residents will be charged applicable taxes. Offer not valid in Quebec. This offer is limited to one order per household. Books received may not be as shown. Not valid for current subscribers to the Essential Romance or Essential Suspense Collection. All orders subject to approval. Credit or debit balances in a customer's account(s) may be offset by any other outstanding balance owed by or to the customer. Please allow 4 to 6 weeks for delivery. Offer available while quantities last.

Your Privacy—The Reader Service is committed to protecting your privacy. Our Privacy Policy is available online at www.ReaderService.com or upon request from the Reader Service. We make a portion of our mailing list available to reputable third parties that offer products we believe may interest you. If you prefer that we not exchange your name with third parties, or if you wish to clarify or modify your communication preferences, please visit us at www.ReaderService.com/consumerchoice or write to us at Reader Service Preference Service, P.O. Box 9062, Buffalo, NY 14240-9062. Include your complete name and address.

STRS18

Get 2 Free Books,
Plus 2 Free Gifts—
just for trying the Reader Service!

HARLEQUIN *Desire*

YES! Please send me 2 FREE Harlequin® Desire novels and my 2 FREE gifts (gifts are worth about $10 retail). After receiving them, if I don't wish to receive any more books, I can return the shipping statement marked "cancel." If I don't cancel, I will receive 6 brand-new novels every month and be billed just $4.55 per book in the U.S. or $5.24 per book in Canada. That's a savings of at least 13% off the cover price! It's quite a bargain! Shipping and handling is just 50¢ per book in the U.S. and 75¢ per book in Canada*. I understand that accepting the 2 free books and gifts places me under no obligation to buy anything. I can always return a shipment and cancel at any time. The free books and gifts are mine to keep no matter what I decide.

225/326 HDN GMWG

Name _____ (PLEASE PRINT) _____

Address _____ Apt. #

City _____ State/Prov. _____ Zip/Postal Code

Signature (if under 18, a parent or guardian must sign)

Mail to the **Reader Service:**
IN U.S.A.: P.O. Box 1341, Buffalo, NY 14240-8531
IN CANADA: P.O. Box 603, Fort Erie, Ontario L2A 5X3

Want to try two free books from another line?
Call 1-800-873-8635 or visit www.ReaderService.com.

*Terms and prices subject to change without notice. Prices do not include applicable taxes. Sales tax applicable in N.Y. Canadian residents will be charged applicable taxes. Offer not valid in Quebec. This offer is limited to one order per household. Books received may not be as shown. Not valid for current subscribers to Harlequin Desire books. All orders subject to approval. Credit or debit balances in a customer's account(s) may be offset by any other outstanding balance owed by or to the customer. Please allow 4 to 6 weeks for delivery. Offer available while quantities last.

Your Privacy—The Reader Service is committed to protecting your privacy. Our Privacy Policy is available online at www.ReaderService.com or upon request from the Reader Service.
We make a portion of our mailing list available to reputable third parties that offer products we believe may interest you. If you prefer that we not exchange your name with third parties, or if you wish to clarify or modify your communication preferences, please visit us at www.ReaderService.com/consumerchoice or write to us at Reader Service Preference Service, P.O. Box 9062, Buffalo, NY 14240-9062. Include your complete name and address.

HD17R3

Get 2 Free Books,
Plus 2 Free Gifts—

just for trying the Reader Service!

YES! Please send me 2 FREE Harlequin Presents® novels and my 2 FREE gifts (gifts are worth about $10 retail). After receiving them, if I don't wish to receive any more books, I can return the shipping statement marked "cancel." If I don't cancel, I will receive 6 brand-new novels every month and be billed just $4.55 each for the regular-print edition or $5.55 each for the larger-print edition in the U.S., or $5.49 each for the regular-print edition or $5.99 each for the larger-print edition in Canada. That's a saving of at least 11% off the cover price! It's quite a bargain! Shipping and handling is just 50¢ per book in the U.S. and 75¢ per book in Canada*. I understand that accepting the 2 free books and gifts places me under no obligation to buy anything. I can always return a shipment and cancel at any time. The free books and gifts are mine to keep no matter what I decide.

Please check one: ☐ Harlequin Presents® Regular-Print   ☐ Harlequin Presents® Larger-Print
                    (106/306 HDN GMWK)   (176/376 HDN GMWK)

Name   (PLEASE PRINT)

Address   Apt. #

City   State/Prov.   Zip/Postal Code

Signature (if under 18, a parent or guardian must sign)

Mail to the Reader Service:
IN U.S.A.: P.O. Box 1341, Buffalo, NY 14240-8531
IN CANADA: P.O. Box 603, Fort Erie, Ontario L2A 5X3

Want to try two free books from another series?
Call 1-800-873-8635 or visit www.ReaderService.com.

* Terms and prices subject to change without notice. Prices do not include applicable taxes. Sales tax applicable in N.Y. Canadian residents will be charged applicable taxes. Offer not valid in Quebec. This offer is limited to one order per household. Books received may not be as shown. Not valid for current subscribers to Harlequin Presents books. All orders subject to approval. Credit or debit balances in a customer's account(s) may be offset by any other outstanding balance owed by or to the customer. Please allow 4 to 6 weeks for delivery. Offer available while quantities last.

Your Privacy—The Reader Service is committed to protecting your privacy. Our Privacy Policy is available online at www.ReaderService.com or upon request from the Reader Service.

We make a portion of our mailing list available to reputable third parties that offer products we believe may interest you. If you prefer that we not exchange your name with third parties, or if you wish to clarify or modify your communication preferences, please visit us at www.ReaderService.com/consumerschoice or write to us at Reader Service Preference Service, P.O. Box 9062, Buffalo, NY 14240-9062. Include your complete name and address.

HP17R3

Get 2 Free Books,
Plus 2 Free Gifts—
just for trying the Reader Service!

HARLEQUIN® Romance

Whisked Away by Her Sicilian Boss
Rebecca Winters

A Proposal from the Italian Count
Lucy Gordon

YES! Please send me 2 FREE Harlequin® Romance Larger-Print novels and my 2 FREE gifts (gifts are worth about $10 retail). After receiving them, if I don't wish to receive any more books, I can return the shipping statement marked "cancel." If I don't cancel, I will receive 4 brand-new novels every month and be billed just $5.34 per book in the U.S. or $5.74 per book in Canada. That's a savings of at least 15% off the cover price! It's quite a bargain! Shipping and handling is just 50¢ per book in the U.S. and 75¢ per book in Canada*. I understand that accepting the 2 free books and gifts places me under no obligation to buy anything. I can always return a shipment and cancel at any time. The free books and gifts are mine to keep no matter what I decide.

119/319 HDN GMWL

Name	(PLEASE PRINT)

Address	Apt. #

City	State/Prov.	Zip/Postal Code

Signature (if under 18, a parent or guardian must sign)

Mail to the **Reader Service:**
IN U.S.A.: P.O. Box 1341, Buffalo, NY 14240-8531
IN CANADA: P.O. Box 603, Fort Erie, Ontario L2A 5X3
Want to try two free books from another line?
Call 1-800-873-8635 or visit www.ReaderService.com.

*Terms and prices subject to change without notice. Prices do not include applicable taxes. Sales tax applicable in N.Y. Canadian residents will be charged applicable taxes. Offer not valid in Quebec. This offer is limited to one order per household. Books received may not be as shown. Not valid for current subscribers to Harlequin Romance Larger-Print books. All orders subject to approval. Credit or debit balances in a customer's account(s) may be offset by any other outstanding balance owed by or to the customer. Please allow 4 to 6 weeks for delivery. Offer available while quantities last.

Your Privacy—The Reader Service is committed to protecting your privacy. Our Privacy Policy is available online at www.ReaderService.com or upon request from the Reader Service.

We make a portion of our mailing list available to reputable third parties that offer products we believe may interest you. If you prefer that we not exchange your name with third parties, or if you wish to clarify or modify your communication preferences, please visit us at www.ReaderService.com/consumerschoice or write to us at Reader Service Preference Service, P.O. Box 9062, Buffalo, NY 14240-9062. Include your complete name and address.

HRLP17R3

Get 2 Free Books,

Plus 2 Free Gifts—

just for trying the
Reader Service!

♥ HARLEQUIN®

MEDICAL ⎯∿⎯ Romance™

YES! Please send me 2 FREE Harlequin® Medical Romance™ Larger-Print novels and my 2 FREE mystery gifts (gifts worth about $10 retail). After receiving them, if I don't wish to receive any more books, I can return the shipping statement marked "cancel." If I don't cancel, I will receive 6 brand-new larger-print novels every month and be billed just $5.34 per book in the U.S. or $5.74 per book in Canada. That's a savings of at least 15% off the cover price. It's quite a bargain! Shipping and handling is just 50¢ per book in the U.S. and 75¢ per book in Canada*. I understand that accepting the 2 free books and gifts places me under no obligation to buy anything. I can always return a shipment and cancel at any time. The free books and gifts are mine to keep no matter what I decide.

171/371 HDN GMWP

Name _____ (PLEASE PRINT)

Address _____ Apt. #

City _____ State/Prov. _____ Zip/Postal Code

Signature (if under 18, a parent or guardian must sign)

Mail to the **Reader Service:**
IN U.S.A.: P.O. Box 1341, Buffalo, NY 14240-8531
IN CANADA: P.O. Box 603, Fort Erie, Ontario L2A 5X3

Want to try two free books from another line?
Call 1-800-873-8635 or visit www.ReaderService.com.

*Terms and prices subject to change without notice. Prices do not include applicable taxes. Sales tax applicable in N.Y. Canadian residents will be charged applicable taxes. Offer not valid in Quebec. This offer is limited to one order per household. Books received may not be as shown. Not valid for current subscribers to Harlequin Medical Romance books. All orders subject to approval. Credit or debit balances in a customer's account(s) may be offset by any other outstanding balance owed by or to the customer. Please allow 4 to 6 weeks for delivery. Offer available while quantities last.

Your Privacy—The Reader Service is committed to protecting your privacy. Our Privacy Policy is available online at www.ReaderService.com or upon request from the Reader Service.

We make a portion of our mailing list available to reputable third parties that offer products we believe may interest you. If you prefer that we not exchange your name with third parties, or if you wish to clarify or modify your communication preferences, please visit us at www.ReaderService.com/consumerschoice or write to us at Reader Service Preference Service, P.O. Box 9062, Buffalo, NY 14240-9062. Include your complete name and address.

MED17R2

Get 2 Free Books,

Plus 2 Free Gifts—

just for trying the Reader Service!

MYSTERY W**O**RLDWIDE LIBRARY®

YES! Please send me 2 FREE novels from the Worldwide Library® series and my 2 FREE gifts (gifts are worth about $10 retail). After receiving them, if I don't wish to receive any more books, I can return the shipping statement marked "cancel." If I don't cancel, I will receive 4 brand-new novels every month and be billed just $5.99 per book in the U.S. or $6.74 per book in Canada. That's a savings of at least 25% off the cover price. It's quite a bargain! Shipping and handling is just 50¢ per book in the U.S. and 75¢ per book in Canada*. I understand that accepting the 2 free books and gifts places me under no obligation to buy anything. I can always return a shipment and cancel at any time. The free books and gifts are mine to keep no matter what I decide.

414/424 WDN GMWM

Name	(PLEASE PRINT)	

Address		Apt. #

City	State/Prov.	Zip/Postal Code

Signature (if under 18, a parent or guardian must sign)

Mail to the **Reader Service**:
IN U.S.A.: P.O. Box 1341, Buffalo, NY 14240-8531
IN CANADA: P.O. Box 603, Fort Erie, Ontario L2A 5X3

Want to try two free books from another line?
Call 1-800-873-8635 or visit www.ReaderService.com.

*Terms and prices subject to change without notice. Prices do not include applicable taxes. Sales tax applicable in NY. Canadian residents will be charged applicable taxes. Offer not valid in Quebec. This offer is limited to one order per household. Books received may not be as shown. Not valid for current subscribers to the Worldwide Library series. All orders subject to approval. Credit or debit balances in a customer's account(s) may be offset by any other outstanding balance owed by or to the customer. Please allow 4 to 6 weeks for delivery. Offer available while quantities last.

Your Privacy—The Reader Service is committed to protecting your privacy. Our Privacy Policy is available online at www.ReaderService.com or upon request from the Harlequin Reader Service.

We make a portion of our mailing list available to reputable third parties that offer products we believe may interest you. If you prefer that we not exchange your name with third parties, or if you wish to clarify or modify your communication preferences, please visit us at www.ReaderService.com/consumerschoice or write to us at Reader Service Preference Service, P.O. Box 9062, Buffalo, NY 14269-9062. Include your complete name and address.

WWLI17R2